In the Name

of the

Crown

In the Name of the Crown

Anthony Matthews

Matador
9 Priory Business Park,
Wistow Road, Kibworth Beauchamp,
Leicestershire. LE8 0RX
Tel: 0116 279 2299
Email: books@troubador.co.uk
Web: www.troubador.co.uk/matador
Twitter: @matadorbooks

ISBN 978 1785891 939

British Library Cataloguing in Publication Data.
A catalogue record for this book is available from the British Library.

Typeset in 11pt Minion Pro by Troubador Publishing Ltd, Leicester, UK

Matador is an imprint of Troubador Publishing Ltd

To my grandmother, Amalia,
who raised her family during the Second World War in great
difficulty. She never wavered in her love for me and I stand in awe
of her dignity and fidelity to the Crown and nation of my birth.

Prologue

"Edward, so good to see you again. I am sorry it has to be such an occasion," said Baron Belasyse to Sir Edward Villiers, as he slowly hobbled over to his old friend, leaning heavily on his walking stick.

"Likewise. I wish our great sovereign King Charles the Second had lived more than his fifty-five years. It makes me think my time is soon; we are going to have a few more funerals to attend," said Villiers.

"Sadly that is true," said Colonel John Russell shaking hands with his old friends.

The three elderly knights of the realm sat down at the Olde Cheshire Cheese Inn on Fleet Street in the City of London. A roaring fire providing a warm welcome on this cold and frosty February afternoon in the year of our Lord 1685. The Thames had once again frozen over and London shivered. Black, oily smoke trails from the many coal fires cast a shadow over St. Paul's Cathedral, the high scaffolding, covered in sail cloth disguised the building, as the Strong brothers and their teams of stonemasons hoisted perfectly cut blocks of Portland stone ever higher. Sir Christopher Wren's masterpiece was taking shape.

"Gentlemen, what may I get you?" asked the proprietor, noting the bearing and dress of the three former members of the late King's secret service.

"Roast pheasant with asparagus, shoulder of lamb and some of those new-fangled fried potatoes," replied Belasyse.

"Sounds good and blue cheese after, along with some wine from Chateau Haut-Brion landlord," said Villiers as the three old soldiers made themselves comfortable at a table in the corner of the dining room.

"I have heard King James will ask you to be a privy councillor in his government," said Russell cautiously.

"I believe so," said Belasyse.

"But, um, well that will affect your position with Parliament; after all you are a ..." Villiers didn't want to say it.

"I know, but I think he still remembers my mission for his brother all those years ago," said Belasyse, "and wishes to reward me for it."

"It is incredible that you returned from your mission, John. You never did tell us the whole story and we didn't want to pry," said Russell.

Belasyse had known Villiers and Russell as young men and had fought alongside them during England's horrendous civil wars. He trusted them totally; they were bound together for life.

"Perhaps now is the time. Once I defended our nation upon earth; soon heaven will take me from it," said Belasyse, as the pleasant sound of the finest red wine being poured into crystal glasses, along with the warm fire, set a mellow tone.

"In the days of old when knights were bold or in our cases bald," said Belasyse, to the amusement of his lunch guests. Then a serious look crossed his face. "I will tell you what really happened across the ocean and the lessons we should learn, so we may have a better nation for all who dwell within," as Villiers and Russell listened to their mentor who, despite his years, was to be offered high office under the new King.

They looked at Baron John Belasyse of Worlaby with admiration, at this calm, measured and brave man, knowing they were hearing the missing part of the story that they had helped to write.

"I'll tell you about that mission; after all, you helped me fulfil it, though the outcome was not quite as I portrayed it," said Belasyse as Villiers and Russell frowned.

"But you killed the proscribed men," said Villiers.

"Well, um." Belasyse paused, admiring his good friends who had helped him all those years ago on a journey of revenge for the King of England.

"I'll tell you the truth. I did not lie to the King, I was just creative with my story," and he took a sip of the delicious wine.

"You're not telling us that Baron Belasyse fooled the King of England are you?" asked Colonel Sir John Russell, aghast.

"Well let me, err, explain," he said with a crafty smile, as the roasts arrived and the elderly knights of England enjoyed their lunch as Belasyse told them the extraordinary story. Villiers and Russell listened intently, incredulity written all over their faces.

CHAPTER 1

Monarchy on Trial

Bang! Went the judge's gavel on the wooden block and Westminster Hall settled down. The assembled crowd looked around the magnificent thirteenth century building. It had seen the trials of the famous and infamous. Queen Anne Boleyn, Guy Fawkes and his associates involved in the Gunpowder Plot, and now Charles the First, King of England, God's anointed representative on Earth. This was new ground.

John Cooke, prosecutor, stood up and eyed the King with malevolence.

"In the name of the people and the House of Commons, it is charged that Charles Stuart, present King of England, did engage in a wicked design to overthrow the rights and liberties of the people. He has traitorously and maliciously levied war against the present Parliament and the people therein represented. To erect and uphold himself an unlimited and tyrannical power, to rule according to his will. He is a tyrant, traitor, murderer and an implacable enemy of the Commonwealth of England," he barked, his words echoing around the hall. Some of the jury nodded in agreement at the charge, others looked around, bewildered.

The King took in the spectators uneasily and said nothing.

"You have heard the charge and we require an answer in the name of the people of England," said Bradshaw, president of the court.

"It is a lie, not half, not a quarter of the people of England. Oliver Cromwell is a traitor," shouted Lady Fairfax from the public gallery. Captain Axtell of the guard saw some members of the audience agreeing, "Shoot the whore; justice, justice, execution, execution," he screamed at the crowd, urging his men to do the same.

"I would know by what authority, I mean lawful authority, I am called here. I stand more for the liberty of the people than any who come here as my pretended judges," said King Charles.

"You must answer the charge!" said Bradshaw. "We are satisfied with our authority. If you had been pleased to observe, you would have known that the Parliament is here assembled and the people of England, of which you are elected King."

Charles bristled with anger. "England was never an elected kingdom, but hereditary for near these thousand years. Remember I am your King, your lawful King. I have a trust committed to me by God; by old and lawful descent, I will not betray it to answer a new, unlawful authority. Therefore, resolve me that. I see no House of Lords here, only some seventy persons and I do not recognise but eight of them. This does not constitute Parliament whatsoever. Let me see a legal authority warranted by the constitution! I require sir, to see it."

"Hear, hear," shouted many in the audience, "God save the King," and the rising hubbub filled the hall.

"It is not for a prisoner to require," said Bradshaw.

"Sir, I am no ordinary prisoner," replied the King in full voice, his stammer gone on this grave occasion.

"Order, order; you must answer the charge," shouted Bradshaw, looking desperately at Oliver Cromwell, whilst banging the gavel as hard as he could on the desk in front of him. The spectators could not believe that a King of England was on trial. It had never come to this, no matter how much the sovereign and his people disagreed; this was a step into the unknown and perhaps, a step too far.

"The court will adjourn," shouted Bradshaw and the commissioners filed out. Captain Axtell of the Parliamentary guard had his men point their muskets at the onlookers. "Just try something and I'll drop you like dogs."

"This is developing into a joke," said Colonel William Goffe, as the jury gathered in an ante chamber. "We have been at this too long and the King has refused to plead. We must move to sentencing immediately."

"I couldn't agree more," said Oliver Cromwell. "We must be decisive in this matter or we will look weak and it could drag on indefinitely. We have negotiated in good faith for far too long. Now is the time to draw a line under this affair. Let a warrant be drawn up for the King's execution and I tell you we will cut off his head with the crown upon it." Goffe looked at Cromwell; good idea.

"I will have the warrant to execute him written up right now," said Cromwell, motioning to the Secretary of the court.

"But if we put our hands to this it will mean the death of God's anointed King," said Colonel Dixwell, concerned who would run the country if they executed the King.

"Exactly," said Colonel Goffe.

"But he has three sons and they might come for revenge someday; that should worry all of us," Dixwell said, hoping for reason in the matter.

"Let them," said Goffe. "We command forty thousand troops and the most formidable Navy there is. Two of his sons are in exile, we hold the other hostage, along with a daughter. They have no money, no military forces. The Royalists are finished."

"Perfectly put. We will formulate a law to abolish the monarchy and all of you better back this stance or else!" said Cromwell. "Now let us get on with it," and they all filed back into Westminster Hall.

"As the prisoner at the bar refuses to plead, this may be taken as pro confesso and evidence of his guilt," said Cooke.

"So be it. This court does adjudge that he, the said Charles Stuart, guilty as a tyrant, traitor, murderer and a public enemy, be put to death by the severing of his head from his body," said Bradshaw. "Remove the prisoner."

"If I am not suffered to speak, imagine, what justice can the people expect?" said the King as he was led away. Then he hesitated; there was a tall man, dressed in a dark brown cloak with a scarred face amongst the spectators who looked familiar, but the guards pushed him on, insulting and spitting at him. The hall emptied and the scarred man walked briskly away down Tuthill Street, as the commissioners for the Army began to settle the affair once and for all.

"Gentlemen, time to sign whether you like it or not!" said Oliver Cromwell, nodding at the preacher Hugh Peter and Colonel Goffe to start intimidating some of the jury who hung back at the entrance to the door. Dixwell joined the queue. "Remember this: any man who does not answer to the charge cannot, in common law, be found guilty," he said to Cromwell, who gave him a bitter smile. The vellum parchment lay on a small table, beside a pot of ink and a quill.

As the commissioners lined up to sign the document, Captain Axtell and his troopers stood against the wall daring them not to sign. Once they had, each man sealed it with his signet ring in red wax, knowing they were ending over one thousand years of English history at the stroke of a pen.

"William, may I have a word?" said Colonel Edward Whalley. "I have signed, no matter what the consequences. I believe in this, but I would mention that the King still has many supporters and there were some in the court who looked very out of place. For the death of the King will, at some stage, provoke revenge; we should be aware of that. We must be on our guard for a rescue attempt."

"And who will try?" said Goffe.

Whalley thought for a moment. "His sons for one."

"They are in exile, or prisoners; we have discussed that and the matter is closed," boomed Goffe, sounding like the stalwart puritan officer he was.

"There is also the Sealed Knot. They're out there waiting for a chance."

"Chance for what?" said Goffe, his temper and voice rising on the freezing January morning.

"To rescue the King," said Whalley, thinking carefully. "Do you remember the siege of Newark? It went on for months; we could not capture the city. Then, thank God, the King ordered it to surrender to save further bloodletting. Do you remember the commander, the tallish man, with a sabre cut to his face? What was his name?"

"Belasyse, Baron John Belasyse."

"Yes, that's him. Do you remember what he said to us? What was it? Yes: 'I will not tire, I will not rest, I will not give in, for I stand for the monarchy, albeit not in the greatest of hands; I stand by it as I do Jesus Christ, for it is my soul.' He is a member of that secret society. He is determined and resolute. The spymaster John Thurloe has made it one of his priorities to capture him but with no success yet," said Whalley.

"I'll see he is dealt with. Leave him to me and he will meet the devil, not Christ, as quick as I can personally arrange it," said Goffe, his face full of menace.

CHAPTER 2

A Noble Death

It's a crisp, cold January morning in the year of our Lord 1649. The dew has frozen over the grass in the park by St. James's Palace, London, making it look like a silver meadow. The crows squawk in the leafless trees, the sun shines on the icicles making them dance. King Charles the First, by God's grace, the King of Scotland, Ireland, Wales and England, has been a close prisoner these last months. None of us could rescue him. I, Baron John Belasyse, officer of the King, know that. Some members of the House of Commons, with the contrivance of the Army, have put the King on trial, if you could call it that. No one believed he would be released if he were found innocent. Some eighty members of the House of Commons from over five hundred were commissioned, the rest imprisoned or dismissed. Told to find the King guilty, then sign the warrant to execute him, or else! I wait, hoping for a miracle.

Belasyse lent on the fence by the Chapel Royal, next to St James's Palace. *What has my country sunk to? Women assaulted for wearing make-up, theatres and taverns closed, country sports abolished and martial law established. Even football has been forbidden and now our King to be executed. For seven long, terrible years I fought for him. I did not love him; he had too many faults for that, made too many mistakes and appointed bad advisers. I fought for him out of loyalty and principle, for what would replace him and the institution of the monarchy? The Puritan zealots! The sovereign was part of my culture, the history of England and it comes to this day, oblivion. The crowd begins to gather; none of us can really believe it has come to this.*

It's ten in the morning now, and his Majesty is at prayer. The crowd has swollen and starts to wail as the King emerges from his ministrations with his staff and armed guard from the Chapel Royal. To many, the monarch was divinely ordained and this was the moment of his martyrdom. Matthew Tomlinson, chief guard, along with Colonel Hacker and his escort form up. With drums beating and flags flying, they make their way to the Palace of Whitehall, across the park his father King James had landscaped and filled with exotic animals. Mounted troopers hold back the crowds, in case anyone should try to interfere or effect a rescue. Across the upper floor of the Tudor gateway with its chequerboard façade, to the Banqueting House of Whitehall Palace. The King suddenly hesitated; there, on the first floor outside one of the windows, was a scaffold draped in black cloth. A tall man, dressed in the same with a mask over his head, waited. The executioner! In front of him was a small wooden block; an axe rested upon it. The King, seeing it, gave an inward shudder. There was no going back now.

Belasyse followed the crowd through the gateway to the front of Horse Guard Yard and saw the King, who was wearing a doublet with the Order of the Garter sewn on the left hand sleeve. He could also make out that the King was wearing two shirts: one, a lace undershirt, and a padded over-shirt. *Clever; he won't shiver in the cold, lest his accusers make it out for fear.* A black-banded hat added to the sombre atmosphere. The King entered the Banqueting House and admired the magnificent ceiling for the last time, painted by Sir Peter Paul Rubens celebrating the Stuart dynasty and his father's achievements.

Many in the crowd were crying as they saw their King for the last time and Belasyse made his way through them; the rapier by his side and hand-tailored clothes make him out to be a gentleman and people moved out of the way. As he approached the scaffold, he spotted Captain Axtell at the first floor window, his leering, uneducated face full of hate. He swears at the King, mocking him and ordering his men to do the same. This is what governs England now.

The King looked out of the window to the open court and wine cellar beyond, wistfully looking at the gulls, free to fly to wherever they wish. He has a little bread and a glass of claret; the scaffold needs more work before it is ready. Then the doors to the Banqueting House opened.

"Sire, their royal highnesses," said Tomlinson, and in rushed Prince Henry and Princess Elizabeth. The King jumped out of his seat, pleased to see two of his children for the last time.

Princess Elizabeth started to cry uncontrollably. "Father, father, are these men going to kill you? Please say it isn't true, please," she begged, tugging at his coat.

The King placed his son on his knee and gathered his daughter to him. "Now listen to me, both of you," said the King. "Henry, Elizabeth, they are going to cut off thy father's head. Do you understand? They will cut off thy father's head. Sweetheart," continued the King, "do not let them make you king so long as thy brothers Charles and James do live. Please promise me that, my son."

"I will be torn to pieces first," said Henry with great determination. This impressed the King greatly, pleased to see such courage in someone so young. "Elizabeth, tell your mother the Queen, that my thoughts have never strayed from her and I will love her to the end. Give my blessings to her and your brothers, fear God and never abandon the Anglican Church. I forgive these men for what they will do to me, but you must never trust them." The King then took off the jewel from around his neck and placed it into his son's hand and stared into his eyes and with great gravity said, "Remember."

"I am very sorry, sire, the time has come," said Colonel Tomlinson, opening the doors.

"So be it," said King Charles and ushered his distraught children into their governor's arms. The King walked across the room, bare of the fine furniture and paintings he had collected over the years, and hardly stooped as he stepped out of the window onto the scaffold. At last, an end to all this; the axe man stands, waiting, impassive.

"Sire, the time has come for your martyrdom," said William Juxon, Bishop of London.

The King walked to the edge of the scaffold, casting his eyes over the crowd, kept at some distance from him so no one could attempt a rescue or hear his last words. A double line of musketeers put paid to that. He spoke softly to Tomlinson and the Bishop. "I forgive all persons who, out of spite and malice, have brought me here. As for the people, I truly desire their liberty and freedom as anybody whomsoever, but I must tell you, that means they must have a government and laws which guarantee their life and property. A sovereign and subject are clean and different things. Yet you claim to be better than I, and I say, the people will never enjoy themselves and it is for this reason that I am here. For if I wished to change the law by the power of the sword, I would not be here and therefore I am a martyr for the people and the Anglican Church. I go from a corruptible Crown to an incorruptible Crown, where there can be no disturbance, no disturbance at all," said the King.

"You have exchanged a temporal Crown to an eternal Crown; a good exchange," said Bishop Juxon to the King, with all the compassion he could muster. King Charles turned to the executioner. "I will put my hair in a cap and pray upon the block; when I thrust out my hands, you may do your duty."

"If it please your Majesty," he said, tucking a wisp of the King's hair into the cap and lifting the axe from the block. The King prayed a while, then thrust out his hands and down went the axe. A groan rose from the crowd, *as to one when you lose your wife or child*, thought Belasyse; *a sound I would not wish to hear again as long as the Lord allows me to live.*

The crowd rush forward to dip their handkerchiefs in the King's blood, the martyr's sign of deliverance. The axe man holds up the King's head and the crowd goes silent, but he says nothing, for there is nothing to be said.

Belasyse walked slowly to Westminster Abbey, aghast at the death of his monarch. The crowd dispersed, stunned, for the future is military dictatorship. Then he saw Colonel Tomlinson and blood coursed through his veins, quickening his steps.

"Sir, may I have a little of your time?" said Belasyse, stepping smartly in front of the Parliamentary officer.

"Please be quick, sir, for I have had the worst day of my life," said Tomlinson, heaving with shock.

"I think all good men would agree with that. I would ask who keeps the warrant that sealed the late King's fate," asked Belasyse as nonchalantly as he could after the momentous event.

"Colonel Hacker, sir; he keeps it at his house in Cheapside. There were some fifty-nine signatories. He said he wanted to keep it for posterity, but why would you want to know that?" asked Tomlinson.

"For, as you say, posterity; oh and twenty gold sovereigns for your silence in this matter."

"But the monarchy will be abolished by Parliament," said Tomlinson, noting the rapier and fine tailored clothes of a Royalist.

"But not by the people. The King is dead and right now we have a new one in exile. Our martyred king has three sons and three daughters and I would not want to be one of the men on that list when they return. I am more than pleased to leave you alone, or I could shoot you right now!" said Belasyse, staring directly at Tomlinson.

"If you did that, you would also die; there are many soldiers hereabouts."

"I will gladly die in the service of the King, even the new one, so you think about that Tomlinson; want to see your wife and children again?" asked Belasyse, a snarl on his face. "Because you won't unless you give me your silence about that list! There are many who will oppose your ruthless military rule and right now two of them are watching your every move and we would be more than pleased to kill you!"

Tomlinson eyed the passing crowd; many looking at him, conspicuous in his scarlet jacket and lobster-tail helmet. He shuddered at the Baron's scarred face. A sabre had gouged his right cheek and shrapnel marks on his head made him a seasoned commander. The moustache and spade-shaped beard, along with his right hand on a double-barrelled pistol were the finishing touch. Then he spotted two men, a few yards to the left and right of Belasyse, staring at him, their backs to the wall of the privy garden, anger on their faces and hands on their swords, ready for action. The narrow gate of King Street to his right, a dead end behind him and the small entrance to Whitehall on his left. He was trapped; this man knew his business and had chosen his moment well.

"I watched the proceedings. We will hit back; we can find you, you're known. Do you want to spend the rest of your life looking over your shoulder? Do you?" said Belasyse bluntly.

"No I don't. You have my silence," Tomlinson said grudgingly, noting the cold, frightening look from the Baron, who produced a small leather pouch of sovereigns. Anyway he was horrified that the army had done this, it had gone too far. Let him have the moment, always good to have friends in both camps.

Belasyse moved swiftly through the crowd, stopping and retracing his steps a few times, to check for any pursuers. He strode past the church of St. Margaret's, full of stunned worshippers. Across the front and side of Westminster Abbey, into Dean's Yard, checking over his shoulder as his companions moved past him, looking carefully for any Parliamentarian troopers.

He passed the Abbey green and the Westminster school, hearing headmaster Busby saying prayers for the late King. Through the arched entrance into the cloisters and along to the chapter house, with its depictions of exotic animals, now whitewashed on the Puritan government's orders. He stopped, looked around and listened for a few minutes then knocked on the simple oak plank door on the right side of the entrance. Belasyse checked the cloisters again and admired the door, *made in 1050, built to last, just like the monarchy.*

A pistol barrel poked its head over the top of the door and Sir Edward Villiers checked him.

"Welcome on this day of the King's martyrdom," he said in a low, sad voice.

As Belasyse entered, a large cannon candle lit up the room and he saw Colonel John Russell astride a red velvet-topped stool, head in his hands. He looked up, weeping.

"Gentlemen, the deed is done. Now we must look to the future and the ascension of his Majesty King Charles the Second. I got one interesting piece of information out of Colonel Tomlinson. There are fifty-nine signatories on the warrant to execute his Majesty and it is kept by a one Colonel Hacker at his house on Cheapside," said Belasyse.

"Well done, John," said Villiers. "We should remember that."

"Let's go back to our estates and lay low. There is nothing we can do for now. We need to get over this and plan for the future. Cromwell won't live forever. Not only that, the people will not tolerate the Army ruling the nation for long and the zeal of the religious fanatics that now govern us will wane. Patience is the key here. We must survive; the future of the monarchy may depend on it."

"Agreed," said Villiers and Russell together, furiously writing the name of Colonel Hacker and his address in their notebooks. They all stood up and embraced, wondering if they would ever see each other again.

"I'll stay behind and cover. Be careful, both of you, the city is heavily patrolled," said Belsayse, checking once again for Parliamentary soldiers. "All clear, and may God protect you both," and off they went, looking furtively in all directions as they walked out of the cloisters and across the green behind the Abbey walls, to an uncertain future in Republican England.

Belasyse walked back to the cloisters, ensuring his friends were well on their way. They had agreed to assist the King's son in exile in France, but he was a mere adolescent. What does the future hold in this world turned upside down? His heart sank; *please, good Lord, help your servant, for I am alone and scared.* Sitting on the low wall opposite the Pyx Chamber, a remnant of the first Saxon church. He clasped a Bible in his hand, acting as if he was waiting for a service or communion to commence, and he read. 'Come unto me all ye that labour and are heavily laden and I shall give you rest. Be strong and of good courage, fear not, nor be afraid of them, for the Lord thy God is by thy side. It is he that doth go with thee; he will not fail thee, nor forsake thee. Belasyse felt a warmth fill his soul. I shall not stop, I shall not give in, I will die for what I believe in,' and he hardened his heart against his enemies.

Belasyse heard the soft steps of a man walking cautiously from the herb garden. "In pectore?" he asked.

"Ut ego sum," said the man judiciously, in a strange, foreign voice.

"Over here," he said, motioning the stranger to the small room Villiers and Russell had left from. The man was short, very thin and a pale clammy white, as if he had never seen the sun. Some five foot tall, with large black eyes. He was dressed in a green olive cloak and matching hat, with black felt boots, brown gloves and a small leather bag over his left shoulder. As he entered the small room, Belasyse joined him, closing and locking the door carefully. The stranger removed his cloak and gloves, revealing a single ring of gold on his left hand.

The surface was decorated with an image of Christ on the cross. He wore a scarlet cassock tied with white cords and he took from his pocket a scarlet mozzetta which he put over his shoulders, and a scarlet zucchetto which he placed on his head. Then, a pectoral cross on a chain, which he hung around his neck. He took from the bag a small bottle of wine, a chalice studded with gems and a silver casket, which he carefully opened, placing a wafer of unleavened bread on the velvet cushion on top of the stool.

"My son, it is time to confess to holy God and take Communion," said the strange man. His eyes darted around the room and eyed the door anxiously, for he knew the consequences if he was caught.

"I, Baron John Belasyse, do swear in the presence of almighty God, to hunt down and kill all those who signed the warrant to execute King Charles the First, by the grace of God, King of Ireland, Wales, Scotland and England. For however long it takes, wherever they may reside and may our Lord have mercy on them, for I shall have none," said Belasyse between clenched teeth.

"You know it says in the Bible, thou shalt not kill," said the stranger.

"I do, but it also says in the Bible, 'for vengeance is mine sayeth the Lord's and it shall be mine, for I am the Lord's servant.'"

The man gave a knowing smile. "Now join with me in reciting the Lord's Prayer."

"Pater noster qui est in caelis," said the men together, before the bells of Westminster Abbey started ringing for the last time, lamenting the death of their benefactor and hiding the two men's prayers. As messengers rode the breadth of the nation informing the people of the execution of their sovereign and the abolition of the monarchy. The ambassadors of European nations wrote their reports of a new power in England and the death of God's anointed King.

CHAPTER 3

An English Breakfast

"Squad, present arms," commanded the duty sergeant, looking straight ahead as regulations required, though those regulations seemed to be slipping every day. *Who controls England now*, he thought, *with Oliver Cromwell dead and his clueless son in command? We need a leader who can inspire us and who was that going to be?* He looked up at the immaculately clad officer. *I wonder if it will be General Whalley?*

Whalley dismounted, handing the reins to Sergeant Wharton and strode up to the door of the command centre of Lower England. He knocked, opened the door and removed his black hat.

"Hallo General, I am surprised to see you here," exclaimed Goffe who was sitting at the end of a long oak table hunched over the map of his command.

"I am here because dark clouds are gathering in London," said Whalley, shaking hands with his son-in-law, noting Goffe's desk was stacked with reports of incidences concerning Royalist agents and sympathisers. Whalley took the top one and read it. "We need to talk; there are major problems confronting us," he said shaking his head at the latest report of another Royalist spy. Goffe went to the front door.

"Sergeant Wharton."

"Yes, sir."

"I want no visitors, whoever they may be, until this afternoon. I am in conference with Major General Whalley."

"I understand, sir. I will hold any persons in the officers' quarters if anybody arrives seeking you, sir. There is only Mr Peter and Colonel Dixwell due and not until later this afternoon, sir."

If General Whalley has come on an unannounced visit there must be a crisis afoot, thought Goffe.

Goffe closed and bolted the door. He had married Whalley's daughter Frances and brought little in the way of a dowry, but told him, 'I marry for love, sir, not money,' and that comment had formed the bond which would bind them together for life. As a member of the House of Lords and a major general, he was one of the most important men in the nation and now that would be put to the test.

"Well, sir, I can see there are problems on your mind," said Goffe.

"Let us have a glass of sack and I will explain." Both men moved to the withdrawing room, Goffe pouring two glasses of the richly flavoured Spanish wine.

"Richard Cromwell, successor to his father as Lord Protector, has resigned," said Whalley. "Thurloe believes that someone with a close grasp of Parliamentary affairs is revealing all of our problems to the King in exile. He knows not who, but believes those people are plotting a return of the monarchy."

"That maybe but they will be without Belasyse as we have arrested him and he is being held in the Tower."

"That is great news!" said Whalley excitedly.

"We took it upon ourselves to rid this nation of the monarchy as a burden to the people and the public purse. Charles Stuart, that man of blood, raised his standard against his own people and therefore was responsible for the wars that brought the death of tens of thousands of people and now we have captured one of his greatest adherents," said Goffe.

"But the rest of the Sealed Knot elude us, though he is being encouraged to talk and Thurloe told me he may have a surprise soon," said Whalley.

"Excellent. We must eliminate all persons who threaten us. When Belasyse breaks we should have him executed," said Goffe.

"So be it," said Whalley, nodding his approval.

"We can be proud of our success in closing down brothels, stopping drunkenness and licentious behaviour. We have freed up public land for the common man, encouraged all persons of whatever social rank to pursue lawful commerce and attend university. Our enemies are crushed, our trade and power stretches across the globe," said Goffe.

"Correct," said Whalley. "But ultimately the army rules the nation and we the generals command it, is that the right way? We cannot run the country like this forever, Parliament must come into its own someday and the army defend it."

"That may be, but not yet. We still have Royalists, Catholics and others who deny the Republic to deal with, and they must be, if necessary by the sword," said Goffe bluntly.

Whalley stared at the fire, thinking deeply. "I have heard our colleague General Lambert has been cashiered by Parliament, so he has in turn dismissed them. There is chaos across the country. The army has lost its head and has no one to lead it. General Monck has some seven thousand troops, mainly in Scotland and the border regions. His army is the best equipped, paid and trained of all. He is therefore the most powerful man in England. We should, on behalf of the Commonwealth, meet him and along the way ascertain the views of the other generals. We need a leader. I would point out, William, it will not be me, for before you ask I do not command enough support," said Whalley.

"Let us go to London, meet the general staff and convince them the Republic must remain in perpetuity. I will have Belasyse executed. Then visit General Monck and convince him to stand for God's chosen cause," said Goffe determinedly. Whalley looked out the window at the vegetable garden, there was going to be a coming together again; war was looming.

"Listen, Peter, I am fed up with your constant hatred and envy against anyone who is wealthy," said Colonel Dixwell. "Will you never get it into your ignorant, stubborn head, we are not all born equal. There has been and always will be people richer than others, its way of the world. Levellers like you should be aware of what has happened to your type. You should be thankful for what you have, a ministry, or has Dunkirk and Flanders become embarrassed with your vitriol?"

"If you think you scare me and snobbery makes you better, you're wrong, Dixwell. Your disjointed and riddled with monies we the people should 'ave and you are an enemy of the good old cause," snarled Peter in defiance. "We know what to do with God's enemies; we have had them enslaved. Eighteen thousand Covenanters shipped out of Britain and how many wrenched papists from Ireland? As many, if not more." Peter's unkempt appearance belied a fanatic preacher, gifted with rousing speeches in the name of the Republic.

"If you think selling British people as slaves to the Indies and butchering the Irish makes you a hero in my eyes, you are beneath contempt," said Dixwell, staring at the rail thin preacher beside him.

The two men looked at each other with mutual hatred as the carriage made its way to the command centre.

"Halt," said Sergeant Wharton. "Papers please, gentlemen."

Peter handed his pass to the duty sergeant in a split glove, which was worn and dirty. Wharton noticed, then he saw the name Hugh Peter and looked up in awe. Here was a real man of the people, who roughed it with the men; a minister to the council of state. A man respected by the rank and file. He had returned across the ocean to help in the war against the King and had convinced many others to do so. He practised medicine and preached to the men without regard for rank or social position. He would not accept his pay until the troops had theirs. His eve of battle speeches had roused the soldiers to victory on many occasions. He knew; he had been there. A man to look up to and respect. He reached for Colonel Dixwell's papers; here were soft white leather gloves, a trimmed moustache, a quilted leather jacket and embroidered caramel britches. He saw a functionary and no more.

"Please wait here," said Wharton, motioning them to the officers' mess at the entrance to the headquarters. "There is ale or cider for refreshment. General Goffe is in conference and must not be disturbed, though he should be finished soon."

"Good afternoon, sir," said Colonel Dixwell. "I do apologise for disturbing you, but I have some matters of importance I wish to share."

"Good afternoon, Colonel," said Goffe. "You have met General Whalley before, I believe."

"Yes, a pleasure to see you again, sir," said Dixwell without enthusiasm, surprised to see both generals at the headquarters. He offered his hand to Whalley, who took it with both of his, showing his need for any friend at this time.

"Gentlemen, I will be brief," said Dixwell, looking at both men anxiously whilst taking the seat offered by Whalley next to the long oak table. "As Governor of Dover Castle and Member of Parliament for the town, I keep a close eye on the movement of persons and goods in the port, as it is the main crossing between England and the Continent. You have asked me to inquire about and seize any correspondence between persons in England and the supposed King in exile. Three days ago, two letters were discovered, destined for Charles Stuart. Having examined them I am convinced that Baron Belasyse is having letters smuggled from the Tower and the Sealed Knot are assisting him."

Whalley and Goffe's eyes locked.

"So why haven't you arrested them?" asked Goffe in exasperation.

"For the simple reason that they bribe the guards. As many of the troops have not been paid, often for months at a time, the temptation to take the money is inevitable," said Dixwell.

Whalley stared at Dixwell and knew he was right. Many of the men were deserting, having not been paid; their families were hungry, rents were not collected, the economy was a mess.

"Sounds reasonable, Colonel. So the Sealed Knot are acting as the messengers for Charles Stuart?"

"Yes, sir, I am sure of it. Unfortunately we can't take apart every ship sailing to Europe. There is a multitude of hiding places in each vessel," said Dixwell with resignation in his voice.

"Good point," said Whalley. "Have all passes of the postmen examined and the signatures checked. I will have their estates searched again and speak with our mutual friend Thurloe and see what he can reveal."

"Sir, I have had all the passes checked and Thurloe swore he did not sign them, but each one has his signature on them, in the blue black ink he always uses."

"That's strange. I trust him implicitly," said Whalley, frowning. "Who could be forging his signature?"

"I am making further inquiries, sir, and I will keep you informed. Just one more thing, gentlemen," said Dixwell, who hesitated, looking around the room for inspiration.

"Get to the point, Colonel!" said Goffe, irritated at the government functionary's 'it's not my fault' attitude.

"Yes, sir. I have grave news for you, General Whalley. Parliament has passed a motion dismissing you from all military posts; it is not yet common news." The two generals' jaws dropped.

"If I may be direct, gentlemen, I, along with yourselves and others, signed the death warrant of King Charles the First. The nation is inexorably moving to change and many are demanding the recall of the late King's son. If that happens we're are all done for; we will lose our property and positions and face death if he returns," said Dixwell and rose to leave, saluting the two generals.

Whalley gave a thin smile as a goodbye and slowly closed the door.

"So why did he not arrest any of the postmen? Bad luck or just hedging his bets?" said Goffe. "I also wonder if Thurloe is telling us everything. He's right though; we have wives, children, estates and you're Oliver Cromwell's cousin. We must stop this; everything we have fought for and thousands have died for stands on what we do now. We must, or we will all pay," said Goffe, gripping the table and staring straight at General Whalley.

"Morning, William," said Whalley.

"Morning, sir," said Goffe. "Ahh breakfast; no matter what new discovery comes from the plantations, like tobacco, horrible and strange thing, breakfast tops the lot."

"What's that?" he asked his wife Frances, staring at the browned, red blob on his plate.

"A fried tomato fruit; it goes very well with English breakfast," said Frances Goffe knowingly.

"I honestly don't think the English will add that to one of the great meals in the nation," said Whalley suspiciously.

"Maybe, maybe not. The children are under instruction in the parlour for reading and writing today."

"Three breakfasts?" he said quizzically.

"Yes, we have a guest – our old friend from Massachusetts, Mr Hugh Peter the preacher. He is finishing his morning sermon for your men."

Before Whalley could open his mouth, the door knocker rapped and in walked Hugh Peter, as always slightly unkempt, the band around his hat tied with several knots to remind him of passages in the scriptures for his sermon. *Hugh Peter*, thought Whalley, he *has come a long way from being minister of the church in Salem, Massachusetts. Chaplain to the council of state, sitting on no less than seven committees, for social, political and religious reform, he has done well. A man deserving of respect.*

"Well, well, this is a great surprise and pleasure," said Whalley, pleased to have an old comrade in arms at his base. "You know my son-in-law William Goffe."

"Yes I remember you well General. I have not seen you both since last year, at the funeral of our Lord Protector. What a sad day that was," said Peter, shaking Goffe's outstretched hand, red-faced and flushed after delivering one of his full blown sermons early in the morning.

"Yes, it was definitely a sad day. Now let us have breakfast before it gets cold and what a delight it is to see you again. I would, if I may, ask you, Mr Peter, to say grace for us," said Goffe, pleased to see one of their most important allies still full of passion.

"Of course, a pleasure," said Peter taking the offered seat and eying the sausages, smoked bacon, fried eggs, mushrooms, black pudding and tomato as if it was the Holy Grail itself.

"For what we are about to receive, may the Lord make us truly thankful, amen."

"Amen," said Whalley and Goffe.

"Mr Peter, what have you been up to since we last met?" said Goffe, as Peter started eating furiously and with evident delight.

"After being minister in Dunkirk and preaching in Flanders, I am back in England. Ahh, a fried tomato now that is interesting. I knew they were being grown in England and potatoes too."

He looked up. "I hope you both are not faltering in God's work," said Peter, eying the generals for their reaction.

"We're not," said Goffe. "But it seems that others are. Richard Cromwell has resigned and I have heard he is making preparations to leave for Europe. The fleet compter is full of Royalist sympathisers, the Government is paralysed, infighting and discord are pushing the one thing we fear the most," said Goffe, lowering his knife and folding his hands.

"And that could be the return of the Stuarts to England. You must kill all our enemies especially that lord, what's his name and then rally the New Model Army to the good old cause," said Peter, chewing on the home-smoked bacon.

"Belasyse, and a correct deduction; we must rally the troops!" said Goffe firmly.

"Right now it is only a chance that the monarchy could be restored, but that is one chance too many. We know what would happen to us all if that were to be the case," said Peter, staring at each general in turn. "We have known each other for, what, some fifteen years and like the good friends we are I have made some plans, in case things turn out for the worse. I have sent letters to trusted friends as to the present problems," said Peter, worried at the direction events round the country were taking.

"May I ask to whom they were sent," said Whalley.

"Certainly, John Davenport pastor to the colony of New Haven and Daniel Gookin. Just to alert them, as trusted men, to your persons, though they will have heard of your zeal in the cause of our Lord and the Commonwealth. Gookin is a captain in the military company of Massachusetts. He is knowledgeable as to the trade routes in the area and therefore its shipping. He is presently at Dunkirk as collector of customs, but I expect him to return to London due to the present uncertainty and he will contact you. He knows the settlements well, having lived there for many years."

"Thank you for your forward thinking, Mr Peter; let us hope it doesn't come to that," said Whalley. "And what of you? How is your wife Deliverance and daughter Elizabeth?"

Peter hesitated, knowing his wife's mental condition was deteriorating rapidly. "Both are well and living with me at my quarters in the Old Palace of Whitehall. Both send their affections. A fine breakfast, if I may say so," said Peter, changing the subject and wiping his plate clean with some crusty bread and devouring it with relish.

"Do tell me about the plantations, Mr Peter. I hear many strange tales and am fascinated. I see the potato, tomato fruit, corn and other fine foods that have been brought here, but I would like to know about its flora, fauna, animals and the natives. A strange land, it sounds so totally different to England," said Whalley, intrigued at Peter's knowledge and experience of places they had only heard of at the edge of the known world.

"That could take some time, but I will acquaint you with the basics," said Peter. "The journey across the ocean is a tedious journey of some eight to ten weeks, or longer, depending on the weather which is always variable, to the port of Boston."

"Near where the Pilgrim Fathers landed?" said Goffe.

"Correct. The principle settlements are Massachusetts and Connecticut, founded by our Puritan brethren some thirty years ago. Along with Virginia, but they are mainly Royalists."

Whalley digested the information.

"How many settlers are there?" he asked.

"There are about seventy five thousand, how many natives I do not know, though many die of smallpox to which they have no immunity and therefore few in number around the coastal settlements.

They are divided into tribes with names like the Massachuset, who gave the name to Massachusetts, the Natick who are praying natives, the tribe who are Christianised, Mohegan – the name means wolf and the Mohawk who have a strange haircut. Most speak a similar dialect based on Algonquian and live in buildings called a wigwam, made of tree bark and sapling wood. The tribes sometimes have clashes with the settlers or fight each other."

"Just like here," said Goffe.

Peter continued. "The outlying seas and inland rivers are a harvest for all. As to the land: bountiful. Venison to eat, hides to sell and turkeys in abundance. So many hares they are a pest. There is a basic thoroughfare called the Boston Post Road from New Amsterdam to Hartford and Springfield, towns in the interior, as well as to Boston in Massachusetts. It partly runs along the shoreline connecting the towns and villages along the way."

"Pray, tell me, what is a turkey?" said Goffe, intrigued, as both generals hung on his every word.

"It's like a chicken but about five times larger and it could comfortably feed a family of six. They roam at will and are easy to hunt; a gift," said Peter enthusiastically.

"A strange and interesting New World you have discovered," said Goffe. "I hope to hear more, Mr Peter, but duty calls. After all I think we all agree we are entering a crucial time for our country. One strong leader is required to pull the nation back from the brink."

"Will you not seek that position yourself?" asked Peter hopefully. "You are a great soldier; I remember your speech after the victory of Worcester, some eight years ago. The troops loved you for it and I am sure would support you in that quest," said Peter earnestly. He had a sinking feeling the nation was turning away from the good old cause and leaning slowly towards a return of the monarchy. A proposition which filled him with dread.

"I don't think I can," said Goffe. "I supported Richard Cromwell and ultimately he was not up to the task," he sighed. "No, the die is cast. We will see General Monck to ascertain his position and seek his dedication to the Commonwealth; after all, he has been loyal. Then rally the Army behind us. Good day to you, Mr Peter, and please do pray for us and our mission," said General Whalley as a goodbye, and went to retrieve his mount, knowing now that both of them had to risk everything to save their way of life. Peter waved him goodbye and turned to Goffe. "Your father-in-law is a good man, but lacks the instinct for what is to come. Kill that lord, find the members of the Sealed Knot and have them and their supporters executed before it is too late. You have little time," said Peter desperately.

"Leave it to me, Mr Peter, I can personally assure you Belasyse and his colleagues will suffer God's vengeance," said Goffe with a ruthless smile.

CHAPTER 4

A Strange Man

Belasyse just heard the gentle knock on the door, with its iron bolts and massive frame, keeping him securely contained in his cell. He was surprised; the jailer was usually as loud as possible for his own amusement, insulting his station, fine manners and cultured demeanour. He waited for the abuse to start. No visitors, not even his wife, as they would be followed by Thurloe's men. But all was quiet, strange. Belasyse looked into the peering hole, used by the guards to check the prisoner had not hung themselves. There stood a well-dressed man of some thirty-five years, with an educated look about him. He had dark blue eyes, long curly golden hair and a rather prominent nose.

"Baron Belasyse?" asked the stranger calculatingly.

"Who wants to know?" said Belasyse languidly, as if he had just finished a three-course meal and a bottle of fine French wine. "After all, if you have come to kill me that is unfortunate, as I have yet to fulfil all my worldly ambitions."

"And I wonder what those might be, Baron?" mused the stranger. "My name does not concern you, only my information. Oliver Cromwell is dead, his son Richard is the new Lord Protector, but has lost his grip on power. Stay calm and wait. I am doing all I can to protect you. Hopefully in time we will get to know each other but, as I am sure you know, trust is a precious commodity. I believe we are of the same mind as regards the throne, which, albeit empty, may one day be filled again," said the strange man, staring at Belasyse for any reaction, whilst pushing a small lemon, dried beef and a bread roll through the peering hole before leaving.

Cromwell dead, hallelujah! Amen, at long last the tyrant was no more. Wait... Richard Cromwell as Lord Protector? Now here was a decent man, not like his father running the country as a dictator. No, Richard Cromwell was a kindly sort, therefore would not last long, and who was the man with the news and how could he get a pass to see me? And he wants me to stay calm and wait; what the hell else was I going to do? Take my wife shopping for a new hat; go to the bloody theatre! All were closed down anyway. Horseracing, dancing, and taverns shut; the only damn thing that wasn't was the Tower of London, which is exactly where he was. Thoughts flowed through his head as he chewed on the dried beef. Uprisings and assassination attempts had come and gone, now nature had done its work and Cromwell was no more. The British did not suffer dictatorships; they argued over football games, laughed and loved, visited inns, went horseracing, danced around maypoles and enjoyed the theatre. They longed for this intolerance to end. As he sat by the fire, with its dancing yellow flames and the crackle of the burning wood, he started to carefully collect the lemon juice. The mysterious man was right; *bide your time, John, bide your time.* He finished the beef and pulled the bread in half, revealing six gold double crowns.

"Good Morning, your Majesty," said Edward Hyde, Lord Chancellor, knocking on the door and entering the King's lounge giving a short bow. "If I may have a moment of your time, sire," and cast a scornful eye on Barbara Palmer. The King rolled out of the couch he was sharing with his mistress, stretched and gave a carefree yawn.

"Most certainly. Any news from London?" he asked hopefully.

"Yes, sire, plenty," said Hyde, emphasising the words slowly whilst eying Palmer with distaste. The King should not involve himself in such frivolities.

"If I might ask for privacy in these matters, sire," said Hyde.

"Darling," said the King, "how about having your hair done. I seemed to have ruffled it, along with your clothes," he said with a wistful smile.

Barbara Palmer slowly raised herself from the couch and gave a sulky look as she left the room, ensuring the King got a good view of her silky smooth thighs. *I have him in the palm of my hand.*

Hyde waited until she had gone, closing the door behind her. *Arrogant tart!*

"As your Majesty knows, the death of Oliver Cromwell has left his son Richard as Lord Protector. I have received correspondence from Baron Belasyse, coded letters smuggled from the Tower, who writes thus – Richard Cromwell has resigned, daily the confrontations grow and the London apprentices are rioting, demanding the return of the King. There is widespread despair across the country; law and order is breaking down. He indicates there is now an opportunity for your restoration. If we are to convince the people to accept your Majesty's return, we must be seen as a viable alternative to the present dictatorship. Therefore it would be prudent that your Majesty and court move to Breda in the Dutch Republic. So as to show the people that your Majesty is living in a Protestant nation.

"Why so? I like France and I would point out that my mother the Queen is French and works daily to recruit an army to help my return."

"For the most practical reasons, sire. A king at the head of a French Catholic army would provoke the most savage reprisals against your supporters in England and would make the nation rise up as one. Belasyse points out such in his correspondence. Sire, England has a fear of Catholics ingrained in it since the Spanish Armada and the Gunpowder Plot; pamphlets have made them out to be the ultimate threat. We know, as educated men, that this is not true. Also, it would be the perfect excuse for the military to tighten its grip. The point is, this is how Catholics are seen, whether we like it or not. Many of your supporters back in England are adherents of that form of Christianity and we must perceive to be opponents of it."

"You're right, but as long as any man obeys the law and is loyal to me, I will not persecute him for his faith. As one of my predecessors said, I will not make a window into men's souls."

Hyde nodded in agreement. "The Republic has a vast military machine, sire. It will not be an armed return, but by the wishes of Parliament and the people of England," said Hyde, counselling the young King.

"So be it," said the King. "Let us go to the town of Breda, but carefully. I don't want the French authorities knowing; after all, King Louis thinks I will be in his debt permanently. Now, what we can offer the people as an alternative to the present system? Tonight, Lord Chancellor, let us dine alone and think, what does England want and need, to settle once and for all the peace and tranquillity of my realm across the sea?" said the King in all sincerity.

"Certainly, sire," said Hyde as a goodbye.

The King had come a long way, hardened by exile, but mercifully educated by it. These long years abroad have made him open his mind to European ideas and made him flexible in thought and deed. He will need all those skills if he is to return and rule with wisdom, thought Hyde.

"Barbara," said the King, opening the door to his dressing room. "I have some three hours to kill before a most important meeting; what can you think of to occupy my time until then?"

"How about a game of tennis, Charles? It's good for you to maintain your body."

"I couldn't agree more," said the King, looking at her violet-blue eyes and undoing the cords of her gown revealing a voluptuous alabaster body. "You're right; a man must keep fit and I have an excellent way of practising it," said Charles with a grin.

"Sire, what plans do you have?" said Hyde, as a servant, the only one they could afford, poured wine, a fruity one, from Carcassonne in Southwestern France. Dinner was cured Bayonne ham with figs, veal in mushroom sauce with roasted onions, sautéed spinach and something new, potatoes, cooked in olive oil and rosemary; all the rage in Europe at the moment. King Charles sat uncomfortably in a small chair, too modest for his size, as thoughts and ideas flowed through his head. Exploring every option he could think of to bring a settlement to his divided people. Hyde sat back; *take your time young man, take your time. We have waited nine long years and this could be the defining moment.* He admired the King, his worn clothes denoting his penury and he had never doubted he would return. But most importantly he had a steady eye due to the desperate days of being hunted after the battle of Worcester. Hyde remembered when Charles had attempted to regain his throne through Scotland, some eight years ago. All the dreams of marching to London to secure his Crown had ended up in an undignified flight from the lost battle. Hunted by the Parliamentary Army, he had ended up hiding in an oak tree. But had learnt some valuable lessons – fear, hunger and poverty – and therefore could understand what his people had been through. The great publicity across Europe was invaluable, no matter how much the reward was for his life, no one had betrayed him, and many were pleased that their King was safe, it had given him a taste of real life few monarchs had had.

"Chancellor," said the King, "I have some ideas. General Monck has the most powerful army in the nation and is trusted by all. Especially as to his principle that the Government should be by Parliament and not the Army. He is the man we should look to. We must contact him, a third party, asking would he support our return. As much as he fought for Parliament, it is because he was forced to do so. He is a servant of the state, not himself; after all, he first fought for my father. Ask him for advice and ensure he will be well rewarded upon our return. Please think on this. I must also produce a declaration for all in my Kingdom; write this down."

"I, Charles Stuart, King of England, Scotland, Wales and Ireland, defender of the faith. To all our loving subjects of what degree so ever. We extend our warm greetings to you all. I do declare it is my will that the peoples of the nation will dwell under my reign in tolerance and benevolence. It is time to heal our divisions. The general distraction and confusion which is spread over the entire nation extends the blood and suffering we have all shared. We only desire to have what is rightfully ours and that all our subjects may enjoy what is theirs, by law and by right. By extending our mercy where it is deserved and required. To those whom may fear our return, we offer a free and general pardon to all (except those excepted by Parliament) and that Parliament is fully supported by the Crown. We offer liberty to tender consciences and will not pursue anyone as of matters pertaining to religion. As to the purchases of property made during our absence, we shall not force any man from his house and shall have any dispute determined by a magistrate or Parliament. The army will receive its outstanding pay in full and may have liberty to return home to their loved ones. All members of the army of General Monk shall be taken on in my service under their present terms and conditions."

Hyde was shaking, tears in his eyes. "Praise be to God for giving you such wisdom, your Majesty. I shall have this written up on the morrow and send a copy post haste, via our friends, to General Monck, then the Speaker of the House of Commons and therefore the whole of your realm. They will see your qualities of mercy and justice," said Hyde.

"I ask for the peaceful transition of power to the king, House of Lords and the House of Commons. We will have only one chance; let us not overplay our hand. There is one point, though," the King said in a low menacing tone. "Remember, apart from those exempted by Parliament."

Belasyse examined the wall of the Beauchamp Tower. *How many people had thought of their fate here? The first prisoner had been over five hundred years ago. There had been earls, dukes and knights of the realm like himself, even King David of Scotland and Queen Anne Boleyn. Some had died, some had gone free on the promise of a ransom, and many had been executed. The King was in exile in France, nearly penniless, and those who had wealth and position seldom made good beggars.* He stirred the fire and added a log, noting the names carved on the wall by the previous prisoners. *They were persecuted like me; let they and the Lord be witness to my suffering*, as the pain from the beating the guards had given him throbbed across his badly bruised back. The beautifully carved inscriptions and statements in Latin told him many of the prisoners kept here were Catholics and the dates told him the reign of good Queen Bess was the time. Although he suspected they called her something else! It had come to this, hunted down for his activities in the Sealed Knot, captured, fined and beaten. Now a close prisoner in the Tower. There was not going to be a trial for him. A hangman's noose and the short drop is what's coming and he stared at the fire; *be strong and resolute in what you believe. Oh god how I miss my wife, her cheerful hallo, gorgeous and soft black hair smelling of herbs, classic roasted beef with red wine, a roaring fire in winter to welcome him home and then as cuddled-up lovers in his ornate four poster bed. The children and their games, teaching them how to ride a horse and their first painting for him. Van Dyke, the celebrated court painter, could not better their efforts.* Tears sprang from his eyes; would he ever see them again?

Clang went the bolt in the door. The jingle of at least a dozen keys told him it was the beginning of a new day. Into the unoiled lock went the key and curses, as the jailer fought to open the door. "Up, Royalist scum." Down the circular stairs to the base of the Beauchamp Tower, across the small green to the chapel of St. Peter ad Vincula, prayers and a long Puritan service. A jog to the Salt Tower where his father's hero, the Jesuit priest John Gerard, had escaped from. The Wakefield Tower, past the ravens hoping for scraps, Mint Street for bread, small beer and mutton. How many secrets did the Tower hold? *First and foremost a prison and I wonder if I am next to die in this forbidding place.* He thought and carefully placed a piece of very tightly wrapped paper into the hollow heel of his right boot and left it by the door for cleaning.

"Belasyse, you upper crust dog, the Governor wants you," said the duty guard, a snarl on his unshaven face and menace in his eyes. Down the circular staircase and over to the Tudor house.

Knock on the door, open, halberdier at the ready, "Sit down here. Name the agents of Charles Stuart and you can go free, you have our word," and in spite of regular beatings, threats and starvation, nothing was going to induce him to talk, nothing.

"Whilst some of our enemies have not been taken, we have you and we will catch the remaining members of the Sealed Knot, let me assure you of that. You seem thinner today, Belasyse; been on a diet, have we?" asked John Barkstead, Governor of the Tower.

"Your humour is like your manhood, tired out and flabby," said Belasyse.

Barkstead struck Belasyse. "Get out! You're lucky; I'd hang you myself, but someone else has got there first," he said with a grin. "Sergeant Jailer, escort this garbage to Traitors' Gate, hire a skiff and take him to the Scotland Yard guard house where Daniel Axtell has a special reception waiting for him," he added with a sneer, slamming the door. Four halberdiers with the duty sergeant marched their prisoner to the exit by Traitors' Gate. *I hope one day to have the regicides here like Barkstead and I will be there to greet them with a blunt axe*, Belasyse thought.

"Baron Belasyse, I see you are off for a just punishment as a spy and traitor to the Commonwealth. Not a fitting end for so fine a soldier. I am sorry it has to end this way. A glorious death in battle would have more suitable than the hangman's noose."

"I do not recall you, sir," said Belasyse, examining the Republican officer.

"I am General Goffe; we fought each other several times in the late conflict."

"I thank you for such sentiments. I would have assumed that if you considered me a gentleman and a fine soldier you would have at least given me the honour of the headman's axe. Any decent officer would have done that," said Belasyse, looking down on Goffe.

"You're a spy and you will get justice as the Republic demands and God wills it," shouted Goffe.

"That sums you up. God wills it; how many crimes have been committed with those words? The name of God has been used to commit the worst of wars, murders and brutality in history. Christ preached compassion and peace. So, who you follow is a mystery to me."

Goffe went red with embarrassment and shame in front of the guard. "Damn you to hell. I will have the pleasure of escorting you to Whitehall myself," said Goffe in a fit of pique.

"Do so. Though why are you here? Maybe to deal with the Governor about his stealing from the prisoners and obtaining money from their families on the promise of good treatment, or are you waiting for your cut? I wonder," said Belasyse. Goffe gave him a look of pure hate, but said nothing. *The rats are killing off all the enemies they can lay their hands on.* He had heard from the troops quartered in the Tower, as well as his unknown visitor, that the Republic was falling and they wanted to clear the decks for a new civil war to justify their tyranny. The guard marched to Traitors' Gate, down the steps and onto the waiting skiff, the Sergeant Jailer watching his every move. He thought about jumping into the Thames and the Sergeant said it aloud, "Don't even think of it, or I'll drop you as I did so many at Marston Moor, Naseby and Worcester," and off went the skiff on the turning tide, the waterman carefully guiding his craft up river to the palace of Whitehall, now quartering soldiers and officials running the Republic. The royal family long gone. Gingerly, he guided his craft into the middle of the river, his oars expertly foaming the water as they moved up the Thames. Slowly, the waterman manoeuvred his craft towards the middle of London Bridge, sweat popping from his head even on this cold winter's day.

"Why don't you row up the side of the bank?" asked Belasyse. "It must be a lot easier than fighting to get us into the middle of the Thames."

"Simple," said the waterman. "On the north bank, by the church of St. Magnus the Martyr, there is a latrine on the bridge. It has some three hundred seats; want to be crapped or pissed on before you get to Whitehall?" he asked. "Also there are two waterwheels driving pumps on the north side and two on the south side driving grain mills. This creates major water disturbance. The craft could capsize and sink; can any of you swim?" They all shook their heads. "In the middle there is a defensive drawbridge. It has the largest gap amongst the twenty arches with no houses on it, so we won't be used as target practice by children throwing household garbage at us. When the tide turns, we have around an hour when the water is stable on both sides of the bridge, otherwise it can be up to a six foot drop on either side. Only idiots shoot the bridge and many have died trying. See that house with the onion towers? It's called Nonsuch House. We go to the left, past the starlings and under. If we crash, here is a three-headed anchor; throw it onto the starling and pull yourself up," the waterman said, knowing they were in his hands completely.

"How long did it take you to learn all this?" said Belasyse impressed.

"It's a seven-year apprenticeship. All watermen have to do this before we can take fares."

Belasyse winked his right eye looking at the waterman and then his foot, whilst lifting his shoe a few inches, ensuring the waterman caught his movements.

"Look behind you, some fifteen waiting for the tide and I am still learning. You can't always predict tides, rivers or anything else for that matter," he said, whilst nodding slowly at Belasyse. The group looked behind and there was a multitude of boats waiting for the moment. One caught Belasyse's eye; there was a man with long curly hair and a prominent nose sitting at the prow of the vessel. Wait a minute wasn't he the man who...

"Hold on tight," shouted the waterman and off they went through the starlings in a flash, assured of their waterman's quality.

"Here we are, Scotland dock by the wharf at Whitehall Palace and that's a shilling and tuppence."

"A shilling and tuppence!" exclaimed Goffe.

"Correct, two pence per person and there are seven of you."

"I am a general of the Republic and have hitched a lift to Whitehall, that's all," snapped Goffe. "Give him sixpence and count yourself lucky I don't have you arrested for your insolence!"

The Sergeant Jailer tossed him a coin, sorry that Goffe was being parsimonious to the ferryman.

"Thank you; a very interesting journey," said Belasyse. "May I ask your name?"

"Joseph Kellogg, sir," said the waterman, winking very slowly with his left eye and furious that he was short-changed and had no return fare.

The escort marched through Scotland Yard to the open court and the guard house, halberds pointing at Belasyse's back to remind him who was in charge.

"Please sign this document for the prisoner, sir," said the sergeant yeoman jailer.

"General, sir, very good to see you again. May I be of assistance?" said Axtell, looking contemptuously at Belasyse whilst signing the execution warrant.

"Yes you can, Colonel; when this rubbish is to be hung give him the short drop so the devil can enjoy the struggle for his soul," said Goffe.

"Yes, sir, it will be my pleasure," said Axtell with a smirk. *What fun this will be*, and he opened the lock on the door to the guard house and pushed Belasyse into a large wooden chair with a pattern of vegetables cut into the base and spectacular carvings of angels on its back. *Looted from the palace so a guard could loll in it.* Axtell attached a metal cuff to him which was bolted to the back of the chair, then a chain and snapped it shut and cuffed him around the back of his head. "I'll hang you myself with an audience of my good friends just like I did at Meelick in Ireland to the papist scum there," said Axtell, laughing in Belasyse's face and slamming the door behind him.

A quick death is all a soldier can hope for, not dangling for ten minutes on the end of a rope being laughed at by a group of fanatics. A few minutes passed as he fought with the chain wrapped around his neck, no luck, then the door was unlocked again and in walked a man dressed in brown britches, a scarlet jacket, iron chest plate and lobster tail helmet. Classic New Model Army officer's clothing. *Just checking the afternoon's entertainment*, but there was something familiar about him. He had long hair under the helmet; did not the Roundheads have short locks and a cut backside? He had a prominent nose and a sack over his shoulder. The stranger put a finger to his lips and walked over to the chair and withdrew a small box from his pocket, along with a glass tube.

"Say nothing. The guards are having ale and beef pie for their lunch; I have to be quick. Colonel Axtell will be rounding up his friends shortly."

The stranger poured oil from the glass tube into the lock and took a hair grip and a small metal file from the box and slowly inserted them, trying to find the levers inside, and picked the lock.

"Here are new clothes and your twin barrelled pistols – they're loaded. In the sack there is water, razor and soap. Do you still have the gold crowns I gave you?" said the stranger.

"Yes, three; I used two for food and lemons in the Tower, one more as a gift," said Belasyse, amazed at the turn of events.

"Good, they will be enough. Now here is the plan. Wash, shave, dress and cut your hair, especially that love lock, it smacks of a Royalist. Here is a map of your route out of Whitehall Palace. There is a side door," said the stranger, motioning to a pile of empty crates and ripped curtains in the far left-hand corner of the guard room. "Here," he lifted up the old curtains revealing a very small door used for bringing in coal and wood for the stove in winter. "I've unlocked it. There is a little alley which leads to the other half of the courtyard; turn right and walk straight ahead after locking the door behind you. The Banqueting House will be on your left and in front of you will be the palace gate; this leads to Whitehall. Don't go exploring – there are some one thousand five hundred rooms and you could get lost. Here are three passes; you will need them. The first is to exit the palace. You must hand it to the duty officer. This pass is to exit London and this one is to travel to Lincolnshire, all in the name of Colonel Stulte Vale."

"Ha Ha. Good one. I hope the guards can't read Latin. I owe you and I always keep my promises. I won't ask who you are or why you do this," said Belasyse.

"Now here is the bad news," said the stranger, taking Belasyse's old clothes. "You will find several letters in the sack confirming you and your colleagues as members of the Sealed Knot, along with your plans. How I came by these does not concern you, what does is one of your members, Sir Richard

Willis, is a traitor. The documents will prove it. Inform all other members their lives are in great danger." Belasyse was shocked, rooted to the spot.

"I know, I am truly sorry, trust is a precious commodity," said the stranger as he left, unlocking the main door, then bolting and locking it from the other side.

Belasyse cut his hair and washed quickly; no time to dwell on the momentous events. Willis a traitor; that explained a lot. How come he was caught red-handed with fifty pounds of gunpowder, trying to kill the Army council? He dressed in the New Model Army uniform the stranger had brought, noting with amazement the passes had been signed by Thurloe himself in blue black ink. Who was this man, and how had he acquired the intelligence of his whereabouts and obtained the passes? He must be at the highest level. *It doesn't matter, get on and get out of here.* He checked the sword and pistols. Just as the stranger said, loaded. He covered himself in the old curtains so as not to dirty his uniform and squeezed through the small door, bringing down some crates behind him and locking it. Down the alley he went and turned right, there was the palace gate, straight ahead as the map showed. He marched smartly up to the barrier and took a deep breath.

CHAPTER 5

A Faraway Land

"'Tis a fine morning, sir," said Richard Sperry, farmer and select man cheerfully.

"That it is," replied John Davenport, first pastor of the Independent Plantation of New Haven, as he made his rounds. "I see you are having a good harvest of fruit this year. Plenty for your family, storage and some for planting and a beehive. Wise of you with no honeybees in this land; pollination and honey is a good combination. I am impressed with your industry and innovation, sir."

"Aye it is so, and thank you, sir," said Sperry. "The land is fair and I have some one hundred and twenty acres, a house for my family and I to live in, which we own and thanks be to God. Also we are free of that damn Archbishop Laud and his King."

"Why do you hate them so?" asked Davenport, interested in hearing one of his supporter's views.

"Why?" barked Sperry, his face reddening as he removed his hat with its rim of sweat, ingrained with months of grime and dust. "Look at my ears, sir. He had them clipped because I refused to go to a Church of England service and grazed my sheep on common land. A right we English have had for a thousand years. Now we cannot, or we pay a fine like the one my ears paid. That is why, Mr Davenport sir!" said Sperry, then realising he had shouted at the most prominent minister in the settlement. Sperry should not have worried; Davenport knew he had a loyal adherent – they both disliked bells, smells, bishops and kings. *We Puritans deal directly with God, not through a rich royal appointee*, thought Davenport. He was pleased; the settlement was far from London and the power of the Crown, especially the Archbishop of Canterbury with his popish relics and Book of Common Prayer, the work of the devil. Here, along with the towns of Milford, Guilford, Branford, even Southold on the Long Island, they had done well. This was Independent New Haven, not part of their neighbour Connecticut. The King of England and his officials had often complained about the governance of the plantations, but his colleagues back in England had dealt with that problem permanently. As he walked to the meeting house, the river lapped contentedly at the edge of the town green. With its four wells, cattle and sheep grazed at the river's side; there was plenty of fresh water and grass. The militia practised their musket and pike drill on the green, as required, six times a year. Back in England notable men and their families were thinking of joining him. Oliver Cromwell nearly had, but now he was England's Lord Protector and had much to do securing the Republic there. Here was a place a man could work his own land, not for a lord or upstart friend of a bishop, who had bought his title by the work of others. Now, time to see the Governor of New Haven and hear the latest news of their brave new world. He had built his city upon a hill.

"Good morning and God's blessings upon you John; are you well?" said Francis Newman, Governor.

"I am, thanks be to God. Now we should discuss the latest news with the council," replied John Davenport briskly.

"Certainly, I will acquaint you with my visit to, as you would say, the lax town of Boston and it's less than godly ways," said Newman guardedly.

"It is so and you know it to be true," said Davenport firmly. "We and seventy proprietors founded this God-fearing settlement, as the Commonwealth of Massachusetts had fallen behind on its baptisms and other duties.

Ever since we met in your brother Robert's barn, some twenty years ago, to compare views and settle upon a plan of civil government according to the word of God, this has been a town true to the laws of our blessed Lord. Unlike Boston, which I hear has slipped from its true beginnings, with its free and easy baptisms and houses of ill repute, amongst other undesirable happenings," said Davenport.

Newman did not need reminding why they had broken away, but he was facing reality. New Haven was being overtaken by Boston and Dutch New Amsterdam. The plan of dealing with England on their own terms had failed; they had no charter. Davenport's intense religious views had put off many who may have settled here. The native supply of beaver, deer and other animals was being brought up by other settlements and diminishing anyway. The agricultural and other products of the colony were barely enough to pay its way. Questions were being raised about their leadership. A total of £36,000 had been brought in to invest. The largest sum by far in New England and they had to make it pay. Not only that, the French had intentions on Canada, or Dutch claims to Greenwich and Saybrook. Disagreements with Connecticut over land boundaries could be settled at a local level or adjudicated in London. With foreign nations, it could develop into something far more serious.

"The council is next door and we should join them and explain the latest developments as to our trade and other issues," said Newman. They opened the door to the main chamber which, albeit only twenty years old, had been raised in such haste it was constantly needing repairs.

"Good morning everyone and God's blessings on you and your households, may this council be in session on the 7th of November in the year of our Lord 1658. Present is William Andrews, John Clarke, Matthew Gilbert, Thomas Kimberley and Robert Newman as the seven pillars of the church. All the rest of the freemen and full church members are about the harvest of fruit and preparing winter food supplies and you speak for them," said Governor Newman.

"Yes we do, sir," they all replied, hoping that after the meeting Davenport's monthly preaching would not last the whole morning.

"I have visited Boston for the following reasons: to ascertain the trading positions of our settlement, and to obtain a supply of coinage. I know we all have a need for more effective trade and therefore look into our application for a charter from London, as well as fending off land claims from Connecticut." Newman stopped. The clatter of hooves disturbed the morning air, a sense of urgency in their noise.

"I must speak with the governor immediately," shouted William Leate to Davenport's wife, almost jumping off his horse and charging up the steps of the Davenport house on Elm Street, looking haggard from a long ride.

"Why, you need a clear head, Mr Leate, if you are to make sense," said Elizabeth Woolly, who was preparing refreshments for the council members. "At present he is in conference with the council," she said, noting Leate's urgency and hoping it was not a native attack.

"So be it. A tankard of ale if I may, Goodwife Elizabeth," he said as his body heaved with exertion. "I have ridden the one hundred and forty miles from Boston in great haste."

"Now take a seat, catch your breath and sup on this fine first brew I have made. Whatever you have to say will come from lips that are steady and only the good Lord could provide." She knew William Leate from Guilford, magistrate and deputy governor, a man not given to panic, which she sensed in his demeanour as he gulped down the refreshing home-brewed ale.

The door of the meeting house opened slowly, almost painfully. The roof was leaking even though Thomas Yale had covered it with sail cloth.

"Ah," said Davenport, spotting Leate's horse tied to the rail on the front porch of his house, its belly heaving and frothing at the mouth, having been ridden hard all morning.

"Praise be to the Lord, and why so dishevelled? What is the reason for such haste?" said Davenport as he joined Leate, noticing his unshaven face and sweat popping from his brow on the cold November morning.

"I have ridden hard from Boston," explained Leate. "It is the devil's work; I must speak with you and Mr Newman immediately, on a matter of the utmost importance."

They all moved into the parlour, sensing the urgency on Leate's face.

"Sirs, I carry dreadful news. Oliver Cromwell our Lord Protector has died."

Davenport stood rooted to the spot, colour draining from his face. "No! These are false words, sir!"

"Sirs, the news has arrived in Boston. I have the letters from the Fairbanks tavern. The commonwealth is threatened," said Leate.

Davenport thought quickly. They didn't need this. Who would buy their produce? Beaver fur hats were the height of fashion in Europe; upset this trade and the colony may fail and many would like that. Oliver Cromwell had been a firm supporter of New Haven and a political ally.

"Mr Leate," said Davenport in a low voice, not wishing to disturb anyone with the news before he had a chance to digest it. "How is the Commonwealth of New England threatened?"

"Oliver Cromwell's eldest son Richard is the new Lord Protector. Oliver was a great leader of men and, as we know, strong-willed. He had to be and Richard hasn't got the backbone, therefore he will not last long. What if the dead King's eldest son Charles returned to England with his Catholic brother James? Would they not look for revenge on those who sent his father to the scaffold and supported the Republic? How many colonialists returned across the ocean to fight alongside Cromwell? This will be noted if they return," said

Leate, worry written all over his unshaven face.

"'Tis simple, sir. He won't return. The people don't want him and neither do we. He has neither the Army, Navy nor the finance. They are in exile in papist France with their stupid pointy bread and snails. I mean, who eats snails?" said Davenport in exasperation.

"Good point, John," said Governor Newman, thinking carefully. "I think it would be wise if I return to Boston and meet with Governor John Endicott as to the situation in England as regards these developments. We should address the council to prevent this news slowly leaking out."

They left Davenport's house and returned to the council meeting, concern in every step. Davenport worried, if there was to be a civil war again, many would return to England as they had before and this would see another weakening of their strength. If the natives were to sense this, there may be trouble. He saw the King as a tragic figure, making up laws as he wished, like the hated ship money and Court of the Star Chamber, along with his belief that God had appointed him to rule. These and other calamities had caused the civil wars in England. The execution of the King and rule by the Army had seen the Puritans in the ascendancy, but all that could change if Leate was right, and he had no reason to doubt him. Massachusetts, Connecticut and New Haven had done much to help the Republic and without Cromwell's protection, there could be trouble ahead. He had settled in New Haven to create a Christian utopia, where the church would be the force to hold the community together, not the rule of a hereditary King or his personally appointed bishops. *Over five hundred people resided in the colony. Life was mostly far better across the ocean, less disease too and no plague; amen,* he thought. *But maybe there was an opportunity; if all of New England declared itself independent, who could stop them?* As he walked home a plan began to form in his mind.

He opened the front door and entered the parlour, hoping his wife had cooked his and his son John's favourite dish of rabbit stew, corn and fried greens.

"Hallo dearest. The meeting is over and I hope all is well," said Davenport, sniffing the air for rabbit stew.

"Just one thing," said Elizabeth smiling, knowing she had cooked her husband his favourite dish. "You know there has been much agitation in England these past years, which is the main reason we left. I hear from friends in Boston that the preacher Hugh Peter wishes to return and visit us here in New Haven; 'tis best that we refuse him. He breathes fire and brimstone like the devil himself. He should stay in England and leave us to our prayers in peace."

Davenport winced; he knew Elizabeth was right. Hugh Peter was trouble, he liked to have a good argument, but would often take it too far and he had celebrated the republican victory in the Battle of the Severn some four years ago. In Maryland, long after the wars in England were over, around fifty men had died in the clash and what was worse, four of the King's supporters had been brutally put to death after they had surrendered, contrary to the rules of war; this may have repercussions if the monarchy returned.

"What have you discussed with the council?" said Elizabeth, always interested in the settlement's progress.

"I have just read letters from Boston and you should sit down," said Davenport softly.

Elizabeth hesitated as she saw the look of worry on her husband's face. She knew him to be a strict minister, who would not compromise over his beliefs. He felt that would loosen the Church's grip and this had made him enemies and stunted the settlement's growth, but it made him formidable; something was up.

"Oliver Cromwell has died and his son Richard succeeded him as Lord Protector. Daniel Gookin writes he is a kindly sort who lacks his father's political skills and will be pushed aside. All are uncertain about the future, therefore could seek sanctuary here. We must be cautious, for revenge has no boundaries," said Davenport.

"We are a faraway land," said Elizabeth, "and we don't even cause a ripple. Now let us concentrate on more important issues. I have the list you wanted. In one week we must organise forty turkeys, ten deer, one hundred pounds of squash, the same of maize, potatoes and cranberries for the dressing, not to mention the pumpkin pie."

Davenport smiled. Yes, Thanksgiving. It was becoming a fixture in New England. A form of harvest festival, every November, to thank God for the deliverance from starvation. First celebrated in 1621 up the coast in Plymouth, Massachusetts. He was told the interesting story by Gookin. After the first harvest, the brother pilgrims had invited the local natives to share the Lord's bounty of this land. They arrived, some ninety of them, mostly braves, to meet these strange folk. With their dark clothes, a musket in one hand and on their day of worship, a book in the other. The chief or Sachem Massasoit and his translator Squanto, asked some of the braves to go out and hunt as there were more guests than expected. They returned with five deer and some turkeys which were spit-roasted by the four remaining women and their servants over iron jacks. The natives were impressed and for three days they feasted and entertained each other with martial skills and gifts. A celebration which was becoming an annual event in New England, he could indulge himself a little. Elizabeth was right; *we are a faraway land, no one will trouble us here.*

CHAPTER 6

Daddy's Home

"George, so good to see you again," said Nicholas Monck excitedly. "How are you and my dear daughter Susannah?"

"She is very well and excited about the forthcoming marriage. She is presently with my wife in Edinburgh visiting friends. I am fine, although a little worried as to the machinations down in London," said General George Monck. "Still, how is Windsor and Eton school? I hope not too close to the capital to be involved in the calamities that affect our nation. Where are my manners? Come hither. You have not changed a bit, it's been years. Still the same young Nicholas, dancing blue eyes, always well shaven and the curate's kindly smile, with charity for all, but none for yourself. God is lucky to have you on his staff! Come to the withdrawing room; it must have been a long journey to Scotland. Warm yourself by the fire, it is well below freezing outside; a mini ice age some Oxford don has said. How about a glass of sack to warm you up? I will have my steward prepare your room," said George Monck, pleased to see his brother after so many difficult years.

"The school is still open," said Nicholas, glad of a comfortable chair, a good lunch and the roaring fire. "But there are Republican officials who check what we teach and usually an armed musketeer on my door. As the provost, I must be doubly careful, as I set the curriculum. We fear the soldiery, George; the whole nation does. You have your intelligence systems, you are well aware of what is happening. Parliament had dismissed Lambert who, in turn, has dismissed Parliament. Just like Cromwell did when they didn't do his bidding. Edward Whalley is seen as Lambert's replacement; another general running the country?" asked Nicholas Monck, worry written all over his face.

"I only follow orders, Nicholas," said George Monck, taken aback at his brother's sense of despair. "And who gives the orders? We can't go on like this. The nation groans under taxation, repression and the depredations of the Army weigh heavily on the people. But let me tell you a story of yesteryear," said Nicholas Monck. "Do you remember some thirty years ago, when our father was dying? We all gathered at home. Mother was crying; we two brothers realising that the link which kept us leading a good, honest and sober life was to be broken. I honestly don't think we realised at the time how important our father was. Providing good sound advice, avoiding mistakes, working to a goal, thrift, love and reverence for our mother. Our father was central to our lives."

George Monck nodded in agreement, knowing how much they had relied on their father all those years ago; it seemed like another world then. Only four people could use a mortar cannon. England had not been at war seriously since the Spanish Armada, over fifty years before, and they had not landed. How had we come to this state of affairs?

"On his death bed he told us a story," said Nicholas. "'To you, my family, I have bequeathed my estate in equal portions; look after your mother, George and Nicholas. We live in quiet and serene times, but you must prepare yourselves for stormy and troublesome ones. I command you, as your father, to honour and obey your sovereign and, though the Crown may hang upon a bush, I charge you forsake it not, for it is the soul of England.'"

George Monck sighed deeply. "You're right, this has to stop."

Then he looked up and stared at his brother. "I would suspect, Nicholas, you have come for your daughter and perhaps another reason?"

"You always were perceptive, George. I have a letter, direct from the King, unopened," said Nicholas, taking the heavy vellum envelope from his curate's cloak.

"That is unwise, even foolhardy, Nicholas. It could cost you. Best to go back to your books," said George Monck, straightening up and looking every inch the general in command.

"It will cost the people a lot more if I hadn't," said Nicholas, a sad look on his face. "I want this nightmare to end; we all do. May God grant you the wisdom of Job, my beloved brother."

With that, he left the general's headquarters to see his daughter.

George Monck undid the purple ribbon on the letter, noting the royal seal in red wax and broke it open. It was handwritten by the King himself.

General Monck,

I ask you, in the name of peace and humanity, to recall all members of Parliament to settle the affairs once and for all, of our great nation. I will ensure that you are amply rewarded for your discretion and loyalty in this matter. I would be delighted to appoint you a knight of the realm and land to substantiate it, along with the sum of one hundred thousand pounds per annum to ensure your comfort.

Signed Charles Rex.

Monck paced the room like a locked cat. Then he stopped, peered into the fire as if seeking inspiration, and threw the letter into it. As it burst into flames he smiled, sat down and wrote.

To Edward Montague of the Commonwealth Navy, Chatham in the county of Kent.

Edward,

I hope all is well at Chatham and you and your family are in good health. The correspondence you have been having with our mutual friend has born the finest fruit. I have some very good news...

"Wake up, Corporal! I'm due at General Lambert's headquarters and it's a long way to Newcastle," barked Belasyse to the slouching guard.

"Yes, sir. Sorry, sir," said the corporal, putting his pipe in his pocket. "May I have your pass, sir?"

The guard noted the Commonwealth Harp and Colonel Stulti Vale written in blue black ink. *That man had a sense of humour*, thought Belasyse; it was getting to him, who was his unknown benefactor? A rat leaving the sinking ship? We need one man with the status to combine loyalty and obedience, and stop further bloodshed and he knew exactly who that should be. He must leave London, get a carriage to Lincolnshire and see his wife and children, then seek out Villiers and Russell. Have a conference and make a plan for the restoration of King Charles the Second. That is, if the passes were valid, his family was still alive and Villiers and Russell were not in prison or dead. So much to do and hope for. Belasyse stared straight into the corporal's eyes; that usually did it and he was not wrong.

"Thank you, sir; you may pass," said the corporal, saluting.

Belasyse walked out of the palace gate, noting the lolling soldiers smoking tobacco and drinking in small groups. *Leaderless*, he thought. *Good, but where are their leaders? I wonder, it seems that some of our birds have flown.* He walked ahead to the entrance of the tilt yard, turned around and looked up. There was the Banqueting House. Ten years ago, more, here stood the scaffold where the King was executed. "I have not forgotten. I have not forgotten at all," Belasyse said half aloud. Then he turned left through the next gate to the street beyond and walked down into the privy garden, now used to graze horses and keep chickens. Belasyse crossed the garden and in the far corner entered the stone gallery with its crenulations at the top of the walls for defensive firing, to the Bowling Green, hopefully to get a skiff to the City and a stagecoach to Lincolnshire.

"Good to see you have had a shave and a change of clothes, sir," said Kellogg cheerfully, whilst sitting on the seat in his narrow boat.

"You know something, I am really glad to see you," said Belasyse happily.

"For a gold crown, I definitely want your custom again and thought, I wonder how long it will be until that gentleman escapes," and Kellogg gave a broad smile. They both laughed.

"Where to, sir?"

"I need to get to Lincolnshire."

"I'll row you down river to Wapping and you alight. There are plenty of fishing smacks plying their trade from that area. All the roads and gates are guarded night and day. That is the best and safest way, with the least questions asked. I will speak with a sea captain I know; he is not above moving unusual cargos about and has many a hiding place on his ship."

"I won't forget this. You mentioned work is tight. I have a ferry concession between the towns of Hull and Grimsby on the river Humber. It's yours if you want and you can keep all the fares for yourself," he said, relieved at the ferryman's knowledge, help and foresight.

"I'll take you up on that; there is too much competition here to make a good living nowadays."

"Good. Ask for me in Worlaby, Lincolnshire. My name is Baron John Belasyse and here is another crown for your journey," tossing Kellogg a golden coin and off they went on the afternoon tide.

"On this day, the first of May, in the year of our Lord 1660, I, the Speaker of the House of Commons, have a declaration from Charles Stuart, addressed to the honourable members assembled here. We, the freely elected Parliament, must think deeply how this country is to be governed."

The newly elected chamber listened with bated breath and the members looked at each other in agreement; could they not find a settlement to the issues that were tearing the nation apart? Not an inch of space was to be had, as all had gathered to hear and see history being made. The house stood, bare-headed, with not a sound to be heard, as the declaration from the King was to be read out. Lenthal thought, as *General Monck commands the most powerful army in the nation and it was billeted in London for the preservation of law and order.* With most of the fanatical Republican generals under armed guard, he was free to speak his mind.

"I present a bill to this house. That the constitution of England lies within the King, the Houses of Commons and Lords. An Act of Free and General Pardon, Indemnity and Oblivion, confirms our lives, estates and possessions. Now is the time to heal our divisions and therefore I ask this Parliament to vote on a bill, offering the Crown to Charles Stuart, that he may return to England and take up the reins of government. Let the house divide," said the Speaker, banging his hammer on the division table with evident relish, glad to be so prominent at this famous occasion.

The members went to vote, nervously eying each other on this momentous day. As they exited the voting booths, the sense of relief was incredible, as if they had confessed their sins to God himself and he had forgiven them.

"Here is the count, sir," said the head teller, handing a note to the Speaker without a trace of emotion.

Every member stared at the man with the woolsack upon

his head, clad in a long black cloak, a white silk band around his neck, black britches and golden cuffs, denoting the gravity of his office. He stood in front of his chair, tension so thick you would need an axe to cut it; men's hearts fluttered and pumped.

"As to the vote on the motion, the eyes to the left, none, eyes to the right five hundred and..."

The outbreak of cheering swamped his words. The chamber exploded in rapture; shouts of joy were heard all over the Palace of Westminster. The powerful Republican Earl of Shaftsbury agreed with the motion. Even Luke Robinson the fanatic, stood up crying, recanting all his past views on the monarchy and promised in future to obey the statues and laws of England and asking forgiveness for his past indiscretions. Grown men cried and prayed in the street as the word of the vote spread. Every ale house from Shoreditch to Fleet Street was filled to overflowing, all ringing with pledges of loyalty to the King when a year ago it was an imprisonable offence or worse. The Republic was doomed. A humble painter climbed up his ladder in the Royal Exchange and painted over the inscription on the niche where the last King's statue had been, which stated, 'The tyrant is gone, last of the Kings'. He then threw his hat into the air and shouted, "God save King Charles the Second!"

With this the whole Exchange joined in with the greatest cheer. Church bells rang out for the first time in over ten years, spreading the word all over the nation. *For all I have seen yet, give me old England, for what is an Englishmen without a King and a Parliament?* Thought the Speaker, *I have done my duty.*

Bonfires were lit all over London and the breadth of the nation, many roasting a rump of beef in derision at the remains of the Republican government. The happiest May Day in years, as the City of London and both Houses of Parliament passed motions that declared the King restored. All pledged their allegiance to the Crown. Parliament voted £50,000 for the royal court as expenses, to enable them to return to England in comfort. The King, at long last, was returning.

"To you, I give my unbridled love, admiration and respect. I have longed for this day, dreamt of it, as God is my witness, nothing, absolutely nothing compares to you. In front of Jesus Christ the redeemer, I love you and never want to be away from you ever, ever again," said Baron John Belasyse to his wife and he started to cry uncontrollably, his whole body shaking. Baroness Belasyse held her husband in her arms. God only knows what he had been through, as the children cried with happiness; daddy was home.

CHAPTER 7

Look West

"May God be praised," said Sir Edward Villiers, as Belasyse and Russell stood at the front door of his manor house, the steward having described the two members of the Sealed Knot to him. They all laughed in sheer relief that they were all still alive, and embraced each other heartily.

"Please, do come in," said Villiers, "and have some fine French brandy I managed to keep from Cromwell's looters. Thank God you are alive. I have been hiding in an old priest hole from Thurloe's agents and prayed you were safe," said Villiers.

"Gentlemen, some more good news. I have been to Colonel's Hacker's house and his wife Isabel gave me the death warrant of our late King, assuming it would save her husband. I think revenge is the order of the day," said Belasyse, relishing the words as his friends slowly nodded in agreement, faces hardening at the thought, whilst sipping their brandies.

As he swiftly walked down Swan Alley, Daniel Gookin knew he faced telling the news they had all dreaded, for it had come from the most reliable source. Gookin rapped harshly on the side door of the church, determined to rescue two of the most important men in the country. The door cracked open a fraction and Minister Seth looked him up and down.

"It's Gookin; quick, we have but little time," he gasped.

John Jones opened the door to let Gookin through and

checked the street with his pistol for stooges, desperately hoping they had not been betrayed.

"Mr Gookin, sir," said General Edward Whalley, urgency in his voice. "What news have you?"

"Gentlemen, I have just returned from Whitehall having spoken earlier with Thurloe. Agents of King Charles are in London and his supporters are arriving daily. It is obvious they are looking for anybody of consequence who helped run the Republic. The King has made it known that he wants no personal revenge and the Declaration of Indemnity and Oblivion says as much."

"So why the round up?" interjected Jones.

"Because the declaration also mentions, except those exempted by Parliament, and that will be us. The Royalists need to bury the Republic. Many in the new Parliament, to ingratiate themselves and hoping for rewards from the King, will betray us," said Gookin.

"So why don't we stay and rally troops that are still loyal to the good old cause and fight it out?" said Goffe, looking at all in the room for support. "Generals Lambert and Harrison are still strong, as is Hugh Peter."

"For the sad, simple reason, that if we did, it would be a bloodbath. The Royalists are in the ascendancy now and most of the Army's leaders are under arrest or, like us, wanted men. We also have families and must not drag them into this fast developing situation," said Whalley to Goffe.

"So it is as I feared; it may not be the King. He will not wash his hands in our blood, but many will, and death is death, no matter who pulls the trigger," said Goffe.

"I will put it to you straight. Thurloe told me to run for our lives, because Belasyse and his colleagues are right at this very moment seeking us out. He has been to Hacker's house and obtained the warrant. They know who to look for," said Gookin in defeat. The room fell silent, knowing the most experienced agent of the Crown, who had escaped his own execution, was now hunting them.

"What of the others?" asked John Jones.

"I only know of a few," said Gookin. "Colonel Dixwell is sick with shock and bedridden.

John Jones Maesygarnedd, your father and others are going to wait and see how the situation develops. There are many who still support our cause. I also have a note from Hugh Peter – it has the address of a friend of his in the New Haven settlement who will help us."

"That's good news," said Whalley with a coy smile, "and I know it to be true."

"How so?" said Gookin, surprised Whalley knew anyone across the ocean.

"Because I have friends in low places," said Whalley.

They all laughed, gallows' humour, knowing now they were the prey. The tables had well and truly been turned.

"We seem to have more friends across the ocean than here," said Goffe.

"Gentlemen," said Gookin. "You have many admirers there. For years we have shared your struggles and you are regarded as heroes; after all, that is why we founded New England."

"If that is the case, we should look west," said Whalley, trying to sound as optimistic as he could in the fast developing crisis. "So, as I see it, the situation is this. The Republic is over, whether we like it or not and we must fear for our lives. It is, subject to any other person's experience, time to leave. Most people look for change, no matter what it brings. That is human nature and we will become a victim of that change. Mr Gookin, can you help us?"

All the assembled looked at him in desperation. They now knew the old order they had tried so hard to destroy was returning with vengeance on the agenda.

"Definitely! I have spoken with Captain Pierce of the Prudent Mary, he is committed to our cause. He has been chartered to bring cargos to the town of Boston, together with some passengers.

His ship lies anchored at Gravesend, some twenty-five miles downriver from here. He will convey us across the ocean and we must leave immediately. I have passes from Thurloe but in these names: General Whalley, you are now Mr Edward Richardson and you, General Goffe, are Mr William Stevenson. Take what you can carry with you. We must leave on the next tide," said Gookin, urgency in his voice.

"But the city gates are closed this hour," said Whalley.

"That they are. I have a skiff chartered and it will row us down the Thames to Gravesend."

"It's unfortunate you do not have a pass to kill the King," mused Goffe.

"Even if we did, he presently has two brothers and two sisters who would be crowned in his stead and I don't think even we would have such fortune," said Gookin, shaking his head.

"So be it. We have tried all we could to give this nation a God-fearing government, good laws based on the scriptures, equal justice and any man, whatever his position, fair pay according to his labour. This is our legacy and no one can deny us that," said Goffe, as a final statement.

"True," said Whalley. "There is one point I would like to make. Prince Charles has two younger brothers, one, James, a Catholic and our enemy, the other Henry who was in our care for over three years. A reasonably experienced soldier who has fought in Flanders and is a staunch Protestant, a man who I think may have some sympathy for us and our cause. At twenty years old, a prince we could look to, if this restoration goes wrong for Charles." The group looked at Whalley with admiration. They packed with urgency, an engraved sword for Goffe, given to him by Cromwell himself after the victory at Worcester. Letters from his wife, gold sovereigns from the sale of his personal effects. Bible, can't forget that. He had realised after the meeting with Colonel Dixwell that the Republic was tottering; now he knew it had fallen. Whalley ran upstairs, throwing his spare boots and general's red sash his wife had made for him into his leather house bags. Then, carrying his goods, he ran down the stairs to the back of the church to the minister's house. Pausing to gather himself, he opened the door to the parlour. There he saw his wife Mary and his children. His heart faltered and sank like a rock in a pool.

"The time has come for me to depart from England," said Whalley, to his family. "It is possible I may never see you again; what has come to pass is that I am a wanted man. My enemies seek to destroy me. I ask you, my dear children, to honour your mother and obey her in all things and be God-fearing like your father." The children started crying and held their father close, he bent down on one knee and clasped them to him, shaking with emotion, then after a minute or so he stood up, tears in his eyes, and looked at his wife. "I desire to speak with you alone, Mary."

"Children," said Goffe, tenderly, horrified at the moving scene before him. "Come with me, I have some presents for you before we leave." The children looked longingly at their father, frightened at what was happening to them, uncertain of the future in the rapidly changing world surrounding them.

As the skiff moved down the River Thames, the group of hunted men looked up at St. Paul's Cathedral, bathed in the light of the fires celebrating Charles Stuart's imminent return. Their thoughts were of the future and the dangers that faced them. The Royalists wanted revenge and they would have it. Too many ills had been done by both sides and the time for settling accounts was at hand. They would be hunted wherever they went. The skiff flew down on the ebbing tide, past the Tower with its high walls and turrets. So long a seat of royal power, once briefly theirs and now returning to the authority of the Crown. *I wonder how many members of the Commonwealth will end up there*, thought Whalley. *Not a place to spend your last days.*

"Good evening, sirs. I have been expecting passengers and you are most welcome aboard my ship," said Captain Pierce, saluting the group. "My boatswain will show you to your quarters; please rest assured of the crew's fidelity in this matter," said Captain Pierce, noting the pistols in the waistbands of the generals, along with their swords. As they walked up the gangplank carrying their belongings, he knew this was all they had to succour them in exile.

"Cast off," he said and the Prudent Mary began her long voyage across the ocean, as Kellogg the ferryman pulled away and stared directly at Goffe, a look of intense dislike on his face.

"May I introduce everyone here?" said Captain Pierce with a flourish.

"General Whalley, General Goffe, officers of the Republic. Daniel Gookin, captain in the military company of Massachusetts. William Jones, son of John Jones Commissioner and Catherine Cromwell, nephew of our late beloved Lord Protector, Mrs Jones, daughter of the first governor of New Haven, and their sons William and Nathaniel. Finally, Mr Marmaduke Johnson. Please everyone sit down and may I assure you all we are of all the same mind and disposition. On that matter, Mr Johnson, what brings you to Boston?"

"First, may I say what a great privilege it is to be in such company of God-fearing people; your reputations precede you. I am but a humble man converting many to the will of our Lord. I have been charged by Mr John Eliot, preacher, with printing a Bible in the language of the natives and converting them to Christ. I have a copy here which is to be printed in Cambridge, Massachusetts and I have been sent by the Corporation of New England to be the assistant printer to Mr Samuel Green."

"Excellent, Mr Johnson, a very worthy mission," said Goffe. "It is your work which brings great joy to myself. There is no greater thing than spreading the word of our Lord."

"If I might trouble you, Mr Gookin, as none of us has been to Boston before, to tell us something of the town and the surrounding area," said Whalley.

"Well, subject to anyone's better knowledge, Boston is the main town in the plantations at present. Settled in the year 1630. There are over three thousand people who inhabit the town and it is some eight hundred acres, formerly attached to the mainland by a narrow neck, which today has been cut, and a drawbridge operates for defence against the natives and any other enemy. The Mill Pond is used to keep fish; the pond freezes in winter and ice skating is permitted, though not on a Sunday."

All the assembled guests smiled; there was definitely no recreation on a Sunday in Puritan Massachusetts.

Gookin continued, "There are some hills, called Fort Hill, Mill Hill and Beacon Hill, for the said reason. Roads are, as in England, named after their produce. Water Lane, Milk Street, Rope Walk, Mill Street, amongst many others. There is a fort to protect the harbour and militia numbering up to five hundred, fully armed, which train on Boston Common, usually every month."

Whalley and Goffe looked at each other. "Interesting, please do continue," said Goffe.

"Across the river is the village of Cambridge where I live. There are around some four hundred people and a fine establishment of learning. Originally called the College at the New Town, today named after a major benefactor Minister John Harvard. His father had a galleried inn in London called The George; he was an acquaintance of William Shakespeare."

"William Shakespeare was an agent of the devil with his licentious life; the writing and performance of such works is an abomination before Christ. Which is exactly why we Puritans burnt down the Globe Theatre as a chapel of Satan," boomed Goffe.

Gookin drew a deep breath and caught Whalley's embarrassed smile and continued. "John Harvard left a considerable library of fine books, numbering some four hundred. As well as seven hundred and eighty pounds. I am sure you are aware, a vast sum.

It has a high standard of discipline set down by governing laws over twenty years ago. But most importantly, Cambridge has a spring with a fine mineral content; it's very good for you."

"Thank you, Captain. If that isn't a sales pitch, what is?" chuckled Whalley, attempting to defuse the situation.

"You are most welcome to stay, gentlemen. I have a large house and five children; instruction from good men like yourselves would be a great honour for them and myself," said Gookin, anxious to show fidelity with the two generals he admired.

"That is a very kind offer. If you don't mind, we will take you up on that, if only until we are settled. We would be very appreciative," said Whalley, hoping that his son-in-law's views were not an embarrassment to all concerned.

"May I ask how Boston is governed and who the principle persons of the town are?" said Goffe circumspectly, realising he had overdone his view.

"It is governed by a council of eighteen, all full members of the Church and a governor, who are freely elected in a secret ballot by selectmen and freeholders who are the eligible voters in the settlement. The prominent persons are Mr John Endicott the Governor, his Marshall General, Edward Michelson and the governor's secretary, Edward Rawson. It is efficient and far more democratic than in England," continued Gookin.

"Land ho! Land ho!" shouted the boatswain.

"I don't see anything," said Goffe, squinting at the horizon.

"To your right, sir, you will see land."

Goffe held his left hand aloft to shade his eyes from the midday sun. "Look just above the horizon for a lantern on Beacon Hill; that is the highest point," said the boatswain. "There is often early morning mist in spring, the temperature rises slowly and the town lies surrounded by water with two rivers flowing into the Boston Sound. But as it is late July it's not needed. So use this telescope and look yonder for a thin mast."

The Prudent Mary sailed slowly into the entrance of Boston Sound, the master wary of the some thirty islands and mud flats. "There are small islands called Deer, Long and Castle, amongst others. They are often used for grazing hogs, but are dangerous for any vessel. Some ships have paid the price and more will be wrecked in the future," continued the boatswain, keen to display his knowledge to so prominent a general. "Upon entering the harbour we will dock between Charlestown and Boston, below Mill Hill, a fine anchorage. There are major benefits here, General. If you're a good worker; a place to call your own. How many people own property in England, sir? Here nine out of ten own their own property or land. If you show good effort and honest endeavour, the council will grant you an acreage. You may build a house for yourself and family, should you have one. It's simple – here you are judged on what you do and say, not your family connections."

"What did you do in the civil wars, sail away?" asked Goffe in a sarcastic voice, unhappy at being lectured by a sailor.

The boatswain stood bolt upright. "People should be judged on their work and character, not their title or their inherited wealth and that, sir, is why I emigrated. I am Thomas Bell, boatswain. I have but a small house on Mill Street; I worked for that house and paid fairly to have it built. I owe no man money, pay my taxes and go to church when I can. I stand for principle, good governance and I work hard. It was my dream to have a home of my own, Mr Goffe, and it came true here. I earnt it, rather than killed for it," said Bell tersely.

"May I shake your hand?" Said Whalley. "I couldn't help but overhear what you said. In five minutes you have summoned up all in what I believe."

"Thank you, General," said Bell, turning to Whalley. My family were not rich or had high office, they were sailors mostly just ordinary people trying hard to make a better life for themselves. My father died in the war, the rest are either married or dead of disease. So I went west. I have been a boatswain for three years and in a year or two possibly a master. Here you get promoted on your ability not your title," said Bell.

"Makes sense to me," said Whalley, eying his son-in-law.

The ship's company could smell the town, flowers, straw, bread being baked and smoke from a fire they had never smelt before, strange, but exciting. All were pleased to be safe and unharmed, the seas were merciless if they wanted to be. The wharf was lined with people, merchants, townsfolk and officials, most had come to hear the latest news of the crumbling Commonwealth and to pass the information on to interested parties in the town. The Prudent Mary glided past the many islands before entering Boston harbour and dropped anchor below Mill Hill. Gookin stepped into the long boat to seek out the council members and ask for their support as regards the two fugitives, asking the generals to wait in their cabins.

"What do you think, Edward?" Said Goffe, concerned they were stepping into the unknown.

"We will be fine here. The monarchy was only too keen to see the back of Puritans and most, if they did not go to Europe, came here and more will do so in the future. We are with likeminded people, have no worry," assured Whalley, confident that their reputations would count for much in this settlement.

"Good morning, Captain," said Edward Rawson. "I hope you had a pleasant crossing and have brought a full cargo."

"That I have and that I do," said Captain Pierce with a smile, glad to be safely ashore after ten weeks at sea. "If I may, sir, speak with you on a matter of great importance to our mutual cause."

"Of course," said Rawson, well aware of Pierce's loyalty.

"Sir, I have some very bad news," said Pierce, who paused for effect. "The monarchy has been restored."

"Oh no," said Rawson and his shoulders slumped in defeat. "We have given so much. Is there any good news?"

"Yes, I believe so. Generals Whalley and Goffe are on board

and hope for sanctuary with us," said Pierce, hoping for the agreement of the secretary. He needn't have worried.

"What a great honour and privilege that is," said Rawson with obvious pleasure. "The most important people so far to visit New England, they are most welcome here in Boston. I will inform Mr Endicott immediately and provide an introduction to the council as to their status and quality," said Rawson, only too pleased to inform the governor as to the new arrivals.

This is why I did not see action, thought Dixwell, his chest heaving as he dragged the coffin upwards, tying the rope around either end, whilst wheezing at the exertion. He stopped again, listening for any sound. There was none, except for his and the horse's breathing. Thank our dear Lord for a full moon and Sunday evening, no one about. He was frightened. There was no doubt the King was returning from exile; the round-up had already started. General Monck had double-crossed them and he had to move fast. Hopefully the story his family had put about that he was sick and bedridden would hold. He had paid off his staff and only the pastor visited him every other day. He tied the rope to the saddle pommel, then around the horse, making a knot. Dixwell looked around, no one out, and he wiped the sweat from his forehead with a cloth. He didn't want to end up on a gibbet and pulled the reins gently, his mount moved slowly forward, the coffin appearing at the top of the grave. He inched it carefully out and onto the hurdle, tying it securely. The last thing he needed was for the coffin to fall off and spill the body onto the road. He took his spade and filled in the grave. As it had only been there a day or two, no one would suspect the fresh earth was out of the ordinary. He had the wheels of the hurdle wrapped in sheep's fleece, for the two-mile journey to his recently sold house. The new Royalist owners thought they had got a bargain from the former Member of Parliament for Dover. Well, they were in for a shock and he walked the horse carefully along the road to the front steps and into the hall. He tipped the corpse out from the coffin. "Sorry," he said to the body and placed it between the parlour and the open back door, gagging at the stench. He poured turpentine over the banisters and first floor landing. Then he hesitated. *It was all over – my comfortable retirement, pension, everything.* He took out two flints from a small steel box and tapped them together several times over a turpentine-soaked rag. It burst into flames. He threw it on to the floor and walked out the front door, not looking back. His beloved belongings sold for a pittance in a Dover auction house; many of the locals knowing what was to happen and sniffing a bargain. He mounted his horse and rode on his way, the moon revealing the tears flowing down his face. He may have got his revenge on a Royalist who had bought his house for a knock-down price, but nothing could disguise the fact that he was on the run, a price on his head, with nowhere to go, no one to help him and agents of the Crown on his trail.

CHAPTER 8

The Royal Displeasure

"Sire, we, the true members of the Houses of Lords and Commons, do humbly beseech your Majesty to return and take the Government of the Kingdom into your hands."

The King exhaled a long breath and put the letter from both Houses of Parliament on to the mantelpiece with his other correspondence. After so many arguments, fighting and blood, the return of the King was done without the shedding of one drop. If Nicholas Monck had not seen his brother, and his brother George had not played such a masterful hand. *That is, if George Monck had a plan at all. Still, no matter, I must have good loyal men at my side. Be careful, but be trustful. We must shape the future without bitterness and recriminations. I don't want to go on my travels again.*

The King arrived in the Palace of Whitehall, London, exhausted after his long journey from the Hague and nine years of exile.

"Sire, just one more meeting, but perhaps the most important," said Hyde.

"And that is?" asked the King, looking as if he had played two games of tennis, one after the other. "Both Houses of Parliament wish to make a quick address," said Hyde, resplendent in his new robes of office as Lord Chancellor of England.

The loyal address was so perfectly put, even the King, after all the speeches he had heard, was in awe.

"Sire, we offer you no flattering titles, but dare to speak the words of truth. You are the desire of the three kingdoms, the strength and balance of the tribes of Albion, for the moderation of extremes, the reconciling of differences, the satisfying of all interests and restoring the collapsed honour of these nations. May God save the King." Both houses took up the cheer, throwing their hats in the air. At long, long last, peace in our time.

Crash went the door, flying off its hinges, splintering as it hit the ground. In charged three heavily armed men, one to the left and one to the right, the other, tall, slim, scarred and in command, stood in the middle of the parlour with an axe in his hands, ready to do battle.

"I thought I might have a pleasant glass of ale here, but as you do not know the meaning of the word 'pleasant', I will settle for your despicable, murdering, filthy carcass," said Belasyse with relish, to Daniel Axtell. Late a colonel in the New Model Army, but now a wanted man. Sitting by the fire, Axtell looked at the musket propped up by the roughly hewn table next to him. *No chance, these men knew their business, unfortunately!*

"Daniel Gibson Axtell, you're under arrest. On the orders of the House of Commons, you are charged with aiding and abetting the murder of his Majesty King Charles the First. You have been excluded from the Act of Indemnity and Oblivion and here is a copy of your bill of attainder you can have as a souvenir," said Belasyse, placing the document on the table.

"Enjoy, for what you have done to others, they shall do unto you," said Sir Edward Villiers laughing, as they trussed Axtell up like a Christmas goose.

"I have an idea; why don't we hand him over to the Irish? I'm sure they would have a warm welcome for you, something on the lines of, your Guy Fawkes this year!" said Colonel John Russell sarcastically.

"Do so if you want; they are papist scum who murdered Protestant settlers and fought against the will of Parliament. They got exactly what they deserved," said Axtell.

"So by way of revenge you looted, murdered and burnt your way around the Catholic villages and towns of Ireland and sold how many as slaves to the Indies?" asked Belasyse, his voice rising at the evil murderer in front of him. "You should have arrested the culprits, but your law is that of 'might is right'. England will pay by having the enmity of an entire people; they will come for revenge one day. You are a barbarian, pure and simple evil."

Axtell smiled. "So what, we won and they lost, badly."

Belasyse, Villiers and Russell stopped, as if hitting a stone wall and stared at the monster in the prison cage.

"Don't!" Shouted Belasyse, as Villiers aimed his pistol at Axtell's head. "He's not worthy of any form of human respect, let alone a quick death. Simple, let the courts decide. Something, Axtell, you have never heard of I suspect." On they went to the Fleet Street compter with its solid brick cells. How many more would they arrest?

"Who ordered the loin of beef?" shouted Pasqua Rosee over the din.

"Over here!" shouted Belasyse.

"My, it's packed," said Villiers, looking around at the throng standing three deep at the bar.

"It's the place to be," said Belasyse, over the noise and hubbub. "The sign of Pasqua Rosee's Head. Meeting and dining place of traders from the Royal Exchange and other such establishments. Trade has picked up; happy people spend and the nation's economy needs the business."

"True; the most fashionable place in town, which makes me feel very old-fashioned indeed," said Russell, giving a mournful smile. "How many more to go, of the ninety-three?"

"As far as I can ascertain," said Belasyse, "of the ninety-three wanted men, twenty-five are dead and forty-five arrested, which leaves twenty-three who have sailed to foreign parts. All to Europe where they roam with the mark of Cain upon them."

"Not all are in Europe," said a smartly dressed man with dark blue eyes, long hair and a prominent nose.

Belsayse jumped out of his chair, mouth open and full of fragrant mutton, which began slipping down his chin.

"My God!" he exclaimed.

"Mine also," said the stranger. "When you have finished your lunch, some of which you are kindly showing me, how about a glass of sack at Whitehall Palace? There is someone I would like you to meet. Let us say four hours after midday," said the stranger, who bowed and strode out of the coffee house as quickly as he had come in.

"Who the hell was that?" said Villiers and Russell in unison.

"That is a question I would also like to know the answer to. Let's say, that man has been my saviour on several occasions," said Belasyse, staring admiringly at the stranger's immaculately clad back.

Belasyse walked up to the gate by the stone gallery, having happily explained on the ride up the River Thames about giving the waterman Kellogg the position of head ferryman to his estate and the towns on the River Humber. The palace guards, striking in their polished helmets and pikes, patrolled with evident pride.

Workmen busied themselves with painting the walls, as carts pulled in through the gate on King Street, loaded with French wines and tapestries for the royal residence.

"Good afternoon, sir," said the guard cheerfully.

"Good afternoon. My name is Baron Belasyse. I am expected and here are my credentials."

The guard called his duty sergeant, who consulted his list and finding his name, looked up.

"Please do accompany me, sir." Off they went up the stone gallery, with its array of paintings and sculptures, full of gawking viewers and the centre of national gossip. Into the labyrinth, guards, servants, ministers and guests moved around as their duties called. A veritable army of hundreds. Belasyse's mind worked furiously. Who is this strange man and what does he do? *I remember the last visit with dread; it nearly cost me my life.* He walked along the gallery to its double oak doors carved with Tudor symbols, glorifying their house.

"Here is Baron Belasyse, sir," said the sergeant to the duty officer, who poked his head around the corner of the door, repeating his name. A man of some forty years appeared, clad in a red tunic and britches, with silver buttons, a white lace shirt, wig and black shoes with golden buckles. He bowed.

"Good morning, Baron Belasyse?"

"That I am."

"Sir, my name is Chaffinch; please do come this way." Belasyse followed him through the withdrawing room and its supplicants hoping for the royal ear, dispossessed cavaliers, ministers of state and hangers on, through the elegantly carved double doors to the bedchamber overlooking the River Thames, where he recognised Chancellor Hyde in conversation with General Monck. Belasyse gave a short bow and followed the servant to a small door on the right-hand side of the room covered in red velvet. Chaffinch pulled a golden key from his right-hand pocket, unlocked the door and they climbed up a very narrow set of stairs. He heard them first – clocks, watches, many ticking away with elegant hands, jewelled numbers and shiny brass faces denoting the time and high tide of the river at Whitehall, the Tower, Windsor Castle and Hampton Court. A venerable collection of time pieces.

"Thank you, Chaffinch, I will take him from here," said a smartly dressed man with dark blue eyes and a prominent nose.

"It's been a journey for both of us," he said smiling fully and offering his right hand. "I think it's about time we were properly introduced. My name is Samuel Moreland. Do come through to his Majesty's closet. I will let him fill you in as to my position and past."

Belasyse's heart jumped. *The King, me. I don't believe it. After all I have suffered and done for his cause. Now I can meet him and pledge my loyalty in person.* Tears sprang from his eyes. *I will remember this for the rest of my life and tell my children what a great honour it was seeing the King alive and restored, a man I have fought for and nearly died for.*

"Thank you, Mr Evelyn, I think the Royal Society is a splendid idea; something we both see as a great step forward in the solving of problems and the advancement of science, away from the restrictions of religious dogma. A thinking club of intellectual men, furthering knowledge for the benefit of industry and the people. Fruit, being your speciality, is of enormous benefit to the health of the nation; the more we can grow the better for all," said the King as a goodbye, pleased that the Royal Society was taking shape.

In the centre of the room overlooking the River Thames, at six foot two, was the man that did count as the most important in the nation. Long curly black hair, thin moustache over full lips, dressed in turquoise britches, white silk morning shirt, a long blue cloak, lined with lynx fur, and a garter star sewn on the top left, was his Majesty King Charles the Second, ruler of Ireland, Scotland, Wales and England.

Belasyse dropped to one knee, "Your Majesty."

"May I present Baron John Belasyse of Worlaby, sire," said Moreland.

"Baron, do come hither, so I may look at you," said the King smiling, and beckoned him forward.

"What you have done for the cause of the Crown ranks high up in the annals of greatness. We shall never forget your suffering in our cause. I know that for my father, you raised regiments of foot and horse at your own expense. Your defence of the city of Newark was dogged and you refused to surrender after all seemed lost. You kept me informed of the situation during our exile, suffered fines and imprisonment for our cause. You have our thanks and gratitude," said the King, offering a velvet-covered chair aside a spectacular baroque table with a symmetrical design.

"Sire, I cannot, but thank you for this praise. It is a great honour and I shall, if I may, share it with my family and staff. Who I may assure your Majesty are loyal. I did and I will continue to do what I hope is in your long-term interest, and that of your Majesty's subjects. At long last we may dwell under your munificence. May I offer my condolences to you in respect of the death of his Royal Highness Prince Henry; truly a great loss for yourself and the nation," said Belasyse.

"Thank you," said the King. "He was a fine man with a great future, a good brother and a great loss to us all. I have not seen you since '45 in Oxford some fifteen years ago," said the King, quickly changing the subject of his youngest brother's death. "And I am well aware you have not known of the identity of your mysterious benefactor for reasons I will now reveal. Sir Samuel Moreland was the deputy to John Thurloe, chief spymaster to Oliver Cromwell of the late and not so lamented Republic, and his successor Richard, who I hear is now on the run in Europe. He is the man who uncovered a plot to kill me, led by the traitor Sir Richard Willis. It is good to know you and your colleagues are all alive and unharmed by his treasonable acts. Moreland has been helping our cause for a number of years. He has Thurloe under arrest and is encouraging him to reveal all he knows about the regicides and other dangerous Republicans. There are some who would gladly start a war again," said the King, staring at Belasyse for a reaction.

"These men offer a rallying point, a chance to turn back the clock. They are the threat that hangs over all of us. May I ask as to the progress in apprehending all those attained by Parliament?" said the King directly.

"Certainly, your Majesty. Inquiries as to the whereabouts of the regicides have been helped by the finding of the warrant to murder your father. If I may inform your Majesty that a Colonel Tomlinson, who showed your father much courtesy and respect, informed me of its existence. He is presently being held in the

Tower. Perhaps something may be done, in this incidence for him," said Belasyse, hoping for a reprieve for Tomlinson, who had been discreet about the threats to kill him.

"Why yes, he is to be a witness for the prosecution in the forthcoming trials of the regicides. After he gives his evidence, I will exercise the royal prerogative and let him re-join his family."

"Thank you sire. Europe, where many of the regicides have fled to, has seen one recent success. Sir Michael Livesey has been recently shot dead in Holland and the search is continuing for the others, sire. Some forty-five have been apprehended and, thanks to your Majesty's generosity, nine now are to be released," said Belasyse, looking at Moreland and the King, who sat back in his chair and picked up a batch of papers from the desk.

"We have learnt much from Thurloe. He has been most cooperative, after a guided tour of the Tower of London and its dungeons by Sir Samuel last week," said the King.

"Thank you sire," said Sir Samuel, basking in the King's praise. "I included the Wakefield Tower, a place, how can I put it, for the extraction of information," said Moreland slowly. Belasyse nodded in agreement; he knew, he had been beaten there regularly and was lucky he had not been racked.

"He has come clean on many issues," continued Moreland. "As to the whereabouts of the regicides, Switzerland and Holland are the main destinations. I have agents actively hunting them down and every ambassador has been informed to this end. There is one interesting piece of information I have discovered. Two former commissioners, Whalley and Goffe, sailed on the 4th of May from Gravesend on the ship Prudent Mary. They and a few other miscreants were on board and Boston Massachusetts was the ship's destination. Therefore, on your Majesty's behalf, I have had this warrant drawn up," said Moreland. He passed a large piece of parchment across the ornate table, dated 22nd September 1660. It had the royal seal at the top, a lion on the left and the mythical unicorn on the right.

A proclamation, it read in bold letters, for the apprehension of Edward Whalley and William Goffe, commonly called colonels, are, amongst others, by an act of this present Parliament, wholly excepted in the act of free and general pardon. They are left to be proceeded against as traitors, for their execrable treasons in sentencing to death and signing the instrument for the horrid murder of the life of our late dear father, of blessed memory. We hereby do require and command all judges, justices of the peace, mayors, sheriffs, bailiffs, constables, officers, ministers of our ports and all subjects wherever within our realm that they be diligent in inquiring, searching and seizing the said Whalley and Goffe. We do hereby further declare, that if any person or persons shall directly or indirectly conceal, harbour, keep, retain or maintain the said men, that they shall incur the royal displeasure.

CHAPTER 9

Wanted Men

Goffe dropped the proclamation to the table. "We're done for!" he said in horror.

"No we're not," said Whalley. "We have been in tighter spots than this, and we have friends here, is that not so?" he asked Gookin.

"Yes you do," said Gookin, "and more than you realise. Have cheer – we are a long way from Whitehall and agents of the Crown."

Goffe knew this, but he wanted to hear it. Boston and its most important inhabitants were well-disposed to them. They had been entertained by the great and good of the town and all had promised to protect them, but that was before this warrant for their arrest arrived. Now the real test was to come. He had witnessed how quickly their support had evaporated back in England and it remained to be seen how many would be true to their word, if the King followed this bill with more practical means. They would find out soon enough if the velvet glove of restoration had an iron fist.

Whalley and Goffe walked up Tremont Street then Boston Common to watch the militia train.

"Ah! Captain Gookin. May we be observers of this military display?" asked Goffe.

"We would be honoured General, and be very appreciative of any advice you may give us. Your military experience may be vital in any action this settlement may be involved in and against any enemy we may face," said Gookin carefully. The two generals observed the militia on the long sloping common. In the centre was a pond, at which the magnificent long-horned Devonshire cattle were drinking, along with sheep on the public grazing land. Down the hill the militia charged, shouting as they went, sixteen-foot pikes held out in front of them as the animals scattered in panic, whilst a further group went through musket-loading and firing practice. After two hours of manoeuvres Captains Gookin and Denision walked over to the two generals to solicit their advice.

"Well, sirs, what do you think?" they said, eager for any ideas to enhance the effectiveness of the militia.

"Well, without meaning any offence, may I suggest this? The pikes are held slightly higher than level aiming at your enemy's throat. Then, just before you close, fire your muskets, breaking up the enemy's line. The musketeers then reload and try to pick off the enemy's officers, or cover your retreat if the assault is repulsed. This will make it easier for the pike men to select a target, as the enemy will have suffered casualties and be thrown into confusion by the musket fire. Knowing how to retreat is as important as how to advance; in fact, more men may be killed in a headlong retreat than a reasonable victory. All the shouting is good for a display, but if possible, the least amount of noise is best."

"Why so?" asked Gookin, surprised at such a statement. So you can hear the commands of your officers and sergeants. Remember, there is so much gun smoke on a battlefield, it is often hard to spot the enemy, so you must be able to communicate in action. Training is very important, but it is no substitute for experience. Use hay and straw as wadding in the cannon when you run out of the real thing. Also use knives, spoons and musket balls in your cannon; it can be devastating. How about that and old nails as grapeshot?" asked Whalley. The two captains admired the general's knowledge.

"With you in command we would be invincible if attacked," said Gookin.

"May I assure you of our fidelity to the town, gentlemen, along with our belief that you should rid yourself of an unwanted King," said Goffe as a thank you. The two generals moved off past the great elm tree used for public hangings.

"Just think, Edward," added Goffe, "over five hundred men trained in the use of arms. Cannon overlooking the harbour entrance. There is a large store of powder on Beacon Hill, muskets, pistols and over five hundred halberds and swords. Raise the militia and it would be very difficult for the King to win back the plantations. Do not Massachusetts, Connecticut and New Haven stand as Puritan theocracies? If we really tried, I honestly think we could declare independence from the Crown. What say you?" asked Goffe, all excited at the prospect of continuing to lead his crusade against the monarchy.

Whalley took a deep breath; he was a realist. The support was tangible, but greater things were at the front of their minds. Did not the French, Spanish and certainly the Dutch make claim to some of the land? Not to mention the natives. England had a powerful military force and the settlers, no matter how many disliked the monarchy, needed its power as a trading ally and a defender of their fledgling settlements. Over time that would change, but right now they needed England more than England needed them, and the survival factor was usually uppermost in people's minds. *Time will tell,* thought Whalley, *let us see if King Charles survives.*

"I have an idea, William. It's Saturday, which is market day in Boston," said Whalley. "There is a fencing master who has erected a platform on the common and challenges any person to outwit him with a sword. He struts upon his stage like a peacock in his pen. You have proved very handy in action, why not challenge him?"

"Now that should teach a blusterer a good lesson," said

Goffe, glad for something to relieve the rounds of introductions and church services.

"Yes, let's make a spectacle. That would also send a warning to any who are undecided about our presence here," said Whalley, and off they went for lunch at Gookin's residence.

"Here we are, sir, the Charlestown to Boston ferry point on the east side of town, around a twenty minute walk to Boston Common, but Mr Gookin here will show you the way. God's speed," said the ferryman, eying up the next group of passengers and cargo for Cambridge. Hopefully with a few rich students for the college; they were the best tippers, he thought.

"I do compliment you and your town. I see much that is different between the settlements and Britain. I feel a sense of freedom and a great opportunity to start afresh and rebuild your life, where each man's good principles are rewarded according to their effort," said Whalley. Gookin looked at him in agreement, he was proud of what he had achieved, rising to some of the prominent positions in Boston, and was pleased to show them the thriving town.

"There are chandlers, carpenters, blacksmiths, skinners and merchant tailors, although they are not at sixes and sevens. All the usual trades from England and, as you gentlemen will know, being a sea port, the associated skills. We do build ships, some small craft, as well as ocean-going. We trade with the sea ports on the coast in Rhode Island, Maryland and New Amsterdam, to name a few. All the way to Jamestown in the Province of Virginia, voyages of some distance. The larger vessels go to the Indies or Canary Islands for spices, liquors and fruits. We even have nutmeg which goes exceptionally well in a pumpkin pie; a favourite and speciality here," said Gookin.

"There are so many pies in England. I have not heard of that one. What is a pumpkin? Sort of bird, is it?" asked Whalley of Gookin, who chuckled, shaking his head.

"Good sir," said Goffe, "I hear you are the finest swordsman in the settlements, although you say it yourself. I myself am not convinced anyone is the best; many of those who have said so are dead on a dozen battlefields. As to you, I think you need a bath as you smell of refuse; perhaps your house is really a pigsty."

"Oh dear me," said the sword master in a doomed voice, "you have just made me a very angry man. Prepare yourself for your demise."

"That I will, but a moment to, as you say, prepare myself."

"Ah, the market on Boston Common; let us regale ourselves of a little local produce," said Goffe to Whalley, satisfied he had roused the man's ardour. Both men walked over to the stalls. A wide variety nestled themselves at the base of Beacon Hill. Flowers and hams were side by side with smoked and salted fish, turkeys, corn, as well as that strange potato and tomato they had seen in England. A veritable emporium of goods and services, both men realised how self-sufficient these pioneers were. After all, they had to be. It was ten weeks or so by ship to the mother country, that is if it arrived at all, and what was that smell, slightly sweet, smoky and delicious?

"Sir, what is that extraordinary scent?" asked Whalley of a passer-by.

"It's a wood called hickory. We use it for cooking pork ribs, sir. Most of the meat is salted for the winter supply of food or sea voyages. We boil the ribs slowly in a large pot for nearly an hour, adding onions and some spices if we have them. Then cover the ribs in a mixture of crushed tomato fruit, a little salt and syrup from the maple tree. Leave it to rest a few hours. Then in a fire pit we place some twenty pieces of this wood called hickory. Across the fire bricks we place iron rods. Then place the marinated ribs on the iron and grill slowly. We call it barbecuing."

"Do you think this will be popular here in America?" asked Whalley, intrigued by this strange cooking method.

"You know it might; a sort of family gathering around a barbecue, but not on a Sunday," said Goffe gravely.

"Could you direct me to a cheesemonger?" asked Goffe of the man.

"A pleasure. At the end of the row is Mr William Phillips; he has a good variety."

"Thank you for your help," and the passer-by went on his way.

"Sir, have you a whole cheese? I would like it wrapped in a linen cloth with a large knot so I may handle it with ease," said Goffe.

"Of course you can, sir, I will wrap a whole cheddar for you. I usually cut them in twelve as to Jesus's disciples, but you are welcome to a whole one," said the cheesemonger, happy to make such a sale. Two shillings and four pence please sir," he said, setting the cheddar on the scales.

"Thank you," said Goffe, and paid the man. "Oh, I see you have a mop to clean the wooden boards you set your stall on. May I borrow it?"

"Certainly, sir," said the cheesemonger intrigued, wondering why his customer would need it. Goffe approached the stand and dipped the mop in a puddle of dirty water then mounted the stage, dressed in old clothes and holding the wrapped cheese in his left hand and the mop in his right. Whilst the shoppers crowded around, noting the bearing of the man who had climbed the steps to the platform and issued a challenge to the fencing master.

"Ha, look at this old fool; back, are we? You even dare to climb my stage dressed as a beggar with a mop. This is going to be good. A silver shilling to the winner, for you are a rustic and laughable as a man. Can you even read or write? Now be gone, before I chastise you."

Goffe did not move, but followed every move of the braggart looking for gaps and weaknesses in his opponent's movement, testing his sword skills.

His whole countenance was totally focused on the fencing

master, who suddenly made a pass at him with his rapier to show who the finest swordsman in Boston was. He got a surprise. Goffe twisted sharply to his left and took the rapier point into the cheese and pressed the mop onto the master's face, giving him a moustache. That did it! The crowd laughed at the unfolding show.

"I'll prove to you who is the finest here," said the furious sword master, and he lunged at Goffe, who stepped smartly to the right and sideways. Again he received the point of the sword into the cheese, whilst the mop made a beard on the master's face.

"Oh!" went the crowd and clapped in awe. Many gathered to see the display, forgetting for the moment their business in the market. The master huffed and puffed, went red-faced in fury and danced around the arena looking for an opening in Goffe's defence. There was none. He frowned in surprise and attacked again. Goffe sidestepped with lightning speed and tapped the mop on the master's head, so the muddy water trickled down his back. Goffe deftly moved away and attacked, smearing the mop over the master's face, who let out a shout of pure anger, as the crowd lapped up the show. He backed off to the side of the ring and laid his rapier down and picked up a broadsword. The crowd went silent; this was a total change. A rapier was the sign of a gentleman and more of an accruement than a weapon. A broadsword had but one purpose: killing! Goffe straightened up and stared at the master.

"Stop, sir, I have merely played with you and have not harmed you whatsoever. If you attempt to come at me I know I will certainly take your life," he said, dropping his old rustic coat and revealing his own gilt-topped and engraved broadsword, a gift from Oliver Cromwell himself.

Dressed in a tunic of scarlet, blue sash and an iron chest plate, there was no doubting his skill or who he was. The firm countenance and speech dissuaded the master from even unsheathing his weapon. He gave a short bow.

"Who are you, sir?" said the sword master, realising he had met his match. Goffe said nothing whilst staring at the humbled man. "You are either Whalley, Goffe, or the devil himself. For there is no other man in New England who can beat me. I am the master here, but I think no longer, for I have been to look a beginner. How do you do that masterful work, sir?" said the fencing master in a kindly way, knowing that he had been well and truly taught a lesson and was anxious to learn. Goffe hesitated and looked at his father-in-law, who nodded. "It is simple. You can train for years, but violent hand to hand combat, year after bloody year, will always give you the edge. By your leave, sir," and they parted through the admiring crowd, many patting them on the back, shouting plaudits and thanking them for their presence, including some of the local militia.

Suddenly two men pushed their way through the crowd.

"Look what we have here – two regicides. You murdering fellows are under arrest. You are wanted men," shouted Kirke, to Whalley and Goffe, his friend Kellond by his side. The two generals froze, eying up the two men, and moved in opposite directions, slowly drawing their swords. The two Royalists hesitated, after seeing the sword display, and knowing their war record, they looked at each other for inspiration.

"I tell you this, if the same situation occurred again I would still act in the same way, for I care not for any King and his bishops," said Whalley to the two Royalists, daring them to act.

"What is going on here?" asked Captain Gookin, advancing through the crowd with four militia men looking earnestly at his side.

"These two men are Whalley and Goffe, signatories to King Charles's death warrant, and they have uttered treasons by attempting rebellion, as well as denying the King's authority. They are under arrest," said Kirke.

"Are they now and who are you?" said Gookin in a commanding voice, anxious to dominate the dangerous situation.

"I am Thomas Kirke, a shipmaster in his Majesty's Navy and this is Thomas Kellond, a merchant, both loyal subjects of the Crown."

"Two lackeys for an absent authority is what you really are," said Gookin, in a slow and menacing tone. "Mr Stevenson and Mr Richardson are two gentlemen who are well disposed to us and they are welcome in the Commonwealth of Massachusetts. Do you have proof positive that these men are who you say they are? Do you have a warrant for their arrest issued by a magistrate?" asked Gookin.

Kirke and Kellond hesitated. They knew of Captain Gookin's powerful connections and with four armed militia men they were outnumbered.

"No matter," continued Gookin, "I will send for the Governor; we will ensure that proper procedure is adhered to. We don't make unsubstantiated accusations on behalf of a King in Boston," he said, trying to gather support, as the crowd gathered menacingly and started taunting the two hunters.

"Get out of here or we will see to you," they started shouting and cat calls followed, as the militia men and Gookin stared at Kirke and Kellond, daring them to take the two generals away. Both men thought discretion the better part of valour and retreated past the new and then old burying grounds, down Sudbury Lane to Kellond's house, cursing their luck.

Gookin ran to the ferry, not before telling the militia men to keep an eye on the two Royalists, they were definitely getting close, too close, and some would be pleased with a reward of a hundred pounds for each man, as well as the gratitude of the King back in Whitehall. That was enough to buy a house and land to go with it. Someone would talk; it was the topic of every tavern and supper party in Boston. The executions of the regicides back in London spurred him on. For he had aided Whalley and Goffe to flee on the Prudent Mary and he was sure the King's agents would find out at some stage, if they hadn't already. Gookin jumped off the ferry and ran along the thick planks of the jetty, across the green, up Wapping Street, past the prized well to his house, unlocking the front door with two quick turns of the key to see the two generals' firm set faces and Captain Pierce at the ready.

"Well," said Whalley, pistol in hand, "We've heard that there are people trying to arrest us."

"Not if I can help it. I have sounded out the men I trust in the militia and the Governor, it seems was not ready for a rebellion yet. The Governor will, at some stage, have to issue a warrant. He can't blindly defy the King's orders, but he can surely delay them. I have sent for an old friend as a guide, Simon Lobdell; he should be here before sundown."

"Then we shall set them a merry chase," said Whalley, as they all went into the backyard and began preparing to flee once again from the King of England's grasp.

"Mr Gookin, I cannot but thank you for your farsightedness in this matter," said Goffe. "May I return the favour if it is possible to do so?" he said, mounting a bay mare. "I will have this horse returned to you as soon as convenient," he said as a goodbye.

"It has been my pleasure to help you gentlemen and do keep the horses as a token of my esteem to you both. I will mind your herd of cattle and other possessions. Now, it is over one hundred miles to Hartford and a further forty to New Haven where John Davenport awaits your arrival. You will find friends on your journey, which will take around a week, God speed," said Gookin and off they went at a gallop into the great unknown, thousands of miles from their homes and their families.

Nobody noticed a smallish, rotund man with inquiring eyes and a squared naval hat at the edge of the common who had watched the entire scene. He knew Kellond and Kirke wouldn't succeed and he walked down Schoolhouse Lane, past the Latin school and the master's house. There he turned left onto the street to Roxbury and nodded to the regulars at the Anchor

Tavern. He walked a little further down on the right and there climbed the ten or so steps into the townhouse.

"May I see the Governor?" asked Captain Breedon of the Royal Navy, to Edward Rawson, secretary to the Governor.

"For what reason, may I ask?" replied Rawson, eying up Breedon, whose loyalty to the Crown was unquestioned.

"It's simple; we have two traitors to the Crown in our midst, namely Whalley and Goffe, and I see no effort on your part to apprehend them. There is a warrant for their arrest which has been shown in these parts for some time now and offers a reward of a hundred pounds each and you have done nothing to enforce it," said Breedon.

"If there is, I have not seen it, nor is it on the front of the townhouse, where all official documents are posted. I assume you have proof as to this document?"

Breedon gave Rawson a direct stare and slowly reached into his coat pocket and produced a copy of the warrant, bearing the royal seal.

Rawson smiled. "The Governor is at his house in Salem, some twenty miles up the coast; do enjoy the journey."

Breedon left in disgust. *Dam impudent traitor*, he thought. Then he saw Kirke and Kellond walking to the townhouse – *good, just the men I need.* "Good day gentlemen. I could not but overhear your steadfast loyalty and your attempt to arrest the two regicides in our midst and would ask if you have had fortune as to your quest," said Breedon, knowing they hadn't, but he wanted to ensure they were serious.

"None, we had them on the common, but the local militia intervened and they fled," said Kellond. "So be it. My name is Captain Breedon. I am sure you have heard of me, a master in his Majesty's Navy. I will report back to the authorities in Whitehall, London as to this. I would ask you two gentlemen, as loyal men, to do all you can to apprehend these two regicides and I will inform the authorities as to your good work in this matter. I will see Endicott when he arrives and will inform you as to the situation. I suspect he will be reticent."

Endicott walked purposefully down the townhouse stairs, leaving Breedon to go to the court room and the marshal general there, which should be entertaining. They were a long way from London and the captain would soon leave. *I won't betray them, but I also don't want a war here; we're not strong enough yet*, and decided to call a meeting of the council as the rumour mill had started and an arrest warrant issued, though let's not rush this.

"You malignant fellow," shouted Edward Michelson, grinning into Breedon's face. "Speak against Whalley and Goffe if you dare, if you dare!"

"I have a warrant direct from London requiring the arrest of these two men. You are either for the King or against him," said Breedon, his voice rising at the intransigence of Michelson, who tore the warrant from Breedon's hand and ripped it to pieces in his face.

"Malignant pamphlet and that's what we do with them," and he proceeded to walk out of the court room. Breedon made his way to his ship at Bendell's Cove, annoyed at the truculence of the general marshal and hubris of the governor. *Don't worry I'll see you in the black book of the King*, and he went to his cabin to wright up a report to the council for foreign plantations in London.

"Here we are, gentlemen, the Independent Plantation of New Haven," said Simon Lobdell, smiling at his charges, glad to have escorted such prominent men from their pursuers to New Haven along the rough terrain of the Boston Post Road without incident.

"We both thank you, Mr Lobdell, and will pray for your good health and fortune. May we be shown to the house of Mrs Jones?"

"Certainly, it is this way on Elm Street."

"Thank you for your troubles, Mr Lobdell," said Goffe, as Whalley gave him two silver half crowns in thanks.

"Leave it to me William, we have friends here, one in particular," said Whalley, as he tied his horse to the fence at the rear of the house. He knocked on the back door, not wanting to be seen entering the front. Suddenly a dog started barking in the house and it ran to the door scratching it with its claws, candles moved about inside, they were discovered. The oak and iron-panelled door was carefully opened and a pistol poked out from halfway down.

"Don't shoot! The late Hugh Peter gave us your details."

"And who might you be?"

"Messrs Stephenson and Richardson. We have been assured as to your quality and hospitality," said Whalley hopefully.

"To that you may be certain of, and gentlemen, it is good to see you again," said William Jones opening the door fully and lowering his pistol. "Do please come in, we have been expecting you."

Whalley and Goffe gingerly climbed the back steps and entered the Jones' household, lit by a roaring fire and various candles.

"I think a round of introductions is in order. General Whalley, I am sure you know this lady."

"Praise to the Lord, Susan, it's been such a long time." And they embraced.

"Reverend Hooke, we meet at last. I have heard much about you. Praise be to God you are well," said Whalley, furiously pumping the hand of the reverend, who was dressed in a smart black suit and stout black shoes with a shiny brass buckle on each foot, the only sign of colour on him.

"Who is this, Edward?" asked Goffe, nervously eying all in the room.

"This is my sister Susan and her husband the Reverend Hooke," said Whalley, smiling with relief that they were in a friendly household. "This man is my son-in-law William Goffe, who is married to my daughter Frances. He is an honourable man of the highest standards, I am very proud of him."

"Mr Goffe, I cannot but thank you for looking after my brother. You are welcome here as family," said Susan firmly, ensuring all in the room knew her view that he was worthy of their protection. "William has written to me often about your courage and fidelity. My niece, your wife, also praising your character. May I introduce Mr John Davenport, one of the founders and chief pastor to the settlement of New Haven."

"Gentlemen, what an honour and pleasure it is to meet you at last. Your reputations of integrity and fidelity to our great cause precede you. I have letters from your families and monies for your usage," said Davenport, shaking their hands and reaching for a leather satchel, producing several letters and two small pouches, jingling with coins. "If I may I invite you to service tomorrow. I am to preach on Christ's charity and hospitality," said Davenport emphasising the last two words.

"I hope we are not imposing upon you and thank you for you kind words of welcome," said Whalley, aware of the need for shelter and friends. "And, Mr Jones, I am so terribly sorry to hear about your father. Mr Goffe and I were distraught. A most detestable occurrence and one we wholeheartedly find as unjust and unmerciful. May we both offer our heartfelt condolences," said Whalley.

"That is most gratifying, gentlemen, we were all shocked to hear about my father's execution and you may be assured of our help and protection here," said William Jones, only too aware what fate would befall him for harbouring the regicides.

"I would hope, Mr Davenport, that you will use all your considerable influence here, and in New England, to ensure these two brave men are protected whilst under our care," said Susan Hooke to Davenport.

"All of you may be assured of that," said Davenport,

determined to play his part in sheltering the men he admired and looked to for advice in maintaining his grip over this Puritan theocracy and independence from the King. "We have amongst us two great men who have, in their own way, fought for the principles in which we all believe. It is my view that whatever has happened in England is England's business. I have not, nor do I, interfere in their affairs; I also say, they should not interfere in ours. Gentlemen, you are welcome in my home and I will do all I can to assist you. May I remind you all that we are risking everything in this business."

CHAPTER 10

Coronation

"Excuse me, sir," said Gladstone, steward to Baron Belasyse. "The ferryman Kellogg asks if he may see you."

"Send him in straight away," said Belasyse frowning.

"He is waiting at the tradesman's entrance, sir," said Gladstone in an unhappy voice.

"Show him to the parlour and prepare two coffees and cake for us." And off went Gladstone with evident pique. Who was this upstart, a mere ferryman having a social coffee with a baron and lord of England like old friends? This former Republic had given the labouring class ideas above their station.

"Mr Kellogg, so good to see you. I hope all is well?" asked Belasyse, wondering why he had not gone through his steward as prescribed by etiquette. "Do sit down." Kellogg bowed and touched his forelock in the ancient sign of respect to his employer.

Both men took a seat and Belasyse looked at Kellogg, noticing anguish written all over his face.

"If I may say, sir, you have been most kind to me," said Kellogg, hesitating over his choice of words, "but I have decided to make a clean break. I am to depart for the plantations and away from the memory of my lost wife and start afresh. You sir run several estates and have high positions in society. You will know more than anyone that sometimes a man must leave everything behind and start again. After the loss of the woman I loved and worshiped, my heart is broken. I need a total change. Sir, I am going. You have been the finest employer I have ever had and I just wanted to say that and may God bring you and your household peace and prosperity forever. For you, sir, so thoroughly deserve it," said Kellogg, with a mixture of respect and kindness.

Belasyse looked at Kellogg, shocked to hear such news. "I know exactly what you mean and I understand; sometimes in life you suffer a sea change," said Belasyse, as they both drank their expertly prepared coffees. "But the plantations? There are strange plants and animals, not to mention the natives. They kill you, I have heard, and then the damn Puritans, no bright clothes and long tedious sermons. Not your idea of fun, I think, let alone the distance and the merciless seas. Are you sure about this?" said Belasyse with a frown.

Kellogg nodded. "I have given it much thought; many have crossed over and succeeded. I have a few contacts there as I have helped load and unload many cargos and passengers from the colonies. It is my decision and I will stand by it."

"So be it. You make your choices in life and live by them. I will help you if you need it and you help me if I need it, is that fair?"

"More than fair, sir."

"I fully understand your reasoning. I will charter a passage for you and your belongings, it's the least I can do. After all, you helped save my life and I do not forget those who have helped me, ever!" said Belasyse, with all the sincerity he could muster. They both shook hands, eyes moistening, as they parted. One going to the New World to start afresh and one staying to see if the old one would stay at peace. Belasyse saw his wife waiting by the door, frowning at the emotional scene she had just witnessed.

"We will advertise a replacement for the ferry service between Hull and Grimsby," said Belsayse sadly.

"I hope it all works out for him. He is a good man and good worker; we need such people."

"If all the people who cross the ocean to the plantations are like him, they will surely prosper. For any new venture needs clear heads and strong bodies, and he surely has both. On Sunday at church we will both pray for him," said Belasyse, staring at the disappearing back of a good and honest servant.

Ding, ding, went the front doorbell.

"Letters for Baron and Henry Belasyse," said the postman, dismounting from this sweat-lathered horse.

"I'll take them. I am Mary Belasyse my father is busy," she said, grabbing the vellum letters tied with purple ribbons and sealed with red wax.

"Don't open my mail, Mary!" said Belasyse, walking from the withdrawing room having heard the horse, as Peter Lely lowered his palate from the portrait he had been commissioned for and admired the baron's stupendous art collection.

"But father," she moaned.

"No," said Belasyse taking the letters. "Postman thank you and have a few ales on me," tossing him a silver sixpence.

"Very generous of you, sir," said the messenger by way of a goodbye, whilst doffing his hat and galloped back to Grimsby.

"Now call your big brother from the garden or I shall tell him about you puffing that tobacco."

"Oh dear, how did you know?" said Mary, blushing.

"Fathers find out. Oh!" exclaimed Belasyse, looking at the purple ribbons, "It's from the King. Mary, call Henry and the baroness and we will see what his Majesty has to say," he said, pleased to show his family the royal connection.

"Father," said Mary in a worried voice, "you promised us never again; the Republic is over, gone, finished."

Belasyse smiled softly and clasped his daughter by the hand. "Now, my dearest Mary, I am staying here on my estates and carrying out duties for the King. Now please, call Henry, so you can read the letter aloud so we may all hear our sovereign's words and, as you say, the nightmare is over," he said, reassuring his young daughter.

At long last all was well. He had been exhilarated over his

escape and thanked God for the return of the King from exile. To see his wife and children alive had made him realise how precious life was. Now he could enjoy the pleasures of peace. He looked out over the garden to see his son hand in hand with a young lady and he smiled to himself, maybe a daughter in law? Grandchildren. The future was bright.

"Father, you have met Susan Armyne?" said Henry Belasyse, leading his girlfriend by the hand from the garden into the withdrawing room. "We are growing quite attached to one another."

"Yes I have and I am pleased to see you enjoying each other's company. May I ask Susan, how is your father Sir William?"

"He is well and sends you his regards, sir," said Susan Armyne, curtsying before a baron of England, hoping the cleavage she was showing would attract the baron's attention as it had his son. She was desperate to the next Baroness of Worlaby.

"Excellent, do please send him my respects. Now, as the family are all here, I wish to say something of great importance. Gladstone, please assemble the staff," said Belasyse. The staff of the country estate of Worlaby gathered slowly, each being summoned from their tasks.

Belasyse paused for effect. "There is something I wish to give to my son and heir Henry." And he opened an ornate cabinet door of the large dresser, a gift from the King; standing at eight foot tall it dominated the room. Belasyse took a broadsword from the rack inside, it had an ornately engraved scabbard and withdrew the dark steel blade placing it in his son's hand.

"Son this is for you. It belonged to your grandfather, then myself and now it is yours. It is a dangerous weapon, make no mistake; it is for war. Use it as the last resort. Defend the humble and those who cannot defend themselves. You must be fearless in the face of your enemies, and protect our women and children, even if it costs you your life. You must never use it to enforce your beliefs or will upon others. Greatness, young man, comes from leadership and learning from your elders. England is the land of your birth; it is your child to protect and nurture, your wife to love and enjoy, your parent to listen to and, if necessary, to change for the better. Never forget that. We have land and wealth, but many do not. Respect all persons who are the subjects of the Crown, no matter what their station. Vanquish all the King's enemies, but show magnanimity; this, young man, will make your father proud and you will have the respect of your peers, but above all you will have wisdom and that will make you an honourable man."

The whole room admired the baron and this showed itself by the bows of the servants and their spontaneous applause. A fair employer is the best employer of all.

"Thank you all for your respect. Please do carry on with your duties," said Belasyse and the staff returned to their tasks. "Now, Mary please do read the letter from his Majesty," said Belsayse, smiling at his daughter out of love and kindness.

Mary opened the parchment, breaking the Royal seal and carefully undoing the knot on the purple ribbon and cleared her throat and read.

Whitehall Palace, London.

To our right, trusty and well beloved Baron John Belasyse,

I have appointed the twenty-third of April next for the solemnity of our Royal Coronation and the day before, being the twenty-second of the same month, for our parading from the Tower of London throughout the same City unto our Palace at Westminster. That you and your family make your personal attendance, where you will be furnished and appointed as to your rank and quality.

Best wishes,

Charles Rex.

"I am sorry, Father, I am mistaken. We lost mother five years ago and we do not want to lose our father. Henry adores you, as do I. We need a father, even though he catches us out," said Mary.

How did he find out about the tobacco? "I thought it may be a call for you to go and fight somewhere again," said Mary, relieved it was not another mission for her father. She had taken it badly when Belasyse had been imprisoned in the Tower. Almost daily, Commonwealth agents had searched the estate, threatening her and Henry. Most of the family heirlooms had been hidden, the rest had been looted by the troops, smashing anything breakable. Then stealing the furnishings and animals for firewood or food.

"As do I," said Baroness Belasyse, skipping into her husband's arms. "We must go to London so I can buy the latest French fashions and a new pair of the turquoise shoes, then we will stay at Whitehall, immaculately dressed, as guests of his Majesty the King."

"Shopping, fashions, shoes, handbags," gasped Belasyse. "What do you think I am, a bank?" he exclaimed.

"No, dearest, but why have cash lie in a vault? After all, we are going to the King's coronation, so you must buy Mary and I a court dress and shoes. Think of it – do you want to see your family look like down and outs? Just think how many will benefit from your largesse – silk weavers, seamstresses, buckle-makers, shoemakers, leather tanners, shop workers, even sailors for transportation; they all have an income. This encourages cross border trade, manufacturing and industry. If you don't spend, men don't work and the children's bowls go empty!"

Belasyse gave a low groan and sank into an armchair.

"Pass me a brandy, darling. I think I need a stiff drink." Then he sat upright and his eyes sparkled. "Now, if I don't have a drink, no one grows grapes, barley, wheat, hops, and the farms don't work. The coopers, brewers and distillers are unemployed, manufacturing bottles for wine and liquors, as well as jugs for ale; in fact, even the foresters are gone."

"Foresters?" the two women said in unison. "How do you work that out?"

"Ahh, foresters grow trees, cut them down, pulp the wood and what do you get?"

"Paper; you can't drink paper," they said loudly.

"True, but you can write on labels for bottles. The finest French brandy," said Belasyse smiling, and poured himself a generous glass and savoured the fumes contentedly. "Henry you have a letter from the King as well," said Belasyse, proud that his son had a letter from his monarch.

"As my son and heir you have responsibilities, you're nearly twenty-one. So let us all hear what his Majesty's chamberlain has written."

To Henry Belasyse of Worlaby, Lincolnshire,

His Majesty the King commands me, Sir Edward Nichols, the Lord Chamberlain, to formally invite yourself, the Baron, Baroness and Mary Belasyse, whilst staying as his guests at the Palace of Whitehall during the forthcoming celebrations, to a private audience, where Henry Belasyse will be invested with the noblest Order of Bath given in the twelfth year of our reign.

Signed,

Sir Edward Nichols.

"I think that's two outfits required, father, not one," said Mary with a cheeky grin.

"Oh no, I think I'll have another brandy!"

People started gathering before sunrise; nobody wanted to miss this grandest of all English occasions. It had been over thirty-five years since the last coronation and there were only a few old folks who could recall that momentous day. King Charles, resplendent in his coronation robes, mounted his beautifully accoutred charger, to ride the three-mile journey to the Palace of Whitehall. The procession from the Chapel of St John in the Tower of London was older than anyone could recall. The Princes James and Rupert followed their sovereign. Behind them, a train of the great and the grand. Dukes, earls, lords and knights of the realm, dressed in their finery, each one wearing their respective chain of office with evident pride. The City of London livery companies had been in overdrive for months, a boom for all, especially the Worshipful Company of Borderers, buying up all the French lace they could lay their hands upon. This this was to be a display to remember for years and it was an opportunity to display their craft. The King left the Tower to Aldgate; over the cobblestones went the procession, down Lime Street to Leadenhall, the spectators cramming every available space. Under a triumphal arch with a figure of rebellion being crushed by monarchy restored.

Past the Royal Exchange, where bands blasted out royal tunes and the crowd shouted plaudits and cheers, "God save the King!" Who bowed to the left and right, hardly daring to believe such an occasion was ever going to happen. Down Cheapside and Fleet Street, everywhere a vast crowd cheered their sovereign. It was as if England had awoken from a great nightmare and all were safe and sound. The King and his entourage entered Whitehall Palace where they would stay for the night and the coronation in the morning.

At last, Westminster Abbey and the west door, the King, flanked by the yeoman warders, dismounted and the crowd went silent. He hesitated, faced his people and bowed. The roar was heard for miles. Inside, the assembled were each seated according to their rank, with a great platform at the north end. The King entered bareheaded, as all must do to be recognised as the lawful sovereign. The floor was covered in a red woollen carpet, the middle area raised to the same height as the great pavement which was decorated with the finest example of Cosmati mosaic work north of the Alps. In the centre, a round piece of onyx, over this was placed the coronation chair and beneath it the great stone of scone. Hanging on the walls were the magnificent tapestries depicting the history of Abraham. The King was dressed in a white undershirt, the cuffs trimmed with embroidered lace, a taffeta of the finest silk, stockings with the order of the garter, the highest award in the nation, tied to his left leg. A surcoat, its cloth woven with silver thread. A mantle of ermine. A feast for the eyes. All the assembled rose and bowed to the King, a sign of their loyalty. The Earl Marshall, having done a stupendous job of organisation, nodded to the three bishops. The proceedings may get under way, as King Charles the Second bowed to the four corners of the Abbey. The dean, appointed by the King, stood by the right hand of his monarch along with the Archbishop of Canterbury, who placed the sceptre in the hands of the King. The symbol of the temporal authority of the monarch. The orb, Christ's universe, and the role as head of the Church of England. They in turn looked at the King, who smiled nervously whilst sitting in the coronation chair, first used to crown King Edward the Second. The Archbishop of Canterbury Juxon looked at Charles and thought to himself, *it is good that I am here to crown you, when I was the one who took your father's confession.*

"Is your majesty willing to take the oath?" he asked.

"I am willing. I, Charles Stuart, do swear to govern the people of this kingdom and the dominions according to their respective laws and customs and to preserve the true religion, so help me God."

The archbishop picked up the flask and poured holy oil into the spoon, a survivor of the republics destruction. He then anointed the King on his hands, breast and forehead. Then the investiture – the spurs, orb, sceptre and sword of state, symbolic of the King's intention to punish evildoers. Finally he picked up the St. Edward's crown from the alter, newly made as the old regalia and crowns had been destroyed on Cromwell's orders.

He took it from the cushion and placed it securely upon the King's head. It was done. From the archbishop onwards, all came to the coronation chair and pledged their allegiance. The news reached outside and the crowd went delirious. Cannons blasted out that the King had been crowned, according to the long and ancient right. Belasyse's wife cried tears of joy, as her husband made his way to the coronation chair. He bowed, withdrew his rapier and placed it with both hands in front of his sovereign in an act of unswerving loyalty. King Charles gave a broad smile and signalled his approval. The invited guests, having made their pledge, proceeded to Westminster Hall across the road for the banquet. There, to top it all, as they took their seats, the twin doors opened and in rode Dymock, the King's champion. He was clad in an immaculate suit of armour, shield and lance in hand, mounted on a great white charger from the royal mews. The assembled guests hushed, as the King's champion rode in to the centre of the hall.

The mare snorting in excitement, as the dignitaries stared at this unusual development. What was this man doing here? Silence pervaded the great room.

"If any person, of whatsoever degree, high or low, shall deny or gainsay our sovereign, Charles, King of Great Britain and Ireland, defender of the faith and heir unto our sovereign Lord Charles, first in name, martyred by the Republic, to be the rightful heir to the imperial Crown of this realm, or that he ought not to enjoy the same, here is his champion, who sayeth that he lieth and is a false traitor. I am ready, in person, to do combat with him in this quarrel to the death, on what day that shall be appointed." With that, he flung down a gauntlet, which made a crash when it hit the floor. All fixed their eyes on him as he slowly rode around the centre of the room. Lance outstretched so that you could touch it if you dared. He stared at the guests and asked a few to challenge him. No one moved or said a word. With this, he spoke to the King. "There is none, sire, who disputes your lawful right." The King thanked him and took a heavy gold cup, a waiter poured wine and the King sipped a little and passed it to him.

"This is your reward for your loyalty." Dymock smiled. He would drink from the same cup as his master. All was well and, with a great round of applause, he joined the sumptuous banquet.

Belasyse said to his wife, "Even Shakespeare could not write such a day as this." As his wife dabbed at her tears, knowing this is what they had fought and nearly died for.

"God save the King!" she cried, as Belasyse held her hand and shouted, "May God bless the greatness of my wife," and he too started crying tears of joy, as so many were in the room. May God be praised it's all over and he held his wife close to him.

"Good afternoon, may I inquire after a passage to New Amsterdam? A one-way ticket for the next sailing?" asked Dixwell, his charming smile covering up his inner panic.

"Certainly, sir," said the official from the Dutch West India Company who consulted his register of shipping. "We have a sailing in three days, sir. There are two styles of transport – first class, which includes fine lodging, food and wines at fifty ducats, or a shared berth and water, where the client would provide their own food, at thirty ducats," said the official.

"I will take the first class option," said Dixwell, taking the golden coins from an ornately stitched leather purse.

"Thank you," said the official, counting the money and writing a further passage in his register.

"May I have your travel permit and under what name shall I book the berth, sir?"

"Davids, James Davids," said Dixwell, handing over an immaculately forged government pass.

"The ship is called The Veilig, the Dutch word for safe, and she sails on the morning tide of the 28th March. Please be here three hours before departure with your baggage for the porters to load. Here is your ticket; please present it along with your permit to depart Dutch territory. I have also included the form to fill out when you reach New Amsterdam, and have a pleasant crossing, sir," said the official, pleased the customer had not tried to haggle over the price. Dixwell left the grand brick building in Amsterdam, headquarters of the Dutch West India Company, which owned the settlement. He noted the wooden crates containing the hides of various animals from the New World, along with bulbs and strange vegetables from the Orient, spices, along with exotic birds from the Cape of Good Hope, all for the thriving European market. A veritable emporium of goods.

I will have a new beginning. It is too dangerous to stay any longer in Europe after Downing betrayed my colleagues. Damn turncoat, he thought, *they would surely be hung, drawn and quartered. A horrible way to die* and he looked around for any stooges of the Crown. He was in no doubt that the King's agents were actively seeking the regicides that had escaped and they were well informed. As an Englishman in Europe, he would stand out. He couldn't speak a foreign language and that would be his Achilles' heel. If the King's men could capture three of the wanted men in one go, they could definitely get him. Barkestead, Corbet and Okey had been tricked into the English ambassador to Holland's residence, then transported to London and executed. He would surely be on the list he knew King Charles had, it was called the black book and it only would take a dozen gold ducats in the right place to see him on a scaffold at Charing Cross. He saw the Dutch settlement as the perfect place to hide. Hanau was a city he liked, but he felt it was time to part with the Old World. *At fifty-five I still have a few more years left and I want to enjoy them in peace.*

With the money he had taken from England after the sale of his possessions, he could buy himself a house, some land and go into business, which had made him a wealthy man in the Commonwealth. New Amsterdam was the last place the King's men would look

CHAPTER 11

It's a Manhunt

"Your Majesty, the ship Guinea has returned from the mission to capture New Amsterdam. I have a dispatch here marked for your eyes only from a Captain Breedon in Boston," said Moreland beaming.

"Excellent," said the King, taking the satchel, and as he read, his smile of satisfaction changed to a frown and then a snarl. "Send for Baron Belasyse immediately!" he demanded.

Belasyse put the letter down slowly and looked at the King.

"Captain Breedon mentions he had made extensive inquiries in Boston for the wanted men some years ago. Now a Joseph Kellogg has provided fresh information. If this is the man I am thinking of, he helped me flee the hangman's noose. Do you remember, Sir Samuel, when you gave me the fake passes written in Latin with the name, goodbye fool?"

"I do, Baron. You have an excellent memory."

"Goffe was on a skiff at the Tower. He had a meeting with Governor Barkstead and hopped on for a lift to Whitehall Palace and refused to pay for the trip, not even tipping the ferryman! Whose name was Joseph Kellogg. I employed him on my staff out of thanks for his help in my escape. Sadly, his wife died of smallpox and he left for the plantations. I trust him."

"If this letter from Breedon is to be believed, Goffe and Whalley have stirred from their hiding place," said the King. "Kellogg has not given his address in case the letter was opened and he could be sought out and killed, so he sent it to Breedon who tells us only that Kellogg recognised Goffe on his ferry somewhere in the plantations. We will meet again for afternoon tea and listen to your deductions as to this information."

"Afternoon tea, sire. May I ask what that is?" asked Belasyse.

"Most certainly. My wife brought the idea with her. You consume a fragrant beverage called tea with or without milk in the afternoon accompanied by delicate cakes; most civilised," said the King, as Belasyse and Moreland withdrew to study the satchel of documents from the New World.

"Gentlemen what are your thoughts?" asked the King, lifting his delicate china cup, its body patterned in gold and purple, the royal colours.

"Sire, there have been so many false sightings over the years and we still get reports of the remaining regicides across Europe," said Moreland. "It could be just another wild goose chase. We have dropped money in the right and often the wrong quarters, although Captain Nicolls who took New York, mentions rumours of a possible rebellion against the Crown."

"Baron, what is your view?" said the King, staring intently at Belasyse.

"From the information we have I surmise thus. Whalley and Goffe fled to Boston over four years ago, where they stayed for some time protected by the locals. With the capture of New York and due to the presence of our forces in the vicinity, both men have fled to a remote place, giving them the space and time, with no distractions, to plan a rebellion. Daniel Gookin is a major player and a man to follow. We can find out from him as to the whereabouts of the men your Majesty seeks," said Belasyse.

"I have here a basic map of New England," said Moreland, "which is mainly scattered villages roughly divided in to plantations, there are a few towns on the coast. It is interesting how the names are the same as if they have transplanted England across the water," said Moreland, intrigued at the settlements across the sea.

"That is understandable," said Belasyse. "When you go on a long journey a sense of familiarity and stability is what the mind needs, so it can be settled and think straight."

The King nodded in agreement and walked over to the painting of his parents by the Flemish artist Van Dyke. *They murdered my father and caused the death of my sister. As much as it is practical, it is also personal. If I am to seem weak, it will encourage the remnants of the Republic to make an attempt to kill me. I have no children yet, which leaves James as my heir. For his sake and mine, I must be strong. I don't want to go into exile again, as nothing more than a beggar to others. Not only that, there will be a war with Holland, therefore my resources will be tied up here. A perfect opportunity to declare an independent state behind my back.* After a few minutes he turned around.

"I am your King, and I will not tolerate treason. I have looked into these men's careers and they have much experience and motivation to move against the Crown. Baron," said the King, "do you think that the two former generals are on the move with insurrection on their agenda?"

"Yes, sire, I do. This is the perfect chance for an attempt at independence."

"If I send an army of, say, four thousand, I will leave myself open to a counter rebellion at home and a Dutch invasion and I will look like a tyrant and provoke them over the edge. Not only that, the word would arrive well before they sailed, thus allowing time for my enemies to prepare and the risk to so large a fleet is incalculable and they know it. This must be done discreetly. Gentlemen, I have arrived at this decision. By the authority invested in me by the House of Commons and Lords, I order you Baron John Belasyse of Worlaby, to sail across the ocean to Boston and seek out Commissioner Samuel Maverick who will assist you. Locate these two men and carry out the court's sentence upon their bodies, which is death in accordance with the law!"

Belasyse took a deep breath and stared rigidly at the King. He could not dispute the sovereign's order, no matter how much he wanted to. He had a settled life and wanted to grow old with his wife, see his children married and teach his future grandsons to ride and play this quaint new game of cricket. Now he would have to obey his sovereign's command and tell his beloved wife he was, once again, going into great danger on his sovereign's behalf.

"It is my duty to obey the monarch," said Belasyse, knowing the King had not called him here just for his advice. It had to be something more, and now he knew.

"And it is my duty to ensure that my subjects are given the support they need. I will have proclamations for your use to ensure all officials obey any of your commands. I have chosen you because you're the best I have," said King Charles. Belasyse thought for a few moments.

"If I may, sire, could any letter sent to the plantations be held in case anyone discovers my mission, but keep one vessel ready for a letter I think will be sent? I don't want to scare the quarry, just confront it, and I have an idea where to start. Sir Samuel, do you have the address of the residences of the families of Whalley and Goffe?" asked Belasyse.

"The homes of the fugitives' families have been searched several times already we know they are across the ocean."

"It's not where you search, it's how you search, Sir Samuel, and I am a hound."

"Good, it is settled then," said the King, smiling at Belasyse's shrewdness.

"Baron, I appreciate you will have some difficult moments with your wife. I am not unaware of the danger you are putting yourself in, and will not be ungrateful. After all, we both have a secret and I have this for your wife." The King strode over to the richly carved baroque mantelpiece in his closet and picked up a cream-coloured box containing a diamond and ruby tiara. "If I may, you should send for her; there are apartments in Whitehall Palace at your disposal. I will also speak with Lady Anne. I am aware this will cause much disruption to you. I want an end to this whole affair; it is like a suppurating wound and must be lanced if we are to move on from the past." The King knew his man. *If he couldn't find them no one could*, and he departed to his private closet to write the necessary documents for the baron's mission.

Belasyse made his leave from the Palace of Whitehall and hired a skiff to Windsor Castle. He had not made this journey before, but now he felt he had to. Through the Henry the Eighth gate to the Chapel of St. George. There, at the altar, was the dean praying.

"Sir, I would, if I may, pray at the coffin of his Majesty King Charles."

"Of course," said Bruno Ryves, the King's personally appointed dean. "Most thoughtful of you. Please do follow me," he said kindly. "Here we are, down the stairs ahead of you, turn left, walk forward maybe ten paces and turn to the right. His coffin rests there; a martyr and saint to the Anglican faith."

"Thank you so much," said Belasyse and took a five-branched candlestick holder from Ryves and proceeded down the stairs to his left, waiting as his eyes adjusted to the dark. He moved ahead a few paces, then to the right, the atmosphere becoming dank and claustrophobic. The candles making flickering signs on the cold, dusty walls, cobwebs of all sizes abounded making the eerie feeling come alive. In front of him was a barrel-shaped vault. He entered and there, lying on the floor, was a simple oak coffin with the words Charles Rex carved onto a tin plate. He gently put the candle holder on top of the coffin and got on his knees. "Sire, it has been these fifteen years and I have not and will not forget. May the Lord give me the strength to finish this business once and for all." Belasyse walked back to the jetty at the foot of Windsor Castle, his shoulders broadening as he thought about the arguments. The generals had to be dealt with, they could raise a rebellion; he was surprised they hadn't already. He would return to London, contact his good friends and start the hunt again. So many challenges ahead, not least telling Anne. But he also had to admit he was a little bored at home and he said to himself, nothing beats outfoxing the fox. His heart beat faster with the thrill of the chase, but what secret did he share with the King?

"You're soaking, John. I told you to take a coat. It's raining cats and dogs," said Villiers, squinting through a rain-soaked scarf as they walked up Cheapside. The market refuse providing a breeding ground for the many rats which caused periodic outbreaks of plague.

"You have told me that already and it's too late. Now gentlemen, watch either side of the door and stay under the eaves; no one will see you there. Make sure you have a good angle to shoot, ensure your powder stays dry and only if I duck, you fire. She has no guests and her children should be asleep. I don't see her as an adulterer," said Belasyse, who adjusted the small pistol in his right boot, ensuring it was covered in the waxed sail cloth.

"Correct, she's mutton," said Villiers and Russell.

They split up, crossed the street and sheltered under the eaves of the houses, standing at the opposite sides of the front door Belasyse was standing in front of. The constant rain covered their sound and ensured there was no one out, not that they would be on a Sunday night as the Sabbath was still strictly observed, even though the King had returned. Belasyse gave them a few minutes to get into position, then rapped several times sharply on the door.

Several minutes passed, then a worried voice was heard. "Who is it? What do you want at this hour?" was the aggravated answer to Belasyse's knocking.

"My name is Minister Richard Head. It's very important,"

said Belasyse in a loud voice so his companions could hear, and they smiled at his humour.

Russell knew why he led them and they were happy to follow. No matter how difficult the situation, he always kept his cool and made them laugh in the face of danger. Belasyse heard the bolts being drawn and he stepped back a pace, whilst placing a two-foot rod of iron on the doorstep. He moved to the side, offering the best line of fire he could in the gloom, just in case. The fires of over thirty thousand houses in London kept the city in a semi smoke-ridden dank, but the rain had cleared most of that for the time being. The soot being washed off the timber and thatched houses created a black oily residue on the street, staining his brown leather boots. The door opened for a moment and Frances Goffe saw a man with a scared face standing in the rain, with a pair of white Geneva bands stuck to his jacket and rain dripping off a wide brimmed hat down his entire body, soaking him through. He forced a kindly smile on his face.

"Err, Minister, what is it?" said Frances Goffe, opening the door and allowing the light from the candles to escape onto the street. No one appeared alongside her; there was no protector! *Perfect,* the three men thought. She hesitated and Belasyse almost jumped through the door, using his chest to push it open, having flicked the iron rod into the gap to prevent the door being shut.

"Good evening, Mrs Goffe. Mrs Frances Goffe, isn't it?" And she knew she had been tricked.

"Who are you and what do you want?" she barked, alarmed at the presence in her house of this unusual man. "I don't know you and your actions are not that of a minister."

"You are completely correct, madam, and I unreservedly apologise for jumping into your parlour, but it is a little wet outside and I did not wish to break down your door. I assume your children are asleep upstairs; there is no need to wake them. My name is Baron Belasyse. I mean no offence to you or anyone in your house, nor do I wish any person here harm."

"So what do you want?"

Belasyse took the document written by the King and placed it on the sideboard by the spinning wheel. Frances Goffe picked up the letter and frowned as she read it.

"I assume you did not come all this way from Whitehall in the rain to show me how important you think you are," she said sarcastically.

"No, madam, I did not. Please be assured of my quality. I am here to tell you that in no way are you responsible for your husband's action in the late King's execution. The searching of your property and the questioning of yourself and friends will cease. His Majesty said that to me personally."

"Thank you," said Frances Goffe stiffly. "The indignities heaped upon myself, family and my friends are unworthy and insulting; not only that, a women on her own, without the protection of a husband to bring up the frightened children. It is a disgrace, which I hope you will convey to the King! You are the ones trumpeting the return of the monarchy but your instrument is, sir, well out of tune."

"That depends on the song you are playing," mentioned Belasyse with his signature smile. "If I may, I feel the persecution of your husband has been unwise and unnecessary. Unwise, because it shows disrespect to a cause many thousands fought for and many still believe in. Unnecessary, as your husband is over the ocean and therefore serves no purpose. Your husband and I faced each other several times in battle and he always conducted himself impeccably throughout the war. If I may be totally honest with you, madam, I wish he had been on our side," said Belasyse, hoping she would act calmly and not wake the children or neighbours. He wanted this visit to be as private as possible. "I appreciate you saying that, Baron; those vagabonds of Moreland's have harassed me long enough.

My home has been turned upside down and my life continually interrupted by those villains. I do not know my husband's whereabouts these four years, and I wouldn't tell you even if I knew," said Frances Goffe, sensing a breaking of the ice. At last, a gentleman. She remembered her husband mentioning his name, what, about ten years ago, and what a formidable man the baron was.

"You have been inconvenienced long enough, Goodwife Goffe, and it is high time it stopped. You are a law-abiding, sober, honest citizen and that is an example to all in society," he said almost apologising. *Let her vent her spleen,* he thought, *then they could get more practical.*

"My husband and I had many frank conversations during the war and afterwards. He made some very good points about the cause he was engaged in. A pity you Royalists wouldn't listen."

"Such as?" asked Belasyse respectfully.

"We are judged on our work, not our worth, our principles, not our status, on what we do, not our father's station."

"Fair points, madam. Having a title should bring integrity, leadership and never looking down on someone, whether they are a king or a gardener. Station should be used to better all persons, not just the man who holds it. Good clothes make a man look smart, but they do not give him good judgement; compromise and reason are the qualities we should look to. That is what everyone, whatever their condition, should strive for. But the two most important things are loyalty and courage and you, madam, are imbued with both," said Belasyse, giving a small bow to the head of the house.

Frances Goffe stood in the middle of the room staring at her adversary. *My God, to hear this gives me more pleasure than I can take,* her enemy, no!

"Baron, may I offer you a pot of ale?" said Frances Goffe, thinking she had chivvied him enough. There is no point in making enemies and the baron sounded like a reasonable man. *If only all the King's men were like him. Some of those Royalists were so arrogant, with their wealth and titles, lording it over their tenants and staff.*

"You are most hospitable, madam, but I have inconvenienced you. Your husband is beyond the reach of even the King and it is time to stop this mischief-making. I will be on my way and do not wish to dampen your furniture or leave a larger pond in your home than I am making with my dripping clothes. I do apologise," said Belasyse, giving a sorrowful look at the increasing puddle in the middle of the room, and moved towards the door and turned to face his adversary's wife. "It is a privilege to meet someone so polite and resilient. Your husband is a most fortunate man. May I present this to you and your house." And he placed a golden guinea on the sideboard.

That will feed my family for at least a month thought Francis Goffe.

"I will have the doubtful pleasure of facing London's lovely weather again," he chuckled, staring intently at Frances Goffe.

"Wait, your Lordship, take this; I have no need of it." And she took a long, dark brown leather coat with a black beaver collar from the rack by the front door. "Sorry if I have been abrupt; it is not easy being a mother on your own and knowing your husband is a wanted man. I just want to be left in peace and get on with my children's future."

"Trust me, madam, I know what it is like being hunted and you may rest assured no one will call on you again. May God bless you," said Belasyse as a goodbye. He took the coat, picked up the rod of iron and walked into the pouring rain on Cheapside not looking back, as Frances Goffe closed the door behind him, rather hoping the tall handsome baron would call on her again. He had charm and however loyal her husband was, he was cold and unemotional. She knew in her heart she would never see him again. He had sailed away leaving her with the children. If it was not for the good charity of friends and her aunt Jane Hooke, she would be destitute.

Frances Goffe bolted the door as Richard Goffe lowered the pistol his father had left him. "We should let Father know the hunt is over," he said with palatable relief from the top of the stairs.

Russell and Villiers joined Belasyse, as they checked the street for the umpteenth time for passers-by. "Now, let's get back to Whitehall Palace. I am wet, cold, in need of a hot bath and a rum toddy," said Belasyse.

Russell brought the steaming pewter mug of rum, lime juice and sugar. "This will revive you. I'll be surprised if you don't get ill, John," said Russell, concerned that his mentor had been out in the rain for hours.

"All is necessary if we are to catch them and I need all the advantages we can get. They will make one mistake, which is a clue by any other name," said Belasyse, sipping on the toddy while soaking in a hot bath.

"Are we ready?" he said, as they changed into fresh clothes.

"Yes, ready." And off they went again into the dripping night on the trail of the King's enemies.

Belasyse checked his pocket watch again and thought to himself, *I wonder if I have misjudged her. I have got my friends on this errand and I hope I'm right.* Then the back door opened a fraction and a very small shaft of light shone through from a single candle and a figure emerged into the night. With practised movement, it scampered to the back gate, waiting for a few minutes to see if there was anyone visible, and to adjust its eyes to the night. *This figure has done this many times*, thought Belasyse and pulled on the ball of twine to alert his friends. Very carefully, he followed, just making out the figure in the gloom. As they moved ahead to the left and right, knowing their duty, not a word passed between them. Up Cheapside, then right on Wood Street then left at London Wall, all the while Belasyse and his companions keeping ahead and to the side of their quarry. The church of Minister John Rowe could be the destination. As they arrived in St. Bartholomew's Close, the figure crouched on the side of the road, listening for any sound apart from the consistent rain. Belasyse did not worry; his boots were lined on the inside and out with wool, he carried no sword and was dressed in dark grey. He would not stand out and his companions were on the other side of the figure, well hidden. A youngster, Goffe's son! The figure pulled gingerly on the rope bell, enough to wake the sleeper, but no noise on the outside. It was probably situated by the minister's bed; clever. The door of the church opened slowly, well-oiled to give away no sound and no candle to illuminate the scene. A quick whispered conversation followed, a package was handed over and the door closed. The figure walked quickly back the way it came and the three men followed in a semi-circle, watching intently until the back door of the Goffe house closed.

"Done," said Belasyse. "Back to Whitehall Palace and bed," and off went the three members of the Sealed Knot to a well-earned sleep at the King's pleasure.

"Did anyone see you?" said Frances Goffe.

"No, mother, I checked twice as father told me and I gave the letter to Minister Rowe as you asked," said Richard Goffe with bated breath, enjoying his position as agent for his father. "Mr Rowe promised to send the letter on in the morning, but he did want a shilling for doing so," said Richard Goffe.

"Cheeky man; he takes a tenth of everything I and your father's friends send him. If he is as poor as a church mouse he says he is, that mouse must have gout with the amount of port he drinks. Back to bed young man and remember, say nothing to no man of this subject; as I have told you before, your father's life is in grave danger," she said to her son as a goodnight.

I wonder where my husband is right now? Across the ocean and far away, sadly. Maybe I should take the family and go over; had not the baron said that no one would trouble me again, but someone would talk; a golden crown would tell a story readily enough. I miss a man; even the simple things like fixing my son's broken bed, trying to use a saw for winter wood and bargaining in Leadenhall Market was difficult for a woman and, thinking of beds, there was no one to warm hers at night. Just having my man next to me made me feel safe and secure. She fought back tears of self-pity. *I must be strong for the children. Even that baron could warm my bed for a night. I wonder what he would be like by my side; he had an annoying, knowing smile. I'll bet he knows a few tricks to liven up a dull winter's night. Stop,* she said to herself, *bad thoughts; he did have that certain type of charm. I bet he has satisfied a few maidens in his time.* She drew back the covers, climbed in and blew out the candle. Moreland's agent noted the time and climbed down the ladder propped up on the back garden wall and went back to Whitehall to write up his report.

"His name is Minister John Rowe. He provided letters of introduction for Whalley and Goffe in Boston. With the information provided by the Sealed Knot, your Majesty, I can deduce that the conduit for money and intelligence is coming from the wife and friends of the surviving regicides. It is being assimilated by the said minister and being transferred to Captain Gookin and thus to the wanted men. I am having all persons mentioned watched and any developments will be reported to you sire," said Belasyse with an authoritative air. The King weighed up the information, thinking carefully.

"I will have all those persons quietly questioned and their activities stopped. Baron, here are the documents you will need for your journey," said the King, proffering a heavy vellum envelope. "And the reward of two hundred pounds in gold for the capture of the wanted men and twenty pounds in silver shillings to help loosen tongues," he said, pointing to a leather bag on the elegantly carved table. "The ship Guniea is being revictuled, and under Captain Carr will return to Boston. You leave tomorrow evening and Prince Rupert has a surprise for you."

"Here, John," said the Prince, "seven pounds weight of the new gunpowder I have created. It is twice as potent as the present type we use. I have ordered the ordinance department at the Tower to let you use the range to try it out with pistol, musket and a musketoon. Is there anything else we can do for you?" asked the Prince, concerned for an old comrade in arms.

"Thank you, but I have all I need."

"These damn Puritans need to be taught a lesson. We should send an army over to remind them who is in charge, damn traitorous wretches," said Prince James.

"No James, we do this my way," said the King. "Subtlety will win this."

"Baron," said the King, "you will not find many friends across the water, but I sincerely hope not too many enemies. I do appreciate you have a difficult journey ahead of you."

"It is not the length of the journey, sire, it is what you learn along the way. In this world of greed, dubious politicians jockeying for power and backstabbing for position, as well shifting loyalties, I am and always will be loyal to the Crown and nation of my birth. Nothing will shake my resolution to this your Majesty, nothing, and for you to ask me to carry out this mission makes me proud to do my duty for my sovereign. I seek no reward and would accept none if it were offered. A man cannot do more than his duty, sire, and he should never wish to do less. God save the King," said Belasyse determinedly, bowed and withdrew from the room. The King withdrew a lace handkerchief from his right-hand pocket and wiped his eyes. "May God shine on him, for no king could have a more loyal subject and a braver man. Will he succeed, Rupert?" asked the King hopefully.

"If he can't then no one can. He can ride, shoot and use a sword better than anyone I know. He is shrewd, ruthless and totally loyal. On the other side of the coin, he faces an over three thousand mile crossing with pirates and others who may intercept the ship. He will have to travel in disguise and his cover could be blown at any time. It is a strange land, only just settled, with strange native tribes who do not speak our tongue and most of them don't want us there. He will have to search thousands of miles and will need all the luck there is. It is his greatest challenge, for if he does find them, those who hide the generals know the punishment for sheltering traitors and they will kill him without hesitation, as would the generals themselves. I honestly don't see how he can," said Prince Rupert, worry written across his face.

"No!" exclaimed Villiers and Russell. "He can't expect you to go to that length."

"What can I do, refuse? I must sail across the ocean to a land of Puritan zealots and disloyal subjects."

"John, would you like us to come with you? We're a team," said Villiers.

"No, this time it is best I work alone, but there is one thing you can do for me. I want you to both promise me you will look after my family if I don't return."

"Of course," said Villiers and Russell, horrified they may never see their good friend again.

"We would do anything for you, you know that. We will call on them, rest assured," said Russell.

"I cannot but thank you. I am caught up in this whirlwind and cannot escape."

They all shook hands as Belasyse went to the King's private apartments to tell his wife he was once again going into great danger on his sovereign's behalf.

"I know that look," shouted Anne Belasyse, Baroness of Worlaby. Belasyse looked at the floor of the withdrawing room, as Cavendish made a hasty exit. He had seen the determined look on the baron's face. The long meeting with the King had not been a social visit and the family's temporary move to Whitehall Palace had but one purpose – to prepare them for this moment.

"Why do you have to do this, why? You promised, never again," Anne shouted, tears streaming down her face, her body shaking in fear mixed with anger. "You should be here to love and protect me. You know the torment we all endured during the wars. Don't you care about me at all?" said Anne through her tears, anguish etched in her delicate face.

Belasyse's shoulders slumped. "I don't expect you to understand, nor should I. A man has to follow the King's orders. In a strange way I am protecting you by ridding this world of the last of the fanatical men who brought our country to ruin. I know it is only words, but I have written this down for you." Belasyse took an envelope from his jacket and placed it in his wife's hands and walked out the front door to the skiff waiting to ferry him to the Guinea, not wishing to prolong the emotional agony for his wife. He had to finish this once and for all.

Anne tore the letter open.

To you, the finest wife our Lord ever created,
The summer has the sun, the autumn its dew
and the world is made sweeter by the life of a woman like you
and if you are cold I shall give you warmth,
when lonely I shall be your companion.
If you are scared I shall protect you and when you are hungry I will
feed you.
At night I will be your lover and in the morning your best friend,
for your fingers have touched my silent heart and taught it how to
sing, for true love is Crown that makes a man a king.

Anne's tears started flowing again and dripping onto the paper, causing the ink to run in little rivulets down the page. She clasped the letter to her bosom and ran out the front door to the street, shouting her husband's name. Belasyse's heart sank again. *My God, what am I putting this woman through?*

"Now, John Belasyse, you listen to me," said Anne, shouting

and grabbing her husband's hands. "You do your duty for our King and do that with every bone in your body. Vanquish all his enemies and ensure these rebels are finished. I want no more war. Then you come back with your love and give it all to me." She shouted with a passion even she didn't know she had. Anne pulled her husband close and kissed him with an intensity that shocked him. Both of them cried, holding each other in a passionate embrace, knowing they may well never see each other again. Belasyse ruled her heart and treasured it more than life itself.

CHAPTER 12

Honest Man

"Gentlemen, may I introduce Mr Richard Sperry, a man of great courage. He is the first person to venture out of New Haven and build his own farm away from the protection of the town, near a lake on the far side of the great west rock. There he will keep you safe until this matter is resolved," said Davenport, urging the two men onto Sperry's waggon. "The King's soldiers are here to ensure there is no Dutch retaliation after the taking of New Amsterdam."

"Thank you so much, Mr Davenport. Your courage and fortitude are a great strength to us," said Whalley in thanks.

The generals looked Richard Sperry up and down; if any man left the enclosed town to build a farm in the wilderness he must be extremely brave, or extremely foolhardy, and only time would tell which one he was. For they were in his hands now and off they went into the great unknown, still one step ahead of their pursuers.

"We all must have faith," said Sperry, as the waggon trundled along the track from the town, rutted and scored by the trees felled for firewood and building. "Without faith a man is lost to the wilderness. I have built a farm and have settled down to raise a family. Back in England I was an apprentice farmer in the county of Bedfordshire. As a young man, I sought to right what I thought were wrongs in our country, but fell afoul of Archbishop Laud and his henchmen. I was sent here by the Earl of Warwick and worked hard as an indentured farmer for his friend Mr Stephen Goodyear for ten years. Then I was granted land outside the town and built my dream." Sperry turned to the generals. "I know it's not much, but it's mine, fairly given, and I work the six days and on Sunday I go to church. I pay my land tax every year, drill with the militia and harm no man. There is neither war here nor do we wish to see one."

"I hope I am not being impertinent, Mr Sperry," said Goffe "but why do you hide us? After all, we are former soldiers from the Parliamentary Army."

"I am loyal to Mr Davenport and help him in times of trouble. That is why I am helping you, because, quite simply he asked me to. You will find things are like that here; we have less of your politics and more practical considerations to deal with. Now, we are some five miles from New Haven and sheltered by the rock. Towards the town and to the south are meadows, therefore a man on a horse can be seen for sixty rods following the trail to this house, so hopefully we will spot any visitors before they arrive. We need to build you a hiding place. Do you remember when you were children, building huts in the woods? Well if you do, we must recreate one for you to hide in. Gentlemen, welcome to my home."

Goffe and Whalley looked at Richard Sperry's farm. Dry stone walls divided up the fields. Logs were stacked five feet high by the side of the house, seasoning for winter fuel. Pear, plum and apple trees in rows of six. Chickens roamed around the saltbox-style house. It had a lean to extension at the back, for cooking and smoking meat, cheeses and sausage, most of which was stored for winter food. Hogs foraged at the river bank with roots, grasses and flowers providing a rich diet. Onions, peas, turnips and carrots grew in the vegetable garden, as his family worked happily in the fields. Both men kept out of their view, ensuring only Richard Sperry knew they were being hidden.

"It's not Windsor Castle, but it's my castle and that is what counts," said Sperry.

Whalley walked slowly and purposefully up to the house with its roughly plastered walls and rudimentary windows. He turned to Sperry and asked, "Sir, is this your own doing?"

"Mostly; I paid the carpenter in kind, seasoned logs, butter, milk and beef. The rest my family and I built with our own hands and the sweat of our brows. No Lord and his gold built this. With honest endeavour, we have the first house my family and I have ever owned," said Sperry with pride, looking at the two men.

A hardworking man and his family had made a home amongst the wilderness. They had a viable, thriving farm. He fed his family, sold his excess or bartered it to provide a future for his wife and children. When he had started with nothing, he now had a home of his own and Whalley lowered his head in respect. "I, with my son-in-law, are hunted men and upon our lives and you risk your own to help us. I cannot but thank you and God for your courage in this matter. We will, with our limited means, do all we can to help you," said Whalley, tears falling down his cheeks showing his relief that this humble, God-fearing man would risk his life to hide them.

"We are, sir, most honoured to be your guest. May God preserve you and your family," said Goffe, thinking to himself, *we are upon the mercy of a humble farmer.*

"Thank you. We have a four-bedroom cottage, not quite a log cabin as some do. The house is not quite the same as in England. We have a brew room, but it doubles as the bathroom and washing room, probably the busiest in the house. The stream I have partially diverted so as to have constant running water. A parlour and kitchen downstairs. You will note the roof is double slanted and at a steep angle due to the snow. May I assure you, it does heavily in winter and I don't want the weight of it to crush the roof. Now, if the authorities do come to New Haven, they will search the locality, therefore we need to find you a hiding place just in case. Only Mr Davenport and I know you are here. I will keep this from my family. You know how children gossip and we all go into town twice a week to the market and church where they are learning to read and write, something that I cannot."

Goffe and Whalley followed Sperry into the woods, their packs weighing them down. Much of it had been cut down for lumber and the land cleared for planting and pasturage. Both men looked up and admired the great western rock, as it was known. They crossed a small stream so dogs could not follow their sent and climbed up the rock face a small way.

"This is a natural cave, let's clean it out, level the floor as much as we can and make a covering for the entrance, as a defence against inclement weather and wild animals. I will provide logs, food every day and there is fresh water from the two streams coming off the rock just to the right of this shelter where you can wash. If you wish to shoot deer, please do so around dusk. That is the best time. I doubt very much anyone is going to hear you. The great rock and distance will cover any sound. I will also leave cheese, ham and other smoked provisions for you in case I am away on business," said Sperry.

"Thank you for your concern," said Goffe impressed at Sperry's resourcefulness and candour.

"There is a tinder box and lint for a fire. Now contact – when I raise a lantern on the chimney it is a warning I have visitors, so beware the lantern on top of my house. The less people know, the less they can tell."

"Is it permissible to fish in the lake and trap them in the streams?" asked Goffe.

"No, don't, remember you are hiding, and so stay in the cave as long as you can. You're being hunted; give your pursuers no opportunity to find you or we will all hang!"

"Do you have a musket we can use for hunting? Our pistols are really only good for close up work," asked Whalley.

"Yes, I do. Most are kept in the town meeting house or with the militia. I have a musket; it took me over two months of constant training to understand how to use it. In England only the gentry knew how, as most of us worked a Lord's land we could not hunt his game on fear of prison, so most of us never knew how to use a firearm, which is why many of the early settlers went hungry. I need a musket for defence against the natives, but the tribe which used to inhabit these parts named the Quinnipiac, are peaceful, though most have died of smallpox or other diseases."

"At least we won't have trouble from that quarter," said Goffe thankfully, worried at the position they both found themselves in.

"I will leave it out twice a week with the food. Now I must go and organise your supplies," said Sperry and left the wanted men to their new home.

"We had better get cracking," said Whalley to Goffe.

"I don't wish to cause Mr Sperry any offence but living in a cave, are we animals? It is not fit for high ranking officers in the New Model Army. It's wrong!" said Goffe, appalled by his predicament.

"Our world has turned upside down and that won't count when the authorities hang us, will it?" asked Whalley and started to build a rudimentary door to keep out the bears and wolves he knew roamed these parts. But William was right; my, how they had fallen. Once commanding a whole county with thousands of troops at their disposal, beholden only to the Lord Protector himself. Now reduced to living in a cave. It remained to be seen how long those agents would keep up the hunt. As he cleared the cave floor of stones and leaves, he cast his mind to England. He wondered if he had made the right decision to run, leaving his family in hope the King would not harm them. So far, Minister Rowe had written that they were well. Both men cleared the cave, each with their own thoughts, knowing now they had hit rock bottom, literally.

Snap went the dry stick and Whalley awoke. He had deliberately placed dozens of them, along with dry leaves around their hiding place to trick anyone who approached. He looked up, whilst reaching for his pistol. He saw a pair of orange eyes glaring in the dark over the top of the barrier to their hiding place. "Up!" he shouted to his son-in-law and drew his pistol and fired just below the space where saw the eyes. The sound of the pistol shot ringing in his ears and bouncing off the walls as both men rushed to either side of the entrance.

"What in heaven's name was that?" said Goffe shaking, still ringing in his ear from the close confines of the cave.

"A cougar, I think," gasped Whalley. "Sperry described them to me. It's like a large cat and may kill us, given a chance." Both men shuddered at the thought of being eaten alive by this hunter and stared out into the darkness, hoping the animal had been scared off.

"I've had enough," shouted Goffe. "I am not going to live like a dog in a cave hoping for the generosity of a few. All my plans are in tatters, my estate forfeited and the hoped for rebellion against the King has faltered. We should call on Jones, Leete and Davenport. I will ask for their favour that we raise the town militia against the Crown. Enough of this living in a cave."

"One moment, young man. I have always listened to your council and, as the elder man, should teach younger people to benefit from measured, sound advice. Are you seriously asking the people of New Haven, some one hundred and fifty able men, to start a war against the King of England?

"Yes I am." Shouted Goffe, his voice bouncing off the walls of the cave and into the valley beyond. "There are enough good men who support us. We could raise some five thousand men, probably more. We both have enough military experience to train and command double that amount. How would the King retake this land, when faced with an army that size? He would be forced to concede as Holland could invade and they are a republic.

"How do you arrive at that conclusion?" asked Whalley, getting worried at the direction the conversation was taking.

"Simple; he would need at least seven thousand troops to retake this land. No one has crossed the ocean with that number, ever, let alone the equipment needed or food. Where could he land? Boston, New Haven, these are Puritan strongholds."

"He could land in Virginia, which is loyal to the Crown," countered Whalley.

"True, but how far would they have to march to get here. Even if he could, when that army landed here the former soldiers we commanded back in England would rise up against him and overthrow the monarchy again. We would be welcomed back as the greatest heroes the nation has had. You can slip into idleness, I for one will not. Perhaps you forgot what we fought and thousands died for. You have accepted the King's return, I have not."

There was a hushed silence, whilst both men thought about what the other had said.

"The people, given the right motivation and leadership, would follow us. We are the ones to provide that," said Goffe, desperately hoping his father-in-law would join him on his quest.

"That may be, but let me play the devil's advocate. There are many persons who are loyal to the King and they are as motivated as us, they will fight. The last battle of our civil wars was fought here. The King's men were defeated and some were shot after they surrendered. They would look for revenge. The King would send an army, join with the loyalists and then destroy us."

"Army, what army? The countryside is full of disbanded New Model Army soldiers, just waiting for a chance to rise again; you know that, and the Dutch in the now New York would aid us." said Goffe.

"The soldiers that protect the King are not those men. The

men we commanded are tired, unarmed and their zeal gone, they seek peace and we both know that. After all, if they didn't, the King would have not returned. The King's forces are largely made up of exiled Royalists. You would give them the perfect excuse to get revenge back in England. Where, I would point out, our families reside. Have you not thought of that?"

"They wouldn't dare."

"You think not? We're known, William. How did Belasyse escape from the execution squad? Someone high up in the system helped him escape. You would be putting our families directly in the line of fire. It's lucky he's not over here hunting us. How about thousands of soldiers recruited from Ireland? A nation we ruthlessly crushed. What would their agenda be? Now, please think of that before we make such a momentous decision," said Whalley, as Goffe walked up and down the cave fuming like a cornered bull. He looked up and Whalley continued carefully. "This is a new country, still finding its way. It has not seen the horrors of war as we have, whether in Europe or, as we both know so well, in England. This land was not born from a King's command, or a conquering general's sword. Let it grow without a cannon or musket shot ringing in its ear. If we do, as you say, raise the militias, how many people, who have fled war, will meet that same fate here? Is that to be our epitaph – warmongers?"

"And I thought it was the young who would change the world. Self-evidently I still have things to learn," said Goffe in resignation.

"William, the young can and will change the world. But they have to know how it works first. We would love these settlers to be citizens and not subjects, but not yet I fear. I think we will have to take the momentous step of giving ourselves in. We must be resolute and give nothing away to any man. All who have helped us must not suffer for their kindness. When I let you marry my daughter, you entered my family and I treat you like my son.

For that I have no regrets and I will stand by you to the end, even if that costs me my life. I swore that at the feet of Jesus Christ," said Whalley. Goffe gave a look of total resignation and they embraced each other, knowing that the King would have his revenge on them after all.

"Mr Sperry," said Whalley. "I have spoken at some length with Mr Goffe and we cannot but thank you for being our saviour, but we have come to a decision that we feel we cannot trouble you any longer and wish to give ourselves up to the authorities, to spare you and the good people who have helped us, the wrath of the King's men."

"So be it, gentlemen. If that is your decision I will not stop you." Richard Sperry took in the scene. Goffe looked beaten and Whalley resigned to his fate. They hadn't shaved or bathed in weeks, their clothes merely rags. Still, it was their decision.

"I will take you, Mr Jones and Minister Davenport immediately."

"Run, two of the King's agents are in New Haven!" shouted Susan Hooke hitching up her skirts and running towards her brother. Then she saw the look over her brother's face and abruptly stopped.

"No, my dear sister, we have decided to give ourselves up," said Whalley despondently.

"Edward, please," shouted Susan, her chest heaving with the exertion of running along the beaten track with a twenty-pound dress and petticoats on, never mind the awkward shoes.

"You have given up? Well. I have not! Mr Sperry is right; now is not the time to do so. Anyway Edward, why do you want to give in? Lost your fire in the good old cause have we? Or maybe it's that women are stronger and more capable of withstanding the pressures of life. Have you lost your zeal in our cause when I and so many others here and in England hoped you would remain strong? A few weeks in the wilderness and you give in. Many pioneers have withstood it for years. Christ never complained when he used a stone for a pillow, had years of trouble and he didn't quit. You're weak, Edward, and a failure as you were early on back in England. Do you remember when you ran away from your creditors to Scotland? Now you're running away again!"

Both men stood like they had been turned to stone, amazed at such an outburst. "That hurt," said Whalley indignantly.

"It was meant to," said Susan. Raising her voice to fever pitch. "Now go, both of you, back to the cave and keep the faith we have in you. Or Edward Whalley do you want to see your sister hanged?"

Whalley took a deep breath, went red with indignation and anger. "Damn!" he screamed and did an about turn and went running back down the Boston Post Road shouting, "Arrh," with embarrassment and shame, as Goffe gave an admiring glance at Susan and went running after his father-in-law, laughing.

"You know something, I wonder if our good Reverend Hooke really knows what an incredible wife he really has, for that is one seriously fine woman," said Goffe panting with exertion. "All a man needs in life is a good woman, clever, hardworking, loyal, and do I miss mine. Only God knows how much I miss Frances." They both stopped to catch their breath, their bodies heaving with exhaustion and sweating profusely. Whalley looked over his shoulder just as well, some two miles back down the road, partially obscured with trees, he caught sight of two riders heading in their direction.

"Quick, run to the west river! Run, William, run!" shouted Whalley in a general's voice. Off they ran, realising now it was for real, as the two riders' horses quickly narrowed the gap. The two sped towards the river and the cover of its banks; the chase was on.

"How the hell did they find us?" gasped Whalley, as they flew down the earthen path and closed in on the small bridge over the west river. Simple American white oak trees, scraped clean and sawn into thick planks. It could take a two-ton cart laden with hams to the market with no problem.

"Down here," said Goffe. "Don't leave any trail." They both scrambled under the bridge and drew their pistols. Luckily the tide was in as they jumped from the grassy bank straight into the river leaving no trace. *Hopefully they don't have dogs with them,* remembering how they used to track down their enemies back in the civil wars. A few minutes passed and two horses thundered across the bridge on their way to Milford and beyond, as both men held their breath, sweating with exertion and fear. The judges stayed under the bridge till nightfall, wet, miserable and scared."I am sure that was the postmen we ran from," said Whalley smiling.

"Please don't say that," said Goffe covered in mud, and both men started laughing. They started walking back to the Davenport household, knowing a change of clothes and a hot meal would be beckoning.

CHAPTER 13

Traitors to the Realm

"Thank you so much for your assistance, boatswain," said Belasyse, walking down the steep stairs to the captain's cabin.

"Good morning, Baron," said Captain Carr. "Here are many small dishes I have asked the cook to prepare from local ingredients to give you an idea of what to expect on the dining table. Here is corn with onions, as bread, potatoes baked and fried, tomato roasted, pumpkin as a sweet pie and a turkey spit-roasted on a jack."

Belasyse looked at the feast before him. If he was to blend in with the locals he must know his food, or "Where is this stranger from?" they would ask.

"What will you do now we are safely over?"

"I will locate this commissioner Samuel Maverick and search out Captain Breedon who has supplied us with much information. Then discreetly scout the town for any intelligence; some who are loyal to the King. Then we sail to New Haven. Best not to be on the road unless I have to and it's quicker by sea. I will go to the governor's house, issue his Majesty's proclamation and see this pastor John Davenport. With the ship and troops having showed the colours to any doubters, the Guinea will return to you. I will go alone with Maverick. I have a reward of two hundred pounds in gold to pay him; an inducement is necessary in these matters. Someone will talk and I will track down these two regicides and return via New York, as there is a strong English garrison there. That, Captain, is my plan. What is your view?"

"Sounds good to me, but you are on your own, Baron, I can't help you. Are you sure you don't want any of my soldiers to go with you?" asked Carr, concerned that Belasyse was virtually on his own in a land he did not know with no prospect of help if discovered.

"No, Captain, and this is why. When I leave New Haven I would like you to literally dress like me and your boatswain like Maverick. The most important thing is to mislead and mystify the opposition, so our real mission is covered."

"Makes complete sense. I will issue orders to that effect," said Carr impressed, as Belasyse tucked into the feast. Carr made his compliments and went to his cabin, drew out the code book and wrote a long letter to the King revealing all that had passed between him and the baron.

Belasyse adjusted his leather jerkin to keep his pistols out of sight. He was dressed in simple thick woollen britches, two undershirts and lined leather boots with a Monmouth cap as protection against the freezing night. The longboat glided across Boston Harbour from the Guinea, which was anchored leeward from Deer Island. The only sounds were the waves gently rebounding off the side of the boat and the occasional gull. The longboat kissed the side of the jetty and Belasyse grabbed the wooden structure, which was covered in a mixture of barnacles and mussels. The salty timbers were slimy with harbour detritus, whilst fat crabs below fed on the discarded guts of fish and slaughtered animals.

"In two days. Ten in the evening," he whispered.

"We will be here," said Carr in the gloom, as the armed longboat moved off back to the Guinea, the half-moon providing just enough light.

Belasyse crouched down on the jetty and waited, listening all the while, ensuring Carr was well on his way before he moved. He looked for a night watchman and saw none. Half crouching he moved along, looking in all directions. Very slowly he started to climb Copp's Hill, the moon revealing the uneven ground and small hollows, the blueberry and other bushes snagging his boots. He noted the graves, none more than a few years old and no rats or other vermin. Belasyse stopped. He spotted a swinging lantern and moved quickly to the side of a house, scattering ground pepper in his wake. He put a scarf around his mouth and the freezing vapour disappeared. He crouched below the magnificent rhododendron bush, as the night watchman walked on, whistling to himself. Belasyse waited for a few minutes. "Ahh, arr," Belasyse froze and inched closer to the house, noticing the fine swan wooden planks protecting the walls. *God, I hope no one is being killed inside,* and he put his left ear to the bottom window. Smack, smack, and he barely contained his laughter and carefully moved down the far side of the hill, past the farm houses. He stopped frequently, checking for anyone out – nothing, just the odd flickering of a candle behind rough curtains and the movement of sheep and cows in their enclosures. He walked up Salutation Street, turning right down the long street from the burial ground, noting the milk pails and discarded whey in vats from cheese-making, ready for the pigs in the morning. He made no sound; the roads were of beaten earth. He carefully examined the front door of each house in the moonlight, his mind working the map Hyde had given him. He noted the good timber used in the construction as well as new bricks; a fine town. Belasyse examined each front door. Suddenly he saw the newly painted iron sign, S MAVERICK. He rang the thin knotted rope and the bell jingled on the inside. A large candle moved swiftly inside and the side window opened fractionally.

"What do you want?" was the cautious question.

"To converse with Mr Samuel Maverick on this issue," said Belasyse, proffering the King's orders.

Maverick took the documents through the window and carefully read them by the firelight; his shocked face said everything. He went directly to open the front door and Belasyse walked into his parlour, pleased to have found the correct house and thankful to be out of the cold. He took in the man in front of him, short, not over five foot, and stubble on his small round face, along with a questionable look, a greasy tanned deer-hide jacket covered in tobacco stains. Most of his teeth were missing and the remainder of his hair was tied in a ponytail, aping the sailors on his Majesty's ships. Belasyse looked around the room – there were no books, paintings, carpets or antiques. This was a man who lived for money and nothing else.

"My name is Baron Belasyse. You will note my rank and orders direct from the King, under whose authority we both act. I would, if I may, see your credentials, Mr Maverick." Maverick stared at the stranger in his house. He moved to a cupboard affixed to the wall and took a small key from his pocket, opened it and took out a rolled piece of vellum and passed it to Belasyse without a word.

Samuel Maverick is hereby appointed by his Majesty King Charles the Second as a commissioner for the liberation of the town of New Amsterdam from the illegal trespass of the Dutch West India Company.

Signed by our hand,

23rd April in the year of our Lord 1664 at Windsor Castle.

"Thank you. You are again working for his Majesty. You note my rank and his Majesty's orders."

"That I do, sir," said Maverick, his head in a whirl at this officer of the Crown along with the mission he would have to undertake. Both men tried to sum each other up. A long dangerous journey lay ahead for both men and they needed to get the measure of one another.

"Initial inquiries have established some of the locals' loyalty to the Crown is suspect, Daniel Gookin featuring prominently."

"Then they should be arrested and punished. Any traitors should face the hangman's noose and not the courts," interjected Maverick, keen to show a knight of the realm he was loyal.

"I would like to point out, Maverick, I fought in the civil wars and you did not, so let me give you a piece of advice. There was right and wrong on both sides. The wars are over, albeit not forgotten. The King wishes for peace here in New England and I will do his Majesty's bidding. I will not punish any man until I have proof positive. Also, we need to move on from the hatred of the past. People will be bound in loyalty, custom, fair laws, freedom of religion and trade. You better understand that and focus on the order the King gave you, assist me to hunt down those two regicides and as a baron of England you bow before me and don't forget."

"Yes, sir, I was just pointing out for your benefit that we may face more opposition that you realise," said Maverick, taken aback by Belasyse's words and bowing before him. "I am loyal sir and have a business importing slaves and make a handsome profit. You just have to get your head around it. Life's basic chores and menial tasks can be done with slave labour and let us, the educated elite, run the system," said Maverick, hoping to impress the baron with his newfound wealth and position. Belasyse said nothing guarding his emotions well, knowing that personal discipline was one of his great strengths and realising he had a questionable man as his assistant, but there was no one else to help him.

"Maverick, we need to find Captain Breedon. He has intelligence on Captain Gookin and Governor Endicott, between them they can provide what information we need. I assume you know where he lives?"

"Yes, Breedon has a house southeast of the mill pond and he likes a flagon of ale at the Salutation Tavern. A good place to pick up gossip and local news. Most of the crew of a ship that calls in Boston will go there. We need to move fast though; if it is known that a vessel of the King's Navy is in port again, it may frighten our talkers away."

"Fair point. Be assured my vessel is well out of sight. Let us visit the tavern, after that Breadon's House and ask him what he knows. Letters will soon arrive from London on a ship which is a day behind us and we need to find out their destination. We will deal with Endicott and Gookin afterwards." Maverick nodded. Belasyse continued, "We then sail to New Haven and settle accounts there. I have two hundred pounds in gold for you as a reward from the King," said Belasyse, hoping this would motivate the man he needed to help him fulfil his mission.

Maverick's eyes opened fully. "As you know, I have met his Majesty and am pleased to act as his commissioner again," he said with a smile possessed only by the genuinely insincere.

"Don't forget, we don't know each other. In case of any trouble, we are strangers who helped each other out," said Belasyse, checking his pistol and dagger as both men walked up North Street to the inn. Both men entered above the sign of the Salutation Tavern. The smell of three legs of mutton roasting on jacks, together with ale, wine and a roaring fire, set a mellowing tone, but the tavern was anything but that. Here were the wharfs, a ship was at anchor and over sixty men were crammed in, with a few women who didn't earn an honest living. *The world over* thought Belasyse, *wine, women and song.* He had seen it so many times in Oxford, Newark, Bristol and a dozen other towns. He knew the deal; where was the one with the least money? He spotted him up at the roughly cut wooden shelving that acted as a bar, short, with rumpled clothing, his remaining hair stuck to the back of his head with tallow, protesting at the cost of an ale at threepence. "Threepence for a flagon of ale?" cried Belasyse with mock indignation.

"Lucky I have finished my business in the market. I'll have two, that is if you don't mind having an ale with me, good fellow, I have just arrived from Providence and am new to Boston."

"If you're buying I'm drinking stranger," said the sailor.

"My name is Richard Head, livestock dealer. I have shipped eighty cattle to the market here and as I have never been to Boston, I would like to know a little about this fair town and need a few ales to clear my throat," said Belasyse smiling at the penniless sailor.

"Let me acquaint you with it. I sail from here as a first mate on the ship Miraculous Providence," said the sailor, pleased to display his knowledge for a few ales.

Two hours later Belasyse had all the information he needed, even if Breedon wasn't there. He caught Maverick's eye, who winked at him over the hubbub, laughter and shouts. The Friday night was in full swing. Both men made their way across the crowded tavern to the exit and made their way to the Captain's house, both of them hoping he was in, which ten minutes later, after knocking vainly many times, they were forced to agree he wasn't.

"What are we going to do?" asked Maverick.

"Easy; we break in. It's below freezing. We go round the back and simply force our way in or someone will notice us loitering out in the cold."

Both men climbed carefully over the rough stone wall and Belasyse went to the back window, took off his coat and wrapped it around his right foot tightly.

"Maverick, fold your coat into four and put it into the water butt then place it over the window. It will make less sound when I break it." Belasyse kicked the sodden coat twice gently and his wrapped foot muffled most of the sound. The simple, small frame, badly glazed, cracked and broke into pieces and he wrapped his scarf around each piece of glass and took them out, placing them well away from the window. He forced the window open and they both climbed gingerly into the house.

"Thank God he doesn't have his dog at home," said Belasyse, pointing to the clay water bowl by the fire. "Now, put your coat over the broken window and I will light a candle. We will look around the house, then settle down and await the captain's return."

It was well past midnight when Belasyse suddenly jerked forward from his seat by the door. He heard the singing, as the captain fell up the steps to his house. Tap tap went the key as the captain tried to get it into the lock and turn it. As he did so, he fell over into the parlour, his dog growling at the two intruders.

"Quick, shut the door, don't slam it," said Belasyse urgently, as the dog charged at Maverick, who turned and ran. Belasyse threw his coat over the running dog, holding it down. "I've got it; the door, shut the door, get the cellar open and we'll leave the dog down there," he hissed.

Maverick shut the door and unbolted the cellar as Belasyse dragged the snarling bundle across the floor and dropped it down the stairs, Maverick spitting at it needlessly.

"Right, that is one problem solved. Now we carry the captain up to his bed, light a fire and have something to eat. After that, settle down for the night because we will get nothing from him now and in the morning we will see what we can get through a very woolly head."

The two men carried the captain upstairs, took off his boots, coat and jacket covering him in blankets, then went downstairs and built a fire in the hearth. Maverick made a bread mix, adding a little maple syrup for sweetness. Belasyse sliced some salted beef, washing it several times, drying it with a cloth and adding some sliced onions, and proceeded to grill it over the fire. The smell whetted their appetites, especially when Maverick added home cured bacon to the grill. Its smoky scent made them both salivate.

With a jug of ale consumed and dinner eaten Maverick stared at the fire, thinking so much you could almost hear the clogs move in his head. "Why did the civil wars happen? I mean, aren't we all English Christians?" he asked, a frown on his forehead.

Belasyse exhaled loudly. "No one has the answer to that, unless you're God."

Maverick looked Belasyse in the eye. "I have spent most of my life here. We couldn't believe that after all the arguments the situation developed into wholesale slaughter."

"Sadly, when men run out of words they reach for the sword, which is the simplest way of putting it. There were many other factors, but you're right on that one. What I hope has happened is that we have realised that in religion you can go too far; it can be used by the educated to tell the uneducated this is what you must do, in the Bible or for that matter any religious book. How many crimes have been committed with the words, God wills it? So the people who read the books, tell those who don't, this is how it should be. There was then a series of wars which have killed or wounded hundreds of thousands and we are back where we started, but I hope, that at a terrible cost, we have learnt that talking, arguing, even shouting is better than killing."

"If that is true why are we here?"

"For the simple reason these men are trying to start another rebellion. Kill them and there will be no more war here or in England. Do you want to see these new, unadulterated lands where you live, ravaged by disease, fire and death? For that is what war is, Maverick. It is horrible! Please, take my word."

"That makes me a lot happier, I can tell you."

Belasyse turned and looked at Maverick. "I will do my duty in this matter, for vengeance is mine sayeth the Lord," he said, relishing the words.

"Fair enough, but the cause," said Maverick.

"I think it started under King Henry the Eighth's reformation. By making himself the head of the Church in England he split the nation on a fundamental issue. Many were opposed to the abandonment of Rome and the authority of the Pope. That resulted in a mess for many, as they did not know what branch of Christianity would triumph. During the reign of King James an attempt was made to blow up the Houses of Parliament and the King, when he was due to open it on the 5th of November. That was organised by a group of disaffected Catholics. You may have heard of a man called Guy Fawkes."

"The reason for the bonfires every year, with an effigy of him or the Pope on top?" asked Maverick.

"Exactly. That failed and the nation was gripped by conspiracy and King Charles lacked the tact and strength to rule with wisdom, as well as some dreadful decisions, caused the wars."

"There were many here raising troops and funds for the Parliamentary cause. I didn't get involved. I just wanted to avoid it all, but the Pope is an agent of the devil."

"That is what I call the ignorant leading the blind, down a one way street to hate. The Pope is human just like you and me; there are good one and bad ones. The male race unites in greater purpose and clarity of thought to kill each other, rather than building bridges of peace. The Republic tried to erase Catholicism and replace it with a fanatical form of Protestantism, an ill-planned tyranny where the Lord Protector is but another name for a dictator. A worse state of affairs than at the beginning," said Belasyse, hoping his long explanation had enlightened Maverick.

"You explain with more clarity than anyone I can imagine," said Maverick. "This whole political scene in England is why I will never go back. Maybe we should abolish religion?"

"I put little store in religion, Maverick. It is faith, which means integrity, justice and mercy. Faith is standing against evil and oppression. Laying down your life, for the helpless, for women and children. Standing for the truth, love and personal freedom, even if it costs you your life. That is faith, and it is what I stand for and, if necessary, will die for."

"You should stay over here; we could do with someone like you."

"I think not," said Belasyse bluntly. "We must be discreet,

quick and clever. If our mission is discovered we will both die; be very aware of that. If we succeed, you're rich and I have done my duty. Now, I think it's time for some sleep, for tomorrow we have a busy day."

CHAPTER 14

Satan brought me a Drink

"Uhrrr," cried Captain Breedon, puking into the strategically placed chamber pot Belasyse had thoughtfully placed by the side of his bed, the stale beer fumes mixed with the smell making the captain throw up again and again. Belasyse heard the tell-tale signs of a very heavy night. He should know, he had had a few of those during his youth. After graduation from Corpus Christi College, Cambridge, he had gone out for a huge booze up at The Eagle Inn next door. He must have spent over six half-crowns standing drinks for all and sundry. He still didn't know to this day how he got back to his lodgings by the old court. When he woke up all hell broke loose in his head and stomach. He swore to himself he would never drink again. Curled up in the embryo position, bowl by the side of his bed, head raging with four blacksmiths' hammers all pounding at the same time, his stomach heaving like ship in a storm. He knew what the captain was going through, although he hoped he had not got a pink sash wrapped around his privates as he had the next day. He still didn't know who the culprit was.

"Captain, I am here as a friend not an enemy."

Breedon looked up. "I'm dying; Satan brought me a drink," he said. The room stank and Belasyse fell ill at the smell and sound of it.

"Let's help him; we need him compos mentis."

"What does that mean?"

"Of sound mind in Latin, for we have some very important questions to ask."

"Wash him, give him new clothes and a very cold, damp scarf around the head and open any window. Let him swill his mouth out. Do not swallow anything, Captain, it will come straight up. A cold wet scarf around the head stops the thumping. Sitting up helps stop the puking and the freezing air takes the hangover partially off your mind. No food for a day; let the stomach recover," said Belasyse, all business-like. Captain Breedon looked at him with bloodshot eyes; here is a fellow sufferer. Belasyse sat down next to the captain. "It will take a day to recover, but I need your help. Your name has been given to us as a loyal subject. We are here to track down Whalley and Goffe. I would like to know everything about the two men and those who have assisted them until this very moment."

Breedon took in Maverick and Belasyse. "Let me have a small kill devil please; hair of the dog and a coffee," he gasped.

"All right, but you will puke again," said Belasyse, wondering why the captain would want a beverage.

"I'll get it. Baron something?" asked Maverick.

"Coffee only thanks!"

The captain winked at Belasyse and waited until Maverick had gone downstairs to his kitchen and he whispered, "I've had enough hangovers in my life. Watch out, don't trust him, whoever you are; he is totally unscrupulous. I want evidence of who you are and I will help in any way I can," said Breedon looking at Belasyse with one eye closed and totally in command of himself.

"We have taken some of your supplies and broken a window. Here is a shilling to have it replaced," said Belasyse, still not sure if the captain was playing a game or not.

"I'll not take your money, whoever you are. I am a Royalist. Are you?"

"I am Baron John Belasyse. Here are my credentials," and took his papers written by the King from his jacket's inner left pocket and Breedon read them.

"I'm impressed. How can I help?"

"Joseph Kellogg sent you a letter confirming the presence of General Goffe, regicide of King Charles the First. Do you know where he lives? I want to be as careful as I can, for his sake."

"No, I don't. He did not leave his address in case he could be discovered and he can't write. He drew a gallows and a noose around a Puritan hat."

"Mmm, I get it. So you, as a Royalist, wrote to the King who then ordered me on this mission. Hopefully another regicide Whalley will be with him. This all fits. May I ask when the post arrives from England, where will it be forwarded from?"

"The Fairbanks Tavern."

"A ship will arrive with post from England tomorrow. There is a letter for Goffe from his wife. It is to be secretly delivered to a Captain Daniel Gookin; follow it and I have a lead. We know through our intelligence system there is a promissory note for ten pounds – quite a sum. Bound for the wanted men to pay for food and other expenses."

"It seems, Baron, you have done your homework. Now, Massachusetts was founded mainly by Puritans, Connecticut by many who felt that Massachusetts was not strict enough in its baptisms. New Haven was founded by people who felt that Connecticut was getting lax in its ways, due to accepting halfway covenant. This is where I have heard these men may be hiding."

"I see what you are saying. Thank you. Do you know anyone loyal we could approach?"

"Yes. Mr Dennis Crampton – a good man; he was whipped for condemning those men. He would assist you, but beware if you're uncovered."

"Ahh, thank you Maverick," said Belasyse passing the Barbadian sprit to Breedon.

"This Captain Gookin keeps appearing in the hunt. Why don't we kill him quietly?" asked Maverick whilst sipping this coffee, hoping Belasyse would remove one of his personal enemies.

"No, he is our lead," said Belasyse.

"We'll kill him after."

"Big mistake. He is a selectman and a captain in the militia. He will be missed very quickly and we mustn't alert anyone to our aims or presence here. Not only that, our quarry would then disappear. Who allows him to operate on behalf of these two men? That is the person who should pay. I am sure he has militia men with him and that could mean a full-scale shootout. Captain, may we rely on your discretion in this matter?"

"Certainly. Shall I alert Mr Kirke? He is my neighbour here in Boston and you're right about Gookin, he is clever."

"No, please don't. I am in no doubt of his loyalty and yours, but I want to inform as few persons as possible; he is a fall-back." And off they went to scout the town.

So, Gookin has collected letters from the Fairbanks Tavern and has wrapped them in new parchment and sent them on their way, via the Tavern to their recipients, thought Belasyse. The postman will collect them after first light and start his rounds. Belasyse and Maverick returned to Breedon's house. Silver shillings made many a person talk.

"Thank you Captain for your advice," said Belasyse. "We have learnt much."

"My pleasure. I am starving," said Breedon, now fully recovered. "There is nothing like a raging hunger to make a man more pliant."

"Or to fix a man's resolve."

Breedon stared at Belasyse – *there is a man and he will need all his strength on this particular journey, although I suspect he has done this before.*

"Maverick, I am off in my minister's garb to make further inquiries. You mentioned you needed to take care of some private matters in town."

"Yes, sir, I have some blankets of mine I need to dispose of, only a few shillings' worth, but I have bills to pay just like everyone else and it's money for old rope."

"So be it. How long?"

"Some three hours."

"Right, I will see you at your residence off the Winnisimmet ferry road at sundown."

"Thank you, sir. I will get my lazy, good for nothing slaves to sweat for a change. No more loitering around for them," said Maverick and off he went to the infirmary, where his slaves had collected the blankets kept from the smallpox victims.

"Keep stamping both feet, rub your legs together and always keep your woolly hat firmly on; most of your body heat escapes through the top of your head," said Belasyse to a red-nosed, shivering Maverick.

"I know, I know, but he is late and we have been here for two hours. I am freezing and hungry."

"Welcome to the standard feeling in the Army," said Belasyse happily and kicked at the parting stone in the fork of the two roads. One going to Springfield and one to Providence. Please, oh Lord, speed this man along! Moreland had discovered the letter sent by Goffe's wife along with the rest of the mail, so it must be there. He jogged up and down thinking of a hot chocolate from Pasqua Rosee's Inn, with a generous tot of rum. *I would give a shilling for a steaming cup right now*, and he kicked the parting stone of the Boston Post Road again, staring in the direction of Boston whilst jumping up and down. "Here he comes!" Each man mounted their mares in a flash, both riding down each of the two roads. Belasyse, dressed in a long caramel-coloured coat and a black hat had placed a woollen scarf around his jaw so only his eyes were visible. The post rider came galloping around the bend. Belasyse, hidden by the foliage, suddenly rode out and confronted the post rider, firing a pistol into the air shouting, "Stand and deliver, your money or your life."

The rider pulled the reins of his horse and stared in disbelief. There were no highwaymen here.

"Dismount or I drop you with zee next shot," said Belasyse, in the best French accent he could muster, whilst cocking the second barrel.

The postman dismounted and stood by his horse, staggered at what was happening.

"Over ere by zee oak tree, face it, allez," shouted Belasyse, and placed his pistol pointing downwards, to the right-hand side of the man's neck. He wrapped a length of rope around the rider's hands, then wound it around the man and tree three times. He took a length of wool from his pocket and gagged him whilst looking around for any other travellers. *Give me three more minutes and it's done.* He rifled the man's pockets, taking any coins. He went through his saddlebags looking at the letters very carefully. His hands located a soft leather pouch and felt the familiar outline of coins. He withdrew it with a, "Merci" and put the pouch into his jacket pocket, ensuring the rider saw. Then he saluted, "Au revoir monsieur!" mounted his horse and went galloping off at full speed down the Providence branch of the Boston Post Road. Five minutes later he broke right when he saw the Charles River and rode through the trees and meadows to the Springfield branch. Just under an hour later, there was Maverick at the rendezvous point.

"Maverick. All is going to plan. You know what to do."

"Yes, Baron, I have your orders and will see you at Captain Breedon's house at dusk."

"Well done Maverick, you're doing a professional job; the King will hear of it," said Belasyse, making him feel as important as he could, as Maverick trotted off to find the postman, and with mock surprise found him tied to a tree. Belasyse stopped in the bank of a small stream and collected large bunches of white flowers including the roots, carefully placing them in his saddlebags, then rode back to Boston to continue his inquiries as to the wanted men.

"Damn highwayman, I don't believe it. Not here. This is only meant to happen back in England. He took my money and the silver shillings for the bridge to be built in Wayland," said the rider as Maverick undid his bonds.

"This is incredible. As you say, we don't have highwaymen here. Let's get back to Boston as quick as we can. Did you get a look at him? Any way we can identify him?" asked Maverick.

"Yes, I think he was a foreigner; he had a strange accent and he was armed with two double-barrelled pistols. He wore a caramel coat, scarf and a black woollen hat," said the rider, frightened at his ordeal with the highwayman and expecting to be eaten by wolves or a bear.

"Anything else stolen? Letters, personal belongings?"

The postman went through the mail. "No, nothing. All the letters and documents are here. I count how many and where to drop them off along the way to Springfield. I have counted them all, nothing is missing, only my wallet and the bridge money. The governor will be furious when he finds out."

"I am glad you are unharmed. He could have easily killed you. Let's ride; it's only some twelve miles back to town. Lucky I was coming on the Springfield Road. I have not seen anyone for hours. He is obviously off to Providence and hopes to get a boat from there."

Belasyse put the coat, hat and scarf on Breedon's fire, as Maverick sipped a warm cider, having spent two hours with the governor explaining how he met the post rider tied to a tree, scared and half-frozen, having been the victim of an armed robbery.

"Well done, gentlemen," said Belasyse. "Good work."

"But you did not take the letter for Goffe," exclaimed Maverick. "We don't know where they are."

"I didn't want to take the letters."

"Why not?" exclaimed the two men.

"If I did it would alert Gookin that the letters had been intercepted by the thief. As they are back in Boston he and the rest of his friends will assume the thief wanted the money and did not care for the mail. This ensures they won't alert them to a possible discovery. It matters not, for I read the address and that is all I need." The two men stared at him – where, where? "To the care of Minister John Russell, Hadley, Western Massachusetts. We've got them," exclaimed Belasyse in delight.

"Well done, sir, masterful work," said Breedon.

"Our business is concluded here. We must make for New Haven with all possible speed. Captain, thank you for all your assistance. The King will hear of it," said Belasyse, shaking Breedon's hand firmly, handing him five pounds of silver shillings as he left and the captain's jaw nearly hit the ground.

"What about Endicott? He should be arrested for treason. He helped the regicides," said Maverick.

"No, he has but a short time to live," said Belasyse, as both men dressed as night watchmen, each with a lantern swinging on a pole, strolled up the long street to Copp's Hill and the longboat to the Guinea.

"How do you know that and why don't we deal with Gookin?" asked Maverick in a sour voice. "I gave Endicott Socrates cup to drink; and don't worry about Gookin, I have a long memory and will see he is summoned to London to explain his actions. By the way, who lives in this house?" asked Belasyse pointing to a house covered in wooden planks.

"John Hull. He is a huge man with a large piece of land."

Belasyse chuckled. "That's a good description."

"I don't get it," said Maverick, frowning as they passed between the gravestones of the burial place.

"I can believe that too!" said Belasyse, laughing as he moved his lantern side to side at the Charlestown ferry dock.

"Captain, we will cast off and make for New Haven with all possible speed. Maverick, what is the distance by road?"

"Over one hundred and forty miles. Even with good weather it will be at least four days before anyone gets to Davenport," said Maverick.

"We should be there in maybe under three, depending on the weather as always," said Captain Carr.

"Excellent. I would hope to be there at daybreak in three days. Is that feasible?" said Belasyse.

"Yes, I believe so."

Belasyse thanked Carr and took Maverick to the quarter deck and they examined the islands of Cape Cod as it was now called. "We will travel all the hours daylight gives us if we are to reach the regicides before they are warned. Now we load our tents, sleeping gear and only five days' dry rations and grain. I want to move quickly. We can forage along the way. We rise at dawn. At this time of year that will give us maybe seven hours of daylight. We do not stop, except to piss and feed the horses, maybe at midday, and no fires; they will alert any human in miles. The smell," said Belasyse, as Maverick frowned.

"But what about water? We hardly carry any," he asked.

"In the small pots. We fill them with snow and place them in between your and then my legs – that will melt it. We each fill our canteen and then do it again for the horses. You lead as the navigator. I will have my musketoon at the ready in case of trouble."

"Err, what is a musketoon?" said Maverick, getting worried they were going to be travelling into the sparsely settled part of the plantations.

"Let me show you," said Belasyse, taking the weapon from his back. "This is how it works. First, always check the barrel has no obstructions. Take the ramrod off the weapon. Take one charge of this fine powder – usually soldiers carry twelve and call them the apostles. Empty it down the barrel, take the ramrod and ram it down twice. Drop three musket balls down the barrel."

"Three!" exclaimed Maverick.

"Yes three, then a wad of silk about two inches long. I prefer it; it will give you a further yard or two range. Again, use the ramrod." Belasyse levelled the musketoon out to sea. "Prime your pan with a little powder and pull the trigger."

Boom went the short barrel and three lead balls flew into the air, eviscerating a passing seagull, so little more than feathers spiralled down onto the rolling waves, leaving a cloud of smoke and a shocked slave dealer. Prince Rupert's powder worked. "Now a musket will take the same time to load as this, but I have three balls to one. I call it the Equaliser. Now you will practise under my tutelage until you can load and fire in the dark, for it may save your life," said Belasyse, happy to put this obnoxious slave dealer through his paces.

CHAPTER 15

Nothing is Usual Here

Hooves pounded the track; officially it was the Boston Post Road. Started over twenty-five years ago, it would not pass for a road in Europe, but this was not Europe. The views were incredible and more beautiful than he could have imagined, thought Belasyse, as he and Maverick made their way into the small town of Guilford from their anchorage. "I note few roofs with thatch in their construction and none in Massachusetts," said Belasyse intrigued, most houses in Britain did.

"Simple – many have burnt down, which has happened to some buildings in Boston. This is why the Commonwealth of Massachusetts banned any roofs under its jurisdiction from having thatch in their construction. Most roof coverings are made of wooden tiles, called shingles," replied Maverick. Belasyse listened to the differences between the two lands, soaking up all the information he could.

"Look at that house on the small rise. Notice the narrow slit windows. From that angle you can cover the harbour and river to see any vessel or canoe approaching, and the lower windows with solid oak louvres to defend against native attack. Whoever had that built expected trouble; its solid block stone," said Belasyse.

"Yes, I see what you mean, all angles could be covered by musket fire."

"I suspect just about everyone could squeeze in, and with

fresh water available they could hold out for days, maybe longer," said Belasyse, impressed, as they rode past Whitfield House and into the small village of Guilford.

"So you heard of the letters and what of them?" asked Belasyse bluntly. "They were addressed to Walter Goldsmith and a James Davids. Minister Davenport thanked the man and gave him two shillings, one for each letter, which is a tremendous amount. He then called his ostler to carry the letters to Hadley, way up the Connecticut River. I am, sir, a loyal subject of the Crown as well as an adherent of the Anglian church, not a good thing to be in these parts and because of my stand I have suffered as a result, sir. I was badly whipped for calling them base traitors. You can find the punishment in the parish registrar, Davenport would have had me hanged if he could. I and others hope you will deal with him sir."

Belasyse looked at Crampton for what seemed like an age. "Well done, Mr Crampton, I have heard of your loyalty. It is important that my colleague and I remain unknown to the populace, you understand. It is refreshing to note your integrity in this matter. I have heard how you helped in the attempt to secure these men some years ago."

Belasyse handed him the small leather bag of silver shillings he had taken from the postman outside Boston. "On behalf of the King, who will be told of your zeal in his service." Crampton bowed in thanks and went to his home much richer than he started out and mightily pleased at his service.

The two men moved off across Guilford Common and on to the Boston Post Road to New Haven.

"That was a gift; he will eat for weeks," said Maverick, annoyed he had yet to get anything as a result of his efforts.

"Being generous ensures service is continued well and you will be well rewarded when we have secured these men. They have pseudonyms; those must be the names the regicides are using. We have our confirmation and will travel to New Haven and set matters straight there. Maverick, where is Hadley?" asked Belasyse.

"It's a long way – at the top of the Pioneer Valley across the river from the town of Northampton."

"The Pioneer Valley? You had better start at the beginning. You are definitely earning your two hundred pounds," said Belasyse with a hopeless smile, realising he knew virtually nothing about the plantations.

"It's like this," said Maverick, glad to show off his knowledge and pleased Belasyse had mentioned the reward. "Most towns and villages here are founded by well organised church congregations from England. The Puritans often argue on minutiae in theology. If there are more than two ministers in a settlement, they often have a falling out, so those who lose or are seemed to lose the argument, up and leave with their supporters, founding a new settlement. To take advantage of the trade in animal skins there is a leapfrogging of settlements and Hadley is the furthest from here and truly exposed. Across the river is an earlier settlement of Northampton, somewhat bigger."

"Why don't the natives attack and destroy the small villages? Is it due to culture or religion?" asked Belasyse.

"The usual things you pointed out in England divide them: land and power. The smaller tribes often welcomed us as protection against their more powerful neighbours."

Belasyse listened intently, as he guided his mare along the Boston Post Road.

"Good day, may I speak with Mr Davenport?" said Belasyse.

"And who may I say is here?" said Abigail Davenport cautiously.

"My name is Head, Minister Richard Head."

"Please do come in, sir," said Abigail Davenport smiling and she eyed Belasyse's finely stitched coat and felt hat.

"May I offer you a glass of sack?" She knew this was a gentleman; his voice and manners gave it away, but his minister's dress was a surprise. Few of the aristocracy took their type of cloth. As she poured the sweet white wine from the round clay pot loved by so many an Englishman, she saw the twin-barrelled pistols in his belt and her heart jumped.

Belasyse smiled and asked in a damning voice, "Do you have any children, Mrs Davenport?"

"Yes, sir," she stammered, frightened. She went into the receiving room and in a panicked voice said to her husband, who was reading various correspondences, "Dearest, there is a Minister Head here to talk with you. He has Puritan dress but he is armed and he is not from here, maybe," she hesitated. "He is one of the King's men."

Davenport looked up shocked, and strode into the parlour of his home.

"Minister Head?" asked Davenport, eying the stranger.

"That is correct," said Belasyse, sizing up one of the most powerful ministers across the ocean.

"My name is John Davenport, the chief pastor to Independent New Haven. May I inquire what you want?"

Belasyse took in the minister's long black gown, black cap and white Geneva bands. Here was a man who would stand his ground and he was in for a difficult time, and he knew it. "Mr Davenport, I am charged by his Majesty King Charles the Second to apprehend all persons attained by Parliament for the murder of his late father, along with any who have aided or abetted them, but I would rather than in any way besmirch your house, ask you to join me in a glass of this excellent sack."

"You are a gentleman, sir," said Davenport carefully, helping himself to a small glass. His heart was pumping so fast his hands started to shake as he noticed the weapons inside Belasyse's coat and knew he wanted him to see them. How had he found out about the regicides? Belasyse thought for a few moments; best to be succinct. "I would point out, you may not like the monarchy but the King's Navy and Army protect this plantation against any enemies you may face and I do hope you appreciate this. I am here to ascertain the condition of this settlement, look into the conduct, people and laws that govern it. So, if I may ask, in the name of his Majesty King Charles the Second, your rank and duties here."

"You will first prove to me, sir, you act in his name."

Belasyse gave him a long, cold, calculating look and he opened his coat and withdrew from the left-hand pocket a vellum parchment rolled and tied with a purple silk bow He untied it and directed Davenport to read it.

I, by God's grace, Charles, second in name, King of England, Ireland, Wales and Scotland, bear witness that Baron John Belasyse acts in the name of the Crown. All persons, whether military or civil, will assist him in any way he commands and carry out his orders directly and with zeal. If any person does not, they will incur the royal displeasure.

Signed in the presence of his Majesty King Charles the Second, Prince James Duke of York, Rupert Prince of the Rhine.

Davenport shuddered. He looked up at Belasyse with a look of respect. He had to find out what he knew as regards the wanted men.

"Now, you bow to a lord of England."

"No, I won't. I only bow to Jesus Christ and you can't walk on water. I am the chief pastor of New Haven, magistrate, selectman and pastor to my flock. I have been here these past twenty-five years, building this settlement from nothing. I have helped feed, clothe and educate the people and their children. This, sir, is no crime, but God's good work. Not only that, I, along with my colleagues Winthrop and Endicott, have built a Christian land from the wilderness," said Davenport, ensuring Belasyse knew exactly where he stood.

"Governor Winthrop is an acquaintance and advisor to his Majesty the King. He has pledged loyalty. As for Mr Endicott he has a meeting with a higher authority. Now," paused Belasyse, "I have it on good grounds that you and other persons here, have hidden Whalley and Goffe, who are attained by Parliament. So, in the name of the King, have you done this?" asked Belasyse.

"I am a man of God, loyal to his scriptures and will help all those who ask for it," said Davenport.

"Including murderers that are not lost but seek comfort in a traitor's lair," said Belasyse.

"I have never betrayed anyone's trust and do my Christian duty to all men, whether I agree with them or not. Remember, hide the outcasts and betray not he that wandereth, for those who do so are not always lost," was the blunt reply.

"All men. I think not, sir. It is my belief that you conceal or have concealed these traitors of the realm. You dispense arbitrary justice as you see fit and run this plantation like a Roman dictator. Is that the work of Christ?" asked Belasyse. "I have made diligent inquiries as to this town and correct me if I am wrong. You wantonly sent money and goods to aid Cromwell's Republic, have made disloyal speeches and lectures, and preached from the pulpit that it is God's vengeance that King Charles was executed. Christ preached compassion and forgiveness, Mr Davenport; where's yours?" said Belasyse firmly.

Davenport gave Belasyse a smile. "If you have any evidence as to your accusations of treason whatsoever, produce it."

"I don't need to, for if I was a liar you would have said so, and by looking into your wife's frightened eyes tells me you have concealed them."

"If you have travelled over three thousand miles to tell me your King is a man to look up to, you are mistaken, Baron. That man breaks the Ten Commandments regularly and makes a mockery of self-restraint, integrity and moral rectitude. Your King has seven illegitimate children and commits adultery like eating breakfast. Vast amounts of taxes are spent on wine, paintings and furniture for the royal residences, instead of improving the standard of living for the common people. Is that right? Look at my wife in the eye and tell her that abstinence, charity, honesty and hard work are worthless. You should take a long hard look at your King, Baron. Does he have any principles he could teach my family and I? Your Queen, a Catholic and a foreigner; if your King loves England so much why didn't he marry one of his own? Or perhaps it was the three hundred thousand or so pounds she brought as a dowry, so he could spend it on himself. He married for money, not love. She plays cards on the Sabbath, the Lord's day of rest, and uses a strange type of eating implement; dearest, what is it called?" asked Davenport.

"A fork."

"Yes, a fork – strange European thing – and she drinks tea in the afternoon. I mean, which Englishman would ever drink tea in the afternoon?" said Davenport indignantly.

Belasyse looked around the withdrawing room, noting the bare walls and little furniture; a room the Spartans would have been proud of. "I note you have few books; any man of intellectual standing has them, but then maybe you burn books you disagree with, do you not? Like the Meritorious Price of our Redemption. You have set yourself up as the sole form of government and justice. That's wrong; trial by jury is the right of all Englishmen and you have engineered many to be executed. You refuse to pay any taxes to the Crown and have tried Quakers, Catholics and others for believing in something you hate, and hate is what Christ preached against. You refuse to allow any other branch of faith but your own, contrary to the law. You're a religious bigot, Davenport. I also note you ignore any law passed by Parliament, unless you agree with it, therefore usurping the authority of the state which you are a part of. There is something called the will of the people, 'demos' the ancient Greeks called it. You will put on your coat and accompany me to the meeting house. I have ordered the council to gather."

"Will of the people!" shouted Davenport. "Not one of the people here can vote in the Parliament in London, so why should they obey those laws when none of us have been consulted or have any influence?" Belasyse looked long and hard at Davenport.

"You cannot choose which laws to obey or ignore, the law is for everyone, whether you like them or not. What about the laws Cromwell ignored when he had over eighty thousand British people sold as slaves and their property confiscated? How about Goodwife Knapp who disagreed with you and got her hung as a witch. I note you do not deny any of my accusations, which self-evidently means you accept the charges. Now, go to the townhouse where the assembled council will be briefed as to my orders," said Belasyse and handed Davenport his coat.

"No, I will not!" shouted Davenport.

"Oh yes, you will," said Belasyse slowly, drawing one of his pistols, "or I will be reading your eulogy."

"John Davenport, minister, William Leete, Governor of New Haven, William Jones, magistrate, council members of this settlement."

Belasyse looked around the meeting house and the assembled crowd. He had come to his decision. No authority could tolerate such dissent. "You have been summoned by myself, Baron Belasyse, on behalf of his Majesty King Charles the Second, under whose authority I do lawfully act. You have all read my commission." Belasyse took a moment to compose himself and picked up his statement, aiming his words at the settlers who had briefed him as to Davenport's ruthless leadership and were now waiting for redress. "I have made a thorough investigation into New Haven from information provided in London and by my own appraisal here. I have made a full report, copies will be sent to his Majesty in London as well as one for your perusal. I have discovered the following irregularities. You have no charter issued and therefore act outside the law, because no one has redress to a higher authority. I quote the following illegal acts: ecclesiastical ministers have no right in law to dominate secular policy, which is the preserve of freely elected officials; the government of New Haven, enacting laws and administering justice repugnant to the laws of England, unequal restraints imposed in matters of conscience and divine worship; trade managed to the detriment of the Crown. The council of New Haven has withdrawn all means of judging their affairs in England, as if they have suspended their obedience to Parliament and the King. You have abolished some of the most fundamental laws of the Magna Carta. For instance, no official shall, on their own unsupported accusation, place any man on trial without producing creditable witness to the truth of it. No free man shall be taken, imprisoned, outlawed, banished, or in any way destroyed, nor will we proceed against or prosecute him, except by the lawful judgement of his peers and the law of the land. Many dissenters, Quakers, for example, have been whipped, even hanged on Davenport's word. Whalley and Goffe, two regicides were lodged at your house, Governor Leate, as well as yours, Messrs Davenport and Jones. This was noted during the month of June in the year 1661, contrary to the law, giving succour to the enemies of the Crown. Therefore, with the power invested in me, I hereby dismiss you, William Leate, from the office of Governor of New Haven, as a threat to the state. For the foreseeable future you are barred from holding any public office. William Jones, in understanding that your father was executed for treason, I have tempered justice with mercy. You have aided and abetted the regicides, by exchanging private bonds, redeemed them for cash in the town of Boston from a one Daniel Gookin, who has received them from the regicides' families in England. You will not take any public office for ten years and are refused entry to England as a disloyal subject.

Finally, the chief mover in this matter, John Davenport. You have shown that religious officials are using their positions to invoke personal rule, contrary to the laws of the land. You have shown breathtaking arrogance and you have brought your position, as chief pastor, into disrespect and disrepute. The vast sum of money brought to this settlement has been squandered and the shareholders have no viable means of return, let alone redress. Therefore I do hereby declare that the settlement of New Haven be abolished and all its land, buildings and persons be subject to the state of Connecticut. John Davenport, all your personal property is confiscated and you are to be banished and forbidden to return to this town and will reside at Boston for the rest of your natural life. To you, the council, you have failed to discharge your duty in respect of fair governance and law. You have not reported taxes collected and failed to stop the abuse of power by John Davenport. I therefore do declare the said council is abolished."

Silence, pure silence, pervaded the room and the look of shock was visible on all the assembled, except Leate. He knew what was coming and wasn't worried; he had kept his house and land. He also was secretly pleased Davenport had been dismissed and the council members looked at each other realising the power that lay in this one man, which was backed up by a twenty-eight gun sloop anchored in the harbour along with fifty regular troops. Belasyse left the meeting house, angry shouts followed him, but the twenty troops he had stand guard in case of trouble would fix any complaint and he crossed the green to the longboat and didn't look back; the future lay elsewhere.

The council members returned to their respective homes and explained the fundamental change that had occurred, as Belasyse went to Davenport's house with twelve troops and took all the documentation. He noted Crampton and a large group at the side of the church who bowed to him as he passed and Davenport walked purposely up to him. "He who is not just, is not right and you are taking away our life's work. You have the power to act in an arbitrary way backed by the King's cannon, but one day we will have our own and we will leave you to be a free people."

"It is best to do things for or with people, rather than against them though I wonder if you can tell the difference." Then Belasyse pointed his finger. "And before you get on your high horse and make yourself out as some kind of hero, why don't you explain to me how you treat women like Mary Dyer. Mm… something to say? I am going to stay here and find those men; they can't be too far, I am sure of it, just watch me," Belasyse said as a goodbye.

"Seek but beware, someone may seek you," said Davenport.

"You are a traitor."

"I am loyal to what I believe and I hope you slowly die of disease," said Davenport bitterly. "So is the devil, and thank you but I don't intend to have a long secession with you; I'm not that way inclined," said Belasyse with a superior smile, as the longboat cast off, the crew laughing at Belasyse's riposte.

"How do I look?" said Captain Carr, tightening his belt.

"Very good. My clothes and hat, and you have the trademark broadsword, and I also like the fake beard," said Belasyse. "Are you clear about the next few days?"

"Yes, sir. Tomorrow, one hour after dawn, with fifty troops, march along the post road to Leate's house in Guilford and pretend to scout the area looking for the regicides. Then make camp there. In the morning, move to the great rocks, west and east. Try to find any evidence of the men and camp again in the vicinity. Day three, move to Milford, thence to my ship and sail to New York and report to Governor Captain Nicolls."

"Perfect. Here are the statements for Captain Nicolls and his Majesty," said Belasyse, handing Carr a leather satchel explaining his investigations into the conduct of the various officials he had met and the decisions he had taken.

"Sir, if I may. Are you sure you should go? Maverick is a questionable man and I doubt his loyalty to anyone but himself. You have a long and dangerous journey ahead. The chance of finding those men is slim. Even if you do, they are undoubtedly armed and supported by the locals who would kill you given an opportunity," said Carr, concerned that his colleague was going on a highly dangerous mission with little chance of success.

Belasyse nodded. "I knew it was next to impossible, but you can't say no to the King. These two men may now know we are after them and Davenport's will send a warning. Sometimes let bygones be bygones is right. But I have my orders, as do you."

Carr agreed, knowing all too well that duty called, and he shook Belasyse's hand. "If there is anything I can do, sir, please do ask," he said, knowing the King's man was all but probably going to his death in the great wilderness that most had not heard of, let alone even seen. Gingerly the Guinea moved in to the shore, just a little east of the village of Milford on Long Island Sound. The gentle sound of the waves hitting the shore and the full moon made for a taut atmosphere, as the two mares were lowered by rope from the ship into the surf. The crew pulled them up to the shore. Belasyse and Maverick loaded their equipment and rations. At five in the morning there was no one outside the village, let alone awake on this frosty morning. Belasyse saluted the crew and both men mounted their horses and made their way to the Boston Post Road a mile ahead of them, and onwards to their quarry, hopefully still blissfully unaware that the King of England's men were closing in.

CHAPTER 16

A Great Soldier

"Morning, sirs," said Richard Sperry, staring inquisitively at the two men.

"Good morning," said Belasyse. "Is that your farm yonder?"

"That it is, sir, and I am proud of it."

"Excellent. I note you have some apple trees; do you have any left?"

"Yes, sir. How many were you looking for?"

"Six dozen or so," said Belasyse dismounting, staring intently at the back of Sperry as he went to the barn at the side of his house. He put the apples into the grain sack Belasyse had proffered to him.

"Three shillings, if I may, sir," requested Sperry, pleased to make a quick sale. "Are you off to Derby to purchase furs?"

"That we are," replied Belasyse. "Are you out here on your own?" he asked, surprised anyone would live outside the protection of the town.

"Yes, sir, I know, many passers-by are amazed I would risk being outside the town defences, but there are few natives hereabouts and the remainder are friendly enough."

"Good to hear. You are off to the market today I think," said Belasyse, noting the firewood, corn and winter greens on Sperry's wagon.

"That I am. It is always good to dress well when offering goods for sale," said Sperry to the well-spoken man who had noted his industry and paid cash.

"Good luck to you and God's speed," said Belasyse and off they went. He handed over an apple.

"Thank you, sir. A bit dry but after months of storage, it's to be expected," said Maverick.

"They were definitely here."

Maverick turned in his saddle. "How can you tell?"

"The blue sash that man was proudly wearing around his waist was only worn by a general in the Republican Army. They were here, no doubt about it. One of them must have given it to him as a gift."

"Why don't we go back and kill him? He is a traitor."

"No! How many people have hidden those wanted men? He is a farmer just trying to build a future in a new land and was probably ordered by Davenport to shelter them. He is also a father. I saw children at the window and I have made enough orphans and widows."

"But he may talk in the market."

"Then we should get a move on," said Belasyse and off they went to the Boston Post Road and the great unknown.

Belasyse froze. Something had made the horses nervous; their ears pricked up. He put down his water bottle and stretched slowly upwards, looking into the reflection of the river in front of him, to see if anything was behind. A few minute pebbles trickled down from the ledge over his left shoulder. His heart started to pump and as his hands moved to the musketoon, years of experience came to the fore. He looked up in a flash and saw the animal's white mouth and whiskers, its ears bent forward. Suddenly the animal jumped, a cougar, bounding down the hill from rock to rock after its prey.

"Stand still, don't run!" shouted Belasyse. Maverick took no notice and ran for his life, fear and adrenalin pouring through his veins. Belasyse moved forward, opening the firing pan in a split second, as the cougar jumped onto Maverick's back, his lumbering pace no match for the four-legged killer. Its sharp claws and weight dragged him to the ground, its jaw opened to grasp his neck and windpipe, suffocating him to death.

Belasyse shouted as loud as he could, the cougar stopped, turning to look at him. Which is exactly what he wanted. The first finger on his right hand pulled the trigger, the flint sparked the charge and fired three one and a half ounce lead balls, propelled with one ounce of Prince Rupert's finest milled powder, through its right eye socket and skull, smashing its pupil to pulp, passing through its brain and exploding through the back of its skull in a shower of blood. It slumped to the ground, dead.

"Jesus Christ, what the hell?" said Maverick, crying with relief, shaking at how close he had come to be eaten. Belasyse walked calmly over to him.

"I told you not to run. A wild animal hunts by chasing fleeing prey. The moment you run, you're done for. The animal will bring you down. You must stand tall, face it, scream, shout and throw stones, anything at it. You must be the big, dangerous man who will fight and kill it. That will make the animal think you will win and it may leave you alone, because we humans can't outrun any four-legged animal that I know," said Belasyse, realising he had a fool as well as a coward as his assistant. Maverick dusted himself down, a look of pure hate on his face; he walked over to the carcass. Blood was trickling from its mouth and right eye, its slim graceful body stretched out, claws still extended in anticipation of another successful kill. Maverick started kicking it in a frenzy of hate, screaming obscenities at the body, cursing and swearing. *What kind of a man do I have to assist me? Kick a man when he is down and a hunter when he is dead, serves no purpose.* "Finished, have we?" said Belasyse sarcastically. "Let us make camp here, feed the horses and have something to eat. There is a good supply of grass if we move the covering of snow, and fresh water as well."

Maverick gave him a sideways glance. "What happens if another cougar attacks us in the night?"

"Simple – we place the carcass you have been beating so pointlessly high up on the ridge. It will scare any others away. These are solitary territorial killers. There probably isn't one for miles and then this." Belasyse grabbed Maverick by the arm and walked him to the horses. "Stand here and drop your trousers, walk in half a circle, peeing all the time as well as on the dead animal, and I will do the other half. Any wild animal will smell man. They know that man hunts and kills them; they will pick up our scent and go. We and the horses will be within that circle of scent, and no fire; we don't want natives to smell one. I can smell smoke for miles, and so will they."

Maverick looked at Belasyse with a mixture of gratitude and shame.

The days went by – Middletown, Hartford, Springfield. Belasyse marvelled at the size of the land with so few people. Good water, grazing, lumber, wild game and turkeys in abundance. No wonder so many had come and more would do so. He consistently scouted the terrain, ensuring they camped away from any human activity. He was in his element, foraging and keeping a sharp eye for anything out of the ordinary. He kept up a punishing pace, ensuring no advance warning could reach the wanted men before they did. Maverick said it could take at least a week and he wanted to be there well before any could arrive. Native tracks doubled as roads and Belasyse would hive off for a mile to settle down for the night. He would shoot a deer or turkey at midday, always one shot; if it were two, someone could discern where the shot came from.

Bang! Went the musket shot and Belasyse just caught its sound on the wind. "Maverick, be alert," Belasyse commanded bluntly. "There is a skirmish ahead, probably on the far side of that ridge ahead of us due to the faint sound." And they cantered up the native track, the trees and foliage covering their sudden movement. Belasyse dismounted, tied his mount's reins to a fir branch and crouched down as low as he could, moving swiftly forward, carefully pushing aside the branches, whilst laying down on his stomach and motioning Maverick to do the same. He pulled his telescope from his pocket and examined the scene below him.

"What do you make of that?" he asked, proffering his telescope to Maverick, who took in the action below them.

"Having been involved in the taking of New Amsterdam, those are regular Dutch troops, probably returning from a long-range reconnaissance patrol and have found out that we have captured the town and are looking for payback. The dozen or so men defending the four wagons are settlers with their bounty of animal furs which will fetch a fine price. Looks like they're done for." Maverick turned to Belasyse. "We should leave them. They're nothing to do with our mission."

Belasyse thought, *if I do, they will die. The Dutch have some thirty troops but look exhausted after months of exploring and mapping. They smell a profit, vittles included. Ultimately, the settlers are the King's subjects and I have sworn to protect them.* He made his decision and mounted his mare. "Maverick, cover me. The range is long, but see if you can drop the nearest one when I attack." With that he started to guide his mare down the slope of the ridge, the snow crunching beneath its feet, due to the ice crust on top, making the descent treacherous, as the settlers desperately held off the advancing Dutch troops.

Boom! went the musketoon and two Dutch soldiers flew through the air as the power of Prince Rupert's powder propelled lead shot into them. Bang! Bang! went Belasyse's double-barrelled pistols and men crumpled before him as he rode swiftly through the Dutch ranks, shooting them down as they took cover behind oak trees from the settlers' fire. Up the ridge and on went Belasyse, looking for their leader, as shot peppered the air around his charging mount, its eyes wide open in fear and alarm. He spotted him, crouching behind a moss covered boulder, a captain, and charged him. The captain turned around, amazed at the sudden attack from the rear and levelled his musket at Belasyse, who was sitting erect in his saddle. He saw the pan ignite and savagely pulled the reins to the left, ducked and drew his broadsword from his back, as the lead ball gouged a hole on the right-hand wing of his capotain hat. He brought down his broadsword in an angled stroke through the captain's neck, decapitating him in one blow, and pulled the reins sharply to the right, as the shots from the Dutch troops rent the space where they thought his horse was to go. He galloped to the settlers' wagons shouting, "I am English; hold your fire!" And he held out his right arm to show he had no weapon, as the regulars cursed the phantom that had killed so many of them.

"I am here to protect you!" shouted Belasyse, noting their haggard faces wrought with exhaustion after holding off the attackers. "Wait, don't fire; they are too far away. Laugh, yes laugh damn you, that's an order," said Belasyse to provoke the Dutch to attack out of shame and anger that a few ragtag settlers held them at bay. Belasyse furiously reloaded his weapons, ramming down three musket balls into his musketoon and reloading his pistols, as Maverick shivered with fright and indecision on the ridge to their left.

"Sir, whoever you are, they are getting awfully close," said Matthewes.

"Don't panic," said Belasyse in a voice used to command. "You couldn't hit a barn door when you are running up hill at a full pace trying to aim a musket."

The Dutch troops screamed in anger and closed in on the defenders. At some seventy yards they slowed and levelled their weapons.

"Fire," said Belasyse and the musketoon tore a hole in the attackers' ranks and the muskets of the settlers did the rest. The Dutch ran from the carefully aimed shot and the settlers cheered. They were going to live, as the sharp acidic smell of powder rent the air.

Steam rose slowly from the dead bodies that littered the ridge, blood trickling slowly into the cold, frosty ground. The settlers took in the momentous events that had saved them from an untimely death. Belasyse noted dirty stubble on their faces, etched with cold and effort at the recent action. Simple homespun woollen britches, greasy stained jackets from partly tanned hides, worn boots and crumpled hats completed the frontier look.

But the clean muskets and apostles round their midriff told a story.

"A close encounter, gentlemen; well done. You are to be congratulated for holding your ground. Please bury these men and keep their arms and horses; they will be a welcome addition to your bounty."

"We will, sir, and may God be praised for sending you to save us," said Matthewes.

"Who are you, sir? Where are you from?" asked the relieved men, as they gathered around their saviour.

"Just call me your guardian angel. I would ask one thing, though."

"Of course, please do."

"I have saved your lives, therefore this," said Belasyse. "Do not tell anyone about my presence here for important private reasons. I am merely passing through."

"Definitely, sir. You can rely on us," said Matthewes, not caring who the man was. Most had reasons to be out in the wilderness and it was not his way to pry. Suddenly he spotted a horseman riding down the ridge and he levelled his musket as Belasyse caught his look and spun round, pistols at the ready. Maverick gingerly rode down the slope toward them, leaning forward in his saddle to move the branches out the way. As he did so he fell over his horse's neck into the snow and they all belly laughed out of relief to be alive and the look on Maverick's face covered in snow as he cursed out loud.

"You're a great soldier, sir," the settlers said as they each shook his hand in thanks.

"Thank you now we should move on and make camp. The sound of this action may attract unwanted interest and we can make a better defensive point, in case the survivors try a return," said Belasyse to the settlers, noting Maverick's musket had not been fired. With the dead buried and captured material loaded, they were mightily pleased that twenty-eight horses and other material had been added to their spoils, and the wagon train moved off.

The party formed the wagons onto a square, placing their own and the captured muskets by their saddles. A fire was lit and a freshly shot deer roasted on an iron jack. Belasyse checked the two wounded men, applying a bandage soaked in vinegar to the wound of one.

"No spirits; it weakens you. Now relax here in the wagon. We will bring you meat and hard tack."

"Thank you, sir, for saving us. That was a display any soldier would be proud of. You must have fought before?" asked Hugh Dudley.

"I honestly don't think that matters anymore, does it? They're over, thank God."

"Very true, sir. I served as a halberdier alongside you at the storming of Bristol and the defence of Newark and I don't regret it for an instant, except the vittles there!" Dudley said.

Belasyse's eyes widened in shock and looked at the man, a tired smile on his unshaven face.

"You mean you found something to eat in Newark?" said Belasyse with a laugh. "If all the King's army was as brave as you we would have won."

"And if I may, if all our officers were as clever as you, there would not have been one in the first place, and you may be assured of my discretion."

"One is most appreciative. Why don't you ferry your goods down river from Northampton? It must be a lot safer."

"Because there is a series of rapids that the ferryman Kellogg said were far too dangerous to shoot."

Belasyse's eyes widened, "Interesting, very interesting, we must talk later," he said and took a seat by the fire, sitting on his saddle as the men cut slices of roast venison and chewed contentedly as the crackle of the flames warmed the group, pleased to be alive after such a close call.

Matthewes cut off several generous slices onto a trencher, added some biscuits and took it to the wounded men.

"Is it usual to go hunting at this time of year because the farming season is over?" asked Belasyse.

"Yes sir," replied John Stewart. "We go on hunting expeditions around the beginning of November for about two months. We can follow the animal's trail in the snow and distinguish what type it is, as well as native footprints if there are any in the locality. Though I would mention, most have or are dying of the pox."

"That's good news," said Maverick cheerfully. "One less problem to be faced."

The group looked at Maverick then each other and said nothing. Whatever thoughts they had, they kept to themselves, as Belasyse looked at Matthewes and slowly winked.

"Gentlemen, we should all go and piss in a circle. I have heard the long howl of wolves and we must stand guard for a two-hour stretch, keeping the fire burning well at all times." Each man was in agreement with this stranger who evidently had seen much action and knew camping and fighting as most men drank ale. They had accepted his leadership without question.

Belasyse and Maverick made their goodbyes, having enjoyed a delicious breakfast of fried smoked bacon, boiled peas with herbs and onions, along with crispy corn bread. They mounted their horses and continued up the track as the settlers made their way to the village of Springfield.

"They're hardy men, these settlers."

"They have to be. There are few stores or tracks and the villages are spread out, so you have to be self-sufficient," said Maverick, red-faced with the fresh morning air.

"It must have been an incredible wrench to leave England," said Belasyse, thinking deeply about the situation the settlers were in. "Back across the ocean you had a sense of continuity, the markets, the old church in every town and village, a butcher, baker, and roads crisscrossed the country. Here, you are going to step up and work as a team or fail." He had seen the poor back in England and had little time for them, living off church charity and spending their begging money on ale and cheap spirits. Here, most were not wealthy, but were making a living as best they could. He had not seen one beggar, but most were not rich and they all worked and made a living as best they could. A grudging respect for them began to form in his mind.

"Stop, don't move," whispered Belasyse, as he spotted men moving between the trees to their right. "But sir, they are natives," hissed Maverick, fingering his musket.

"We don't want to give them an excuse to attack," said Belasyse, putting his left arm across Maverick and extending his right. "Stretch out both arms, the sign we are not holding a weapon; hopefully they will understand and move on."

The four braves got the meaning and moved across them, heading down the hills to their left.

"Probably a hunting party. We will canter along this track for a few hours to put some distance between us."

"What about the settlers?" said Maverick.

"Four braves won't attack such heavily armed men, and their dogs will give them plenty of warning."

"Sounds reasonable. They have no muskets, only the bow for a medium range, but they carry stone clubs and a few metal axes and I wouldn't want to get in a hand to hand combat with them. They can be ferocious," said Maverick nervously and both men cantered up the track.

"We're getting close, Baron," said Maverick. "We will be there tonight."

"Good. How far do you think?"

"Maybe ten or so miles. You have noted the notches on the trees and cartwheels on the track."

"Yes, and the hoof marks. But…" Belasyse stopped and put his hand to his lips and both men drew their weapons. They needn't have worried. The man looked drunk, falling over himself twice before lying motionless in the snow ahead of them. Both men waited to see if he would rise again. Nothing, then Belasyse spotted ravens circling on the wind. The man was dead or near to it and he went to investigate.

Both men looked at the man on the ground. "He is a native of the Pocumtuc Tribe," said Maverick. "The pox has got him."

"I agree; he is covered in scabs and still contagious. Leave him. We should check the village in case anyone is following him," said Belasyse.

"Why bother? They will all be dead or dying and we could be attacked. Best to leave the area immediately," said Maverick, nervously scratching the stubble on his jaw, his eyes darting around.

"I have never seen these natives or their settlements and someone may come looking for him," said Belasyse, his curiosity aroused and noting Maverick's worried disposition. He took in the man's beautifully coloured deer hide jacket and leggings. He was tattooed on his face, a sort of tribal design he suspected, and had his long hair tied in braids. He was fit and a warrior. The healed stab wound to his left forearm showed he had been in action, now he was dying a horrible death of the white man's gift. Belasyse shook his head in sympathy as the man's eyes flickered open and gave him a pleading look. He smiled in welcome to a fellow warrior. They both knew. He bowed in respect and in a flash unsheathed his broadsword and plunged it into the brave's heart, killing him instantly.

"Well done, sir!" exclaimed Maverick. "That's how to treat the natives, send them to their happy hunting ground."

Belasyse spun round and took in his assistant and his grin at what he had just done. *Don't!* Belasyse thought to himself, *you still need him, but by God when I don't!*

"No," he ordered. "You stay here and guard the road. I will scout the village quickly, just to see if any more are heading this way." Off Belasyse went at a canter. If there were any more, he wanted to be at a speed he could outrun anybody. He followed the path and arrived at the village in minutes, and he wished he hadn't. Squash in different shapes and colours by the side of the wigwams, strips of deer meat, cut very thinly and air-drying on racks of wood. Then the dead and dying littering the ground. Bodies putrefying; many had scabs of smallpox still on them. But worst, the village dogs eating a dead woman. He spotted blankets wrapped around many of the bodies. He dismounted and spat on the fire in front of a wigwam. It had been out for days. Belasyse turned a blanket over with his broadsword. 'S Maverick' was stitched on the top right-hand corner and his blood boiled at what his assistant was doing to clear the land. The devil's agent. And he cantered back to the track.

"They're all dead. This one was the last," said Belasyse. "Now we must move. I want to use the remaining daylight to get within striking distance of Northampton."

Maverick took the lead. At long last this baron has seen the true nature of life here. Kill all of the natives, by pox or by lead musket balls and you have all the land you need. He smiled to himself, but he failed to see the look on the baron's face, which, if he knew, was the same one he had had when he arrested Captain Daniel Axtell four years earlier.

Three men on horseback came slowly into view. They stopped, as if to attend calls of nature, looked around for anyone and moved into the trees, some three hundred feet ahead of Belasyse and Maverick, who had climbed a large oak tree to view the town and the river beyond. The three men dismounted, one opened his saddlebags and took out a white cloth and spread it on the ground. Then took out a book, a flask, a goblet and some beads, which the men proceeded to wrap around their right hands and got on their knees. Belasyse knew he was fortunate; the hoof prints in the snow could have given them away and both men descended the large oak.

"Cover me," Belasyse whispered. "I will go around the back behind their horses and surprise them. Only shoot if they draw a weapon." Maverick gave the thumbs up sign and crouched down, observing the group. Off went Belasyse, crouching behind each tree as he slowly made his way behind the three men, staring at the ground, then the men, in case he trod on a twig or branch and gave himself away. He carefully approached between the horses, using them as cover, drew his twin-barrelled pistols and rushed forward.

"Well, well, what do we have here?" The three men froze, seeing pistols pointed at their heads and they looked at one another, knowing that what they were doing was a death sentence in Massachusetts.

"What are your names and no tricks, or I will drop you all. I also have a friend who is watching your every move, so don't try anything. Maverick," said Belasyse curtly.

"Yes, sir."

"Go check the road for anyone."

"Be careful sir, they may be armed."

The three men looked at each other, knowing this could be their end, and each of them looked for a way out. "Who are you? I will check your dead bodies if you don't tell me. Now talk!"

"We carry no weapons, I promise you," said Throw, frightened, noticing the scarred and determined face of the man in front of them.

"We are Clesson, Cornelius and my name is Throw. Please, sir, don't tell the authorities. We have a little money. It's yours if you want. You can have the horses as well. Please just let us go," he said, pleading for his and his friends' lives.

"Let me explain my deductions, then my orders," said Belasyse, looking at the objects on the ground. "Your accent is, shall I say, not local. I reckon I have three Irishmen here, wafers, a wine flask, three rosaries and a Bible. I think I can work this one out and you know the punishment for that, don't you?" Belasyse paused to let the information sink in. "I propose a deal. You keep quiet, we keep quiet. You're here, because in an hour it will be dark, but there is enough daylight for you to take Communion." The three men looked surprised at Belasyse's quick deduction of the scene.

"Show me to the house of Joseph Kellogg, the miller, and I will let you go on your way, but if you don't, I will gladly tell the minister and you will dangle from the gallows by sunrise."

"Yes, sir, it's a deal, you can trust us, I promise you, but Kellogg is the ferryman, not a miller. He lives in Hadley just across the river," said Throw nervously, hoping this armed stranger would not inform the town council of their particular brand of Christianity.

Good, he is here, thought Belasyse. "All right, let us trust one another," and he patted each man down. "Pack and mount up." He motioned them to their horses.

"We will continue to the town," said Belasyse to Maverick. "They will accompany us."

"These men are up to something, maybe some sort of Catholic or satanic mass. We should hand them over to the authorities in Northampton when we leave," said Maverick with evident spite.

"Maverick, I have their names and can use these men as a lever if we need. Take the lead slowly. I want to enter the village when it is dark." And off they went to the top of the Pioneer Valley.

"Put a small sack over your mount's head with some grain

in it, and we move through the village. The snow will cover the sound of the hooves. There will be dogs and we don't want to wake anyone," said Belasyse. "Where is Kellogg's house?"

"At the bottom of the village of Hadley, sir, across the river by the aqua vitae meadow," said Throw, only too keen to show the armed strangers he was cooperating. "Only a few more minutes, sir." The group carefully skirted the village to the south and made their way along the stone walls dividing up the fields. "That is the house, sir," said Throw pointing to the first house across the Connecticut River in the soft light of the moon. "Can you see the smoke trail from the chimney stack?"

"I don't trust them and I am sure they don't trust you," said Maverick.

"They're unarmed and we are, so carry out my orders. Prepare the horses for the crossing," said Belasyse and off went Maverick in a huff. Belasyse waited until he was out of earshot and turned to the men. "You may go. Keep this incident to yourselves."

"We will, sir, I promise and thank you for not reporting us."

"In the name of our redeemer Lord Jesus Christ, in nomine patri et fili et spiritu sancte."

"What in the Lord's name?" exclaimed Throw, with all the admiration he could muster as Belasyse made the sign of the cross.

"Shh, now be about this business," said Belasyse smiling, and rode to the river's edge to prepare the crossing, as the three men went to their homes astounded at what had just happened.

Both men dismounted and walked carefully towards the ferry point Throw had directed them to, down the bank of the Connecticut River, slippery with thick mud. The dancing pattern of the moon on the slow moving river was their only source of light. Belasyse noted the thick rope tied to a large pine tree at the top of the bank as the anchor fitting. It was slung across the river inside iron rings, which were attached to posts hammered into the bedrock of the river. The wooden platform ferry would be pulled slowly across letting the flow of the river do the work, but from this side, probably a donkey walking around a wheel.

"Maverick, you will cross with the horses on the ferry. I will shimmy along the rope. When I reach the other side I will pull on it twice. Load all the equipment and the horses and we both pull the ferry across the river."

"Yes, sir," he said in trepidation.

With that, Belasyse stripped to his underwear, taking the shillings and golden crowns in a leather bag and put them around his midriff, along with his broadsword, and grabbed the rope. *The things I do for the King*, and he hauled himself along; the river was freezing. He lay partially on his back and his arms grabbed the rope in turns propelling himself through the softly moving river, his arms straining at the effort. He eventually felt the mud beneath his feet and pulled himself up the slippery bank to the ferry disembarkation point. *Thank God I have kept my boots on.* The path up was lined with crushed rock, providing a firm grip for the beasts of burden so they would not slip and drop their loads. He undid the rope holding the ferry to its station, making sure it was between the iron ring, and paused a while catching his breath and listening out for anyone out and about. Nothing – just the lapping of the river on its bank and the odd rustle of small animals in the undergrowth. He pulled the rope twice and felt Maverick do the same and he hauled the rope along and the ferry disappeared. After some twenty minutes of hauling the ferry back, he saw both mounts appear out of the darkness.

Damn it! Jesus Christ himself, thought Maverick. *What have I got myself into? I should have killed that baron the first time I got a chance. Here I am in the middle of nowhere crossing a river into a nest of traitors. I need to drop that lord as quickly as I can and run for it with the reward, as well as the endless supply of silver shillings he has. I'll make it look like the natives or locals; no one will be the wiser.*

"Maverick," hissed Belasyse in the dark.

"Here, sir. All's well," he replied, tying to sound as unflustered as he could. *Damn, I should have left him to the Puritans and I soon damn well will!*

CHAPTER 17

Independence

"Minister, I cannot thank you enough for your hospitality," said Dixwell. "I hope I am not inconveniencing you or your family?"

"Not at all," said Russell kindly. "The letters you bring are most welcome and Mr Whalley and Goffe confirm you are gentlemen of the highest standing."

"That is most considerate of you and them," said Dixwell, hoping that Russel would not mind three wanted men under his roof. He was well aware that he had never seen action, but the two generals were set in their ways, he was shrewd and flexible, had charm and money and they may bring trouble to this village; he had to be careful.

"Do you think you were followed or left a trail that could be discovered?" asked Russell looking at Dixwell for any reaction.

"Not that I am aware of. I go under a pseudonym, James Davids, and have covered my movements well." Dixwell hesitated. "I know the King has sent out assassination squads across Europe for us. Three were captured in Holland some years ago and John Lisle has been shot in Switzerland a few months back, but I don't think they know that this village even exists." Russell knew, the ministers of Massachusetts may not always get along, but they all hated the King and his bishops. They used trusted members of each other's congregations to pass around information and keep a look out.

"How about if I tell you of my extraordinary journey over a glass of Madeira," asked Dixwell, knowing he could smooth the relationship with the minister he depended upon.

"That sounds a good offer, as you say; we are at the end of the known world. I have had a large room built under the stairs when I was given word that Whalley and Goffe were to come here and hide. The cellar is the first place any person would look. We would know by the travellers and merchants coming here, if there were agents on the way. Even if they got this far, how would they get you back to London? There are upwards of forty armed men in this village, let alone Northampton across the river, who would protect you," said Russell, quietly confident they were out of reach.

"Do you honestly think we would know?" said Dixwell, concerned that Russell had mentioned the point.

"There are snakes, cougars and brown bears, not to mention the natives to contend with along the way. The King and his ministers will crow about the New York they have and will forget us. The garden has a high palisaded wall around it, enough to cover the height of all concerned. Do please keep conversations to a low volume. Ask my wife or myself for keys to the meeting house. It is used for the various town gatherings and service on Sundays, otherwise it for your use."

The back door opened and Whalley and Goffe entered the parlour, deep in conversation.

"Ahh, gentlemen, I am off to see Samuel Porter who is sick and minister to him. Do discuss any changes you wish to make to your living arrangements amongst yourselves," said Russell who gathered his coat, scarf and Bible and made his way down the long village common, hoping Porter hadn't got smallpox.

"Good morning gentlemen may I ask what you do to pass the time?" said Dixwell guardedly.

"We work hard in the garden," said Whalley.

"It will produce much in the way of fruit and vegetables.

We also mind some fine Sussex chickens, enough to feed us and some to trade. We will be going into the cattle business shortly when Gookin forwards the funds we left with him. On occasions we meet trusted folk and late at night or very early in the morning we go for walks in the hills surrounding the town, especially on evenings with a full moon. We check the accounts of the village and write sermons for the minister and his flock. May I assure you, Mr Dixwell, it is a most comforting retirement from all our troubles."

"Maybe," said Goffe. "But I am determined that we make more of an effort to declare independence from the tyranny of the Crown. His spendthrift and adulterous ways are a detriment to all honest and religious folk. We must not allow ourselves to rot here in idleness. I am making plans to stand against this idolatrous King and I expect your help in doing so."

"Rebellion again?" said Dixwell.

"Yes," snapped Goffe. "Or perhaps your zeal in the good old cause was just for show. I remember you were reticent in signing Charles Stuart's death warrant. Now is your opportunity to show your loyalty to the two generals you see before you. There are many former soldiers who have returned here from the civil wars and are only too ready to follow us."

"Are you sure you are on the right side of the river, General Goffe? We command no army, we have no funds to pay one and are but three men hiding in the most remote part of civilisation and you want to start a war? You're mad! The monarchy is restored and we have to accept that fact."

"Accept it? Accept it?" said Goffe, exploding in anger. "Never. I'll stir in my grave before I will accept a king and his bishops again. Maybe you're just a coward."

Whalley deftly stepped in between the two feuding men. "Enough, both of you, before we get an audience."

"What we will get is a rope around our neck because of this idiot. Where is the army you propose? They're on their farms or in their stores and have had enough of killing. They want peace like the rest of us."

All three men stood facing each other, anger writ large.

"Gentlemen, stop this, you are in a house owned by a minister of God and I don't want any of you planning the death of even the most wicked of people," said Minister Russell, having returned across the green and horrified at the argument he was hearing. "Disunion breeds destruction." And they all went to separate parts of the house knowing the explosive atmosphere could be the ruin of them.

"I do apologise, Whalley, if I have caused any offence," said Dixwell, glad that Goffe had gone for one of his long walks to calm down.

"Please, Colonel, don't worry. We have had to live in a cave on occasions and this fall from grace has hit him hard. We were once governors of several counties in England, with a veritable army of soldiers, secretaries and the power to control a hundred thousand people. Now we find ourselves at the edge of the known world with hardly a pound to our names," he said mournfully.

"I plan in a year or so to return to New Haven, settle down and live a life of quiet contemplation. I have seen the worst that a human can do and wish no further part in war."

Whalley understood. He knew Dixwell wanted nothing to do with their planned rebellion and only wanted to spend his remaining years away from the King's grasp.

"Please, General Goffe has gone for a walk by the river bank and we may converse freely," said Whalley, knowing Dixwell had more to say. Both men strolled into the large garden, with its medicinal herbs and fruit trees.

"Why should we not have a war of independence against the King in England? After all, I do think we would win it. Colonel, all three of us would make a great team," said Whalley hopefully.

"Let me explain my reasoning, sir. Many dispossessed cavaliers had left for Virginia or Maryland after the war. They had lost most, if not everything, they had and felt a new start, away from Cromwell's grasping officials was a better life. We would provoke them into action," said Dixwell.

"If I may," said Whalley, "a very good and logical deduction of events."

"Most kind, sir. I did not fight battles, General, but I learnt how and why generals like yourself issued orders and for what purpose. Listening carefully can often sort out the clever from the fools."

"Correct deduction," said Whalley, anxious to hear more from this evidently clever and wily colonel who had escaped from the King's agents in Europe and made his way unscathed to Hadley.

Dixwell looked pensive and had a draught of his small beer and walked amongst the peach and apple trees, admiring the organisation of the garden. *There are times in life when it is best to conceal one's feelings, but there is also a time to say what you think, straight and true. Whalley is reasonable enough, not like Goffe, a difficult, spiteful man. God only knows how these idiots ruined England; if they had only listened to the ordinary Members of Parliament, the monarchy would have never been restored. The Army can't run an economy. It shoots what it doesn't like and smashes what it doesn't understand.* Minister Russell's dog sensed the mood and jumped up and licked his fingers, half for the salt and half out of compassion. Dixwell reached into his pocket and withdrew some beef jerky left over from his journey; *at least this one is friendly.*

"Whether we like it or not, we must accept that the King is restored and the Republic is over. The majority of the men who ran it are either dead, in prison or like us, on the run. It would be foolhardy to expect the governors and their councils to agree for us to be put at the head of their militias. There may be a chance with the Dutch, but we would look like traitors to many in England."

"But if we did side with Holland, we would be helping a Republic. Remember, my enemy's enemy is my friend," said Whalley.

"That holds true, on most occasions, but by ridding the Dutch control of New Amsterdam the settlements have less competition and are happier for it," said Dixwell. "There is no gold, silver or iron here, not even a mint to make coins. How many munitions are there in the Commonwealths? Not enough to fight a war," said Dixwell with a sad look.

"One other crucial thing – leadership. You, sir, and your son-in-law are highly experienced men, but all three of us are on the run and have been hiding like frightened rabbits for some five years; it's not much to motivate a man to lay down his life. The settlements need the power of the English Army and Navy, as well as their trade. I would think that in a hundred years, when there are a million and more here, who are self-reliant, they could thrive better without a King issuing commands from thousands of miles away. Things will change, but not yet. Peace and trade is what they wish for, not an armed rebellion."

Whalley's shoulders slumped. *This colonel and former Member of Parliament had been the quiet one, but by God, he was the clever one – a shrewd and practical man. If only we had more like him and he was right, you can't run a country with an army; it just doesn't work.*

"When I add up what you have said, you are so completely right it hurts," said Whalley.

"General, if we make some hasty decision, not only we, but many others, will regret our presence here and I don't want that on my conscience," said Dixwell. "We should hide here, keep a very low profile and wait until we have further information from Davenport, Gookin or your sister in New Haven. As I see it, the King's agents cannot find any trace of us and no one is going to get this far."

"To that, I totally agree. I will speak with Goffe and if I may ask you to be, err, absent when I do."

"Of course, sir, I fully understand."

"Ah! Mr Russell, good to see you again. I hope all is well. I think I have resolved the differences between us," said Dixwell, as Whalley left to speak with his son-in-law.

Minister Russell looked hunted. "I see you are enjoying the cakes my wife has baked, Mr Dixwell. I am most fortunate the Lord has sent her; no man could be more content. Are you married, Colonel?" asked Russell, anxious to befriend this cautious, but evidently cultured former officer of the Republic.

"No, sir. I have not been called by the Lord to do so and I suspect, at my age, I might not be so fortunate as yourself."

"Please, Mr Dixwell, age is no barrier and with your years of experience and fine countenance, there will be many a maiden who would only be too pleased to have the company of such a wise gentleman as yourself. For as a man matures with age, he may offer a knowledgeable mind for the protection and education of a lady. What was your occupation in England, Mr Dixwell?" asked Russell.

"I was a Member of Parliament four times and the governor of Dover Castle."

"Ah yes, there is a church in Dover, em… St. Mary in Castro, built by the Saxons next to the Roman lighthouse, which is over one and a half thousand years old."

Dixwell stared at the minister for Hadley. "If I may, sir, continue this incredible conversation over dinner tonight. I am most impressed with your knowledge! I beg your leave, Minister," said Dixwell, incredulous at Russell's knowledge of the eastern corner of England.

As he went through the parlour to the back door, he took a brace of pistols and a broadsword for full effect if he met Goffe, and left the house through the garden, to the side exit. He walked behind the houses on the long common to the river, admiring the tranquillity of the land, down the path to the riverbank, raising his right hand in welcome to the ferryman who was unloading sheep and iron goods for the expanding community. *Another rebellion, I think not*, Dixwell thought to himself, *one was enough.* Sounds good, as does all bravado, but reality told him different. *In time I'll go back to New Haven. I love the shore, fresh crab and seafood. I have my money. I'll live out my life in peace as James Davids, known only to myself, as a wanted man. Though maybe Minister Russell is right; maybe I should marry. Life is often a strange journey and mine is definitely so. Those two can dream about rebellions, it's usually the mass of the people who do the fighting, then lose everything and die, as the leaders go on arguing about who was right to the grave.*

"I do confess this is a fine land, Mr Russell, and God had bestowed his bounty on us in his mercy. I have written a sermon for you on the morrow and, God willing, he will inspire me to drive out any Royalist from these God-fearing plantations," said Goffe, his voice full of passion in the good old cause.

John Russell looked at Goffe with concern.

"Mr Russell, if I may ask you for a little time alone with my son-in-law. I have to speak with him on several matters which do concern us," said Whalley, winking at Russell with his left eye.

Russell left the two men in the parlour. *I'm risking my and my family's life here. I don't need a war to start on my door step. I hope Whalley talks some sense into him.*

"I have spoken with Mr Russell, in whose house we are commanded by God to dwell. I have letters from the council in Boston and Gookin. I have also spoken with Colonel Dixwell and others here in the community. We all have thought about the proposal you have mentioned in declaring independence. I have something to say from my heart and from all who I have spoken to over this issue. In one word, no, there not ready yet!"

CHAPTER 18

A Brave New World

Belasyse pulled the rope bell on the right-hand side of the door of the house Throw had directed him to, setting it jingling, noting the raised porch and small windows, a mix of brick, plaster and wood. He was amazed at the size of the oak planks on the porch; he had not seen any that wide before. The roof at such a steep angle to let the snow slide off, Maverick told him, along with the large chimney, made sense.

"Who is it?" came the muffled reply.

"Let me show you," said Belasyse, pushing a golden crown under the door with difficulty, as woollen cloth formed a barrier in the gap between the door and the floor. He waited for what seemed an age and drew his pistol thinking he had been fooled. The door opened a fraction and an unshaven face squinted at him in the narrow light from the tallow candles in the parlour, flames from the fire making the light dance on the plastered walls.

"Somehow I was expecting you, sir. It must have been a long journey," said Kellogg softly.

"I can assure you it was and hazardous too."

Kellogg opened the small door to his house, so Belasyse had to stoop to enter and Kellogg closed the door rapidly, replacing the cloth.

"It's been a long time," said Belasyse proffering his right hand, and Kellogg took it.

"That it has, and it's good to see you again. I assume you found out about Goffe from Captain Breedon, sir."

"That I did, he figured out your drawing, though I'm not alone. I have a commissioner – a man named Samuel Maverick."

"Samuel Maverick of Boston Massachusetts, but his appointment has expired," exclaimed Kellogg, frowning as Belasyse nodded.

"He has a new one. Do you know him?" said Belasyse, surprised that his name and reputation had reached here.

Kellogg moved within inches of Belasyse's face. "We both have been through much, each in our own way. I saw back in Boston his reputation for slave dealing, ruthless legal practices and methods of clearing Native Americans from the land. He is not welcome in my house. It's as simple as that, Baron. I have two barns at the back, one for vegetables, the other for hay and straw. He can stay there for the night. This is my house," said Kellogg, standing square on, he was his servant no more.

Belasyse took a step back, surprised that his former member of staff spoke to him in such a manner and hadn't bowed to him. That explained a few things though, why so many in Boston were tight-lipped; he was a nasty piece of work and he stared at the fire for what seemed an age, as he felt Kellogg's eyes boring into his back. Then a harsh rap at the back door startled both of them out of their reverie.

"Leave it to me. I'll deal with him," said Belasyse as he strode through the parlour and looked at the back door, a veritable fortress with two iron bolts, one at the top, one at the bottom. He struggled with both of them, the cold having tightened the metal. Finally, with the amused Kellogg looking on, he opened the door to see a red-nosed and shivering Maverick at the foot of the back stairs with the reins of the mares in his hand.

"About time too," he said in evident anger. "I am freezing," and proceeded to drop the reins and walk up the stairs.

"Not so fast," said Belasyse. "The owner of this property has no room at the inn and like a good Christian you will sleep in the manger of his barn."

"Barn? In a barn? I am a commissioner for the King. I am not staying in a barn; that's for slaves," said Maverick, his voice raising in indignation and anger having been out in the cold for so long.

"And how would you know that?" said Belasyse, staring at Maverick. "You're going to, or you can sleep in the snow." A hardened look appearing on his face. "Still, the owner of this property could inform the locals, who would like to know why two agents of the King are in their midst. I command this mission as you are well aware, so take the two mares to the barn, dry them and see they have hay and water. We will bring you some dinner, build a high bed of hay bales, and it's dry, so don't complain. I have slept in far worse conditions, as did my troops. Maybe you are just weak."

Maverick snarled in anger, turned around and headed to the barn, sulking.

"Let us bring him some dinner and blankets, then we can talk. I would like to know anything you have heard about him," said Belasyse. "He is a fawning knave. Unfortunately I was ordered to take him along and he has much knowledge."

"So be it, your Lordship. Sorry if I am inhospitable, I will tell you all I know about him and the men you seek," said Kellogg, offering his advice as an equal. Belasyse looked at Kellogg in admiration. His former member of staff had gone from taking orders to giving them.

"I have a little pottage left and some cornbread; that should do it." And Kellogg took a small cauldron from the larder and half a loaf of cornbread and placed the pot by the side of the roaring fire and the bread in the small side oven to warm up. Then he went up to the spare bedroom and came down with three large homespun blankets and put them by the back door. Kellogg opened it with the words, "I'm just going to get a hen for our supper," and proceeded to the hen coup covered in linen to keep the flock warm and opened the thick iron cage built to protect them from cougar and fox attacks, grabbed a squawking hen and wrung its neck expertly. On the parlour table he plucked the feathers in handfuls before cutting of its head and drawing its guts. He put rosemary sticks from a bunch hanging upside down under its wings. He smeared a little butter over it, then wrapped four thin slices of smoked bacon around the hen, before trussing it with twine and finally placing it on the jack to roast over the fire. They both waited as the stew heated up, saying nothing, each thinking about Maverick and the mission that Belasyse was here to complete, wondering where it would each leave them. Hunted, assaulted or even dead, the prospects were frightening. Kellogg at peace and the Baron within reach of his quarry. The sound of the pot boiling awoke them from their thoughts. Kellogg went to the fire and wrapped a cloth around the cauldron and the bread.

"I'll help you. No point in making two journeys," said Belasyse, and he took a torch from the wall at the parlour window, wrapped it in old strips of linen and dipped it in a jar of pitch and lit it from the fire.

"He gives pox a bad name, nothing more than a spot on a trollops behind," said Kellogg as they picked up the blankets and dinner on the way to the barn. Kellogg grinned at the baron whom he thought was incapable of swearing, which he did a lot of the time, on the river, at his horses and to a few people in town. He respected the man – he was straight, paid well, was loyal to his staff but above all, a gentlemen, never taking advantage of others and dedicated to the principle of the monarchy. *The King is lucky to have such a man. I just wish there were more like him.*

"Maverick, here is your dinner and some blankets for you and the horses," said Belasyse, taking two and folding them over the horses. The torch showing the mares contentedly chewing on the hay, as Kellogg took two sacks and put a few pounds of grain in from the store box and tied them over their heads to add to the feed. Maverick said nothing; he had built his bed between the mares for warmth and the expression on his face said it all.

"Good evening," said Kellogg. "We haven't met. Your rank as a commissioner for the King pulls no favours from me. Here is your pottage."

Maverick walked over slowly and took his dinner saying in a low voice, "I hope that this man is not an enemy of the Crown or a Puritan."

"No, I am not. I am a reborn Satanist and a follower of the devil himself and I dance naked around a fire worshiping him."

Belasyse laughed. "I am sure you have a few naked witches running around after you."

"Nah, I left them jam tarts back in East London."

Kellogg and Belasyse left, sensing the red-hot angry eyes piercing their backs.

"Let him stew. I might need his anger in a day anyway," said Belasyse, as they went back to the house and its roaring fire.

Kellogg went to the larder and shucked four cobs of corn and placed them in a skillet next to the fire with a little butter, he took a cast iron pan added a little broth from a pot by the side of the fire and ladled some over the chicken to maintain its succulence.

"After all that, how about a flagon of ale?" he said.

"That is a very good idea," said Belasyse, and Kellogg took two leather jugs off the buffet and poured two measures of ale from the wooden barrel. "I brew this for sale here. I am the only brewer in Hadley; a good little trade. I think you will enjoy it. Take a seat and I will acquaint you with all I know about Samuel Maverick and I am sorry, sir, I should not have spoken to you like that."

"May I assure you, most of us, in the heat of the moment, say things we later regret and please, no more of this sir. We have known each other for some years and you are no longer on my staff. I would like to consider you my friend and am in need of your help. Please, do call me John."

"Thank you." Kellogg hesitated. It was unheard of for a man of his station to be on first name terms with a lord of England and confidant of the King.

"Thank you, sir, err, John," Kellogg said with an embarrassed smile.

"Before we get down to business, how are you? I have often wondered how life turned out for you."

"I do well. The ferry and brewing are my main income, and I never was much of a farmer. I had my own patch as most of us did back in Deptford. My wife and I tended it a few days a week, vegetables and the like, herbs, and we kept chickens. I sold many a rooster for cock fights – that was a good little number, I can tell you, upwards of a few shillings a month. I was granted land here three years ago and for the princely sum of two pounds, I had this house built."

"But why did you leave my employment? You had somewhere to live and a wage. You were a servant in my house."

"I was a servant in your house sir, now look around you, I am master of my own. I pay rent to no one, work hard the six days God gives me, bow to no man and honour the memory of my wife in church on the seventh."

Belasyse looked at Kellogg with a mixture of embarrassment and respect. "This is definitely a New England," he said and admired the house, the large fireplace which provided light as well as cooking and heating. Flitches of bacon smoking and drying, a jack for roasting meat. Wooden chests for clothes and work goods.

Belasyse noted the only book was the Bible and knew Kellogg could not read or write. He could count though and that's what mattered in business.

"It's true," went on Kellogg. "A man's character is what you are judged on, along with what you say along with what you do.

It is the New World without the baggage of the old," said Kellogg, embarrassed speaking in such a way to his old employer.

"How do you know Goffe was here?" said Belasyse, changing the subject.

"Do you recall that trip up the Thames all those years ago when we first met?"

"Yes, Goffe was with us on the skiff, going to a meeting at Whitehall Palace."

"He wouldn't pay, saying the yeoman warder had paid me enough. I remembered him, a stingy man. I also admit I was hired to take a party of men down the Thames to an oceangoing ship in May, nearly five years ago, just before the King returned, and he was one of them."

"Ahh, that's how they got away. Do carry on."

"Last October, he and three other men were on my ferry. He was one, another was Mr John Russell, the minister here. I did not recognise the other two men."

"Are you sure, Joseph? I do not want to doubt you, but I must be sure."

"No bother. Goffe had a broadsword around his waist and a brace of pistols, as did the other man. The minister had a Bible with him, nothing unusual, but he seemed exhilarated and treated the two men as if they were the disciples of Jesus Christ himself. The fourth man was a tracker, I am sure. He looked very comfortable in his moccasins and kept looking around to see if they had been followed."

"Comfortable in his what?"

"Moccasins – a type of foot garment made by the natives. They also leave no track I can see. I make some six trips a day, each for four pence, cattle, sheep, hogs, men, anyone or anything that pays me, so I see and hear a lot. But one thing stands out. You mentioned years ago that fifty-nine men sealed and signed the King's death warrant. Goffe and another man had gold signet rings. How many men here wear one?"

"So, we have the minister, a tracker and two men; one was Goffe, the other armed man about sixty?" Kellogg nodded.

Belasyse put down his ale. "I don't doubt it for a pound you're right. That other man must be Whalley. This is the perfect place to hide and it has been quite a journey to get here. A quick word in the right ear and we would have disappeared off the face of the earth and the regicides to a log cabin. How did you hear of them?"

"When I arrived here three years ago, the story for the hunt for Whalley and Goffe filtered up to Northampton," said Kellogg. "People talk and the King's reward pamphlets sped the news along. It was obvious Boston was too hot for them, and New Haven. Davenport knows the minister in Hadley, John Russell – they both sit on the board of the Hopkins School."

"There hangs a tale. I do admit when back in London I was dismissive of the people here, but I was wrong," said Belasyse, almost apologising.

"Let me tell you about this commissioner of yours. He moved to Massachusetts many years ago – one of the first Englishmen to do so. He was involved in land purchases from the natives in the Roxbury area near Boston, using blankets as part payment. Six months later, if a couple of dozen or so were alive I would be surprised."

"But wouldn't he catch smallpox himself?" asked Belasyse.

"Oh no, he is too clever for that; he got his slaves to do it. If he lost a few he didn't care because he made far more from clearing the land and Governor Endicott turned a blind eye. The new settlers have no idea of land prices. You should see the writs he issues in Boston if anyone does not pay him," continued Kellogg. "When the King was restored, he converted to being an Anglican and toadied to Captain Breedon and other men who were hunting Whalley and Goffe. He provided a guide for them to New Haven. By doing this he ingratiated himself with John Winthrop, Governor of Connecticut, who recommended him to the King as one of the four commissioners to take New Amsterdam.

Belasyse took a long draught of his ale and stared into the fire whilst Kellogg turned the jack, ensuring the chicken was evenly cooked. He turned to Kellogg, "How do you know all this?"

"When I landed in Boston, I stayed seven months there looking for a position as the ferryman across the river at Cambridge, but with no success. Captain Breedon helped me settle in and got me a job as a labourer in the wharfs, as well as helping deliver goods to various premises in the town. People like a bit of gossip and I found out much about Maverick and his ways. One day in the Salutation Tavern, he sought me out and tried to sell me land he had no right to, saying all the natives had been paid to leave and he was commissioned to sell it. Vacuum dome, something like that, were the words he used frequently, but I don't know what it means."

"Ha Ha, vacuum domicilium. It's a Latin term meaning no legal ownership," said Belasyse. "And why did you come here?"

"I had heard that the town of Northampton was looking for such a person with experience as their ferryman and brewer, as there was none who would risk being so far west. I thought I'll take that job. Once you can jump the drop at London Bridge, everything was downhill as far as I was concerned and I have thrived in the countryside, away from dirty, disease-ridden London. I am lonely, though I hope this mission of yours won't ruin my and this villages tranquillity," Kellogg said, looking kindly on his old employer and benefactor.

"You're a practical man, Joseph. It will take timing, planning and ruthless execution," said Belasyse.

"And luck," added Kellogg.

"No, the minute you add luck to a plan that is the road to failure. If lady luck smiles upon you, so be it. Never trust to luck. Trust to planning, equipment, organisation and professional discipline. That is something we cavaliers did not learn and that cost us all three civil wars. You are only strong as your weakest man and I know that man all too well," said Belasyse.

"I am sure you have not come all this way without a plan."

"Well I am still formulating it. Ultimately I must take them down and we three have led a merry dance with each other, knowingly and unknowingly, for over twenty years and it all ends here. Maybe it was meant to be this way," he said, knowing this was to be the last battle of the Civil War for him and he hoped for all.

"Clash of the titans?" asked Kellogg.

"I think so. The less you know the better. When all is said and done, you will still be here and I don't you want to be picking up the pieces. Are you happy to take me to the market on the morrow? I need to pick up what other information I can."

"What about burying the hatchet with these men?" asked Kellogg hopefully.

"Why would I bury it? I need it for the return journey."

Kellogg laughed. "It's a native saying, to forgive and forget."

"I like it, no I am under orders and I want an end to this once and for all. This entire issue needs to be settled for all time."

"But how will you get them back to London to trial, never mind New York?"

"I am here to execute them, simple as that," said Belasyse, looking Kellogg straight in the eye. "Do please tell me of this town, as I am sure you can work out, as soon as I appear in the market I will be noticed. If Maverick goes out, he will annoy someone, so he stays in the barn. I would like to scout around. If I arrive on your ferry as a dealer wishing to buy furs for New York, it will be my cover – what do you think?"

"Yes, there will be plenty of traders from the surrounding farms and villages. Let's eat the hen. It smells delicious."

"Another ale, John?" Kellogg poured another quart and carved the crispy skin, bacon and succulent flesh along with some corn cobs to the wooden platter. Both men savoured the meal, juicy chicken and herbs with the fresh corn and rich gravy, made an enticing dinner and both ate heartily.

"About Northampton and Hadley," asked Belasyse wiping his platter clean with some cornbread. "The basics I must know to give me a good idea what I am facing."

"The town of Northampton is some nine years old, built here to tap the beaver and other pelts for trade with Europe. Some six hundred souls dwell in Northampton and just over one hundred in Hadley. Lumber, corn, pelts, tobacco and now cattle are the main income."

"Quite successful for the northern most settlement," both men continued, Kellogg describing the land and his hopes for the future, wanting another wife, Belasyse hoping this was the last of the regicides he would have to hunt down and his country and family would be at peace. Both men knew a final confrontation was inevitable and the outcome uncertain.

Maverick struggled to warm himself. *I can't light a fire in this barn, I'd burn the damn thing down, and I hope I will. Stuck up shit, that baron.* Thank God there was no nobility in Boston. The only reason he took this job was the two hundred pound reward. That baron was so rich he didn't need it. All right for some, he hadn't inherited anything and had to work for a living, not order around servants. The money would enable him to have built the finest house in Boston, a residence worthy of his station as a commissioner for the King. So what if that upper crust knob was in command, it was he who could speak the native tongue and had known which road the postman would ride down. Even if the baron was a crack shot, he knew the tracks and had guided them this far to their destination, what could and should not be eaten. *Still, it will be over in a few days and I will enjoy hanging those traitorous scum who have been the cause of my sleeping in a barn with horses.* "Damn shits," he said aloud, which frightened the mare below into emitting a pile of faeces. Maverick groaned and turned away from the smell. *Damn this to hell.*

CHAPTER 19

I Need a Favour

Belasyse checked his pistols for the umpteenth time, so close. He climbed the stairs to his room, having been out in the early morning to reconnoitre. He checked the hair he had stuck on his door was still in place. It had crossed his mind that Maverick might think of an easier way to get the reward. He opened the window and started to make mental notes of Hadley – a long common, the longest he had seen in New England, maidens milking cows and brewing ale, the cooper beating the iron ring over his barrels, soon to be filled with maple syrup and the blacksmith punching out nails for all and sundry, two for a penny; expensive. Still, a man had to make a living and nothing was for free. He warmed to the land. The fields were full of farmers ploughing in preparation for the spring planting. He noted seeds for corn, potatoes, tobacco, wheat and barley. A busy community where all lent a hand. *Do I want to leave a trail of death in my wake?* The names amazed him – Windsor, Guilford, Milford, Northampton – the same as back home. After all, hadn't they just transplanted themselves? Belasyse smiled in respect at Kellogg. He had his own house and a good living. He was pleased for him, he had worked hard for it. New England could teach the old one a thing or two. It was like a son, in a way. One day he will leave home and strike out on his own, it was inevitable really.

"Good morning," said Belasyse.

"Morning, sir," said Kellogg, only half awake.

"I have just the thing for you – coffee!" said Belasyse with a grin.

Kellogg's face lit up. "Just the thing, sir. I haven't had a coffee since I left England. Mm, now that's a delicious smell." His nostrils flared, appreciating the sensual aroma of the pot brewing the strong brown liquid on the fire.

"I have brought you three pounds of beans, raw, so you can roast them in your own time."

"Thank you so much. That will be a pleasure, savoured slowly," said Kellogg. He had only tried coffee a few times back in London, but it was a treat and he had enjoyed it immensely.

"I notice you have no sugar," said Belasyse with an inquiring frown.

"True – sugar beet is pretty well down on the list here. There are also few honey bees in this land. So importing them is not only very expensive, but very difficult. For cakes and puddings we use maple syrup and I have some for our coffee."

"Maple syrup – what's that?" asked Belasyse smiling again at his own ignorance.

"Well there are trees here called the Maple, they grow in abundance. You make cuts in it, like a sword slash, and collect the liquid in a metal container through a small trough cut from the wood. Boil the resulting liquid down until it thickens and that is pretty much it. Do try it; trust me, it is delicious. You can use it to sweeten anything." Kellogg went to the larder and brought over a pewter jug and poured a little of the amber-coloured syrup into a spoon and brought it to Belasyse, who sniffed it, wondering what was the next strange thing he would taste. His eyes clouded over in near ecstasy. "Now that is heaven on a spoon, absolutely delicious," he said earnestly and took two spoonsful and stirred his coffee contentedly, his forehead furrowed in concentration. "Right, let's have a little bread and fried bacon for our breakfast. Joseph, as its market day, see what information you can pick up. If Whalley and Goffe are in Hadley, the minister will need extra provisions for his guests. Maybe you can spot if he is buying large quantities of food. I also suspect he will come for some ministerial duties and here is a shilling for our dinners. Maverick, I have explained your work for the day; you have done very well. Keep working on the horses, they need rest, plenty of fodder and their coats seen to. Please ensure you can do all you can to prepare them for the journey back. Clear?"

"Clear, sir."

"I will bring my mare so as to show I have come from Hartford, dealing in pelts. Do you know anyone who is discreet and could arrange foodstuffs and grain for our return journey?"

"Mm, yes, I know a lady, a Mrs Abigail Rutland. Her husband died recently leaving her alone with three children. She lives on the cart way to Windsor in a log house called Springway. I feel for her; she is young and alone, although Minister Mather calls on her every day," said Kellogg. Belasyse noted the look and his sense of concern.

"Remember this, we all have everything to lose and need to be on guard for any potential slip-ups. I wish for us to be well on the way before morning service on Sunday and both of you with fair reward for the risk and effort you have put in on behalf of the King," said Belasyse.

Both men noted the baron's determined look as they enjoyed the strong fresh coffee with the rich milk from Kellogg's Devonshire cow, as the bacon grilled over the beach fire and the cornbread hardened in the skillet. Belasyse hoped his mission, no matter how dangerous, would leave his old servant and newfound friend in peace to rebuild his life. God knew what torment a man went through when his wife died. How do you explain that? He had buried two himself.

"Baron," said Maverick, "why do I have to stay in the barn? It is for slaves. You evidently don't like the idea of having them, but I find it a good way of working the land and it is far cheaper.

I mean, an indentured servant is fine, but you can't always sell them. That is the advantage of slavery; you buy and sell them as you would cattle. The Egyptians, Greeks and the Romans all dealt in them. It's not like it hasn't been done before."

"Times have changed. I don't believe in the philosophy that one man can own another. You tie a man to you by principal and mutual respect. Any employer should provide the tools to get the job done and pay the agreed amount at the agreed time. That's my way. This house was built by and is the property of the man who did so. It has value by the effort put in by the owner. To use a slave to do so devalues its worth morally. You will get your reward, but money is not everything. Charge after the golden dream of wealth if you wish, but sometimes it is best to stop running and enjoy what you have. Remember that." And he left the house, leaving Maverick to reflect.

Belasyse dropped to the ground, tied his mare to a horse post and scanned the crowd. All were busy buying, selling or both. Many had made the journey to the saturday market, the multitude of carts and horses hauling goods told their own story. The town crier vocally telling the visitors where to buy the best cheeses, hams and seasoned wood, amongst the other offerings on the multitude of stalls. The noise was incredible; he must have spotted over a hundred children, playing catch, tag and, he noticed, football. What is in the water here? He stood to his full height and marvelled at the surroundings. The valley was enclosed by a series of hills with a mountain over his left shoulder. Trees covered the land and the large river was fed by an array of little streams. Spring grass was poking its head above ground; the cattle and sheep will be out for forage soon. Buds had appeared on the trees and shrubs. Life was beginning again after a hard winter. He walked the town, noting the meeting house on a hill of the same name. It had a wooden shingle roof and a modest turret atop, with four windows and a door at the front. Swine ran freely along the paths, a good way of having the garbage removed. The alluvial soil at the river's edge would produce a good supply of wheat and corn.

Then a shock – four wolves' heads upon spikes at the crossroads, with a sign advertising ten shillings per head. Now that was a living! He noted the saw mill and an ordinary on the main street, where a John Webb proudly sold his 'fine local ale'. He saw the house Kellogg had mentioned and walked up to the door, the last vestiges of winter snow making a slurping sound in the muddy slush. He wasn't worried about slipping; he had had his boots dipped in tar, then sand. Springway, carved in white oak, hanging on a metal chain.

Rap, rap, went the knocker. He stepped back and the door was opened by a young woman, fresh faced, with pale cheeks, a cap upon her head which covered her light orange hair, tied in a bow. "Yes sir," she said with a morose voice.

"Madam, my name is Richard Head, a pelt merchant. I wish to buy hard tack, grain and beef jerky. I am looking for some thirty pieces of tack, fifty pounds of grain, if you have as much, along with around six pounds of jerky and two smoked hams. A Mr Kellogg, the ferryman, mentioned you deal in these commodities," asked Belasyse hopefully.

"Ah yes, Mr Kellogg mentioned you would be passing. Please do come in. These are my children; I have three and no husband to mind us," she said in a pleading voice, as the little children hid behind their mother's apron, worried little faces peering at him.

"I do apologise for disturbing you at this most unfortunate time, Mrs Rutland. Mr Kellogg told me you had lost your husband. May I offer my most sincere condolences to you and I hope God will help you in your search for peace of mind. The world is often an unfair place for the good and the meek. May I personally assure I will pray to our saviour."

"That is most kind of you, sir."

"I also need, if you can provide from your stores or in the market, two shovels and I will pay ten silver shillings for your discretion."

"That is a great deal. Why so much for my discretion?"

"Because I do care for children and have two waiting for my return. I also have a good supplier of pelts in a shrinking amount that is being caught. It is advisable to keep the customer happy and not let the competition know. If I could have the goods before sundown; I do not wish to be caught working on the Sabbath."

"I'll have the goods bought and arrange delivery, sir."

"Please, no bother. Mr Kellogg mentioned he would collect them, if that is acceptable," said Belasyse putting the coins on the parlour table.

"Thank you so much, Mr Head. You are a real gentlemen, sir."

"Oh and if I may, Mr Kellogg sends you his kind regards. On Monday he mentioned he would be in town to settle his accounts and asks if you needed any help, like repairing your barn out back. I noticed the roof needs new planking and the yard to be cleared of the winter snow."

Abigail Rutland stared at Belasyse and he knew exactly what was going through her mind.

"That is if it were no imposition, madam. He doesn't wish to disturb you in any way whatsoever."

"It's no imposition, sir. He is most courteous and has been so kind to my children. He is most welcome to render his help," said Abigail, smiling as she opened the door to let him out. *Everyone needed a little help in life and Mr Kellogg was such a kindly man and the children like him. If only I could…*

Poor woman. Three children and no breadwinner. Belasyse walked to the tavern on the west corner of Fort Street. Always a good place to pick up information.

"Tis you and your kind countenance, sir," said David Throw, sitting uncomfortably on the wet bench attached to the stocks.

"And what brings you here?" said Belasyse to the sodden man.

"For condemning the constable's authority, sir."

"In what manner?"

"He commanded me to the meeting house for God's ordnances last Sabbath."

"I can't imagine why you refused," said Belasyse winking. "When will you be released?"

"When it grows dark and I must attend the service or I shall be whipped," said Throw.

"Here is a pound in silver. I need a favour," said Belasyse bending down in the slush and slipping the coins into Throw's top pocket, whispering instructions in his ear. Belasyse moved on to the ordinary; a welcome ale was just the thing. There would be many who had done their business in the market and were ready for a little light conversation.

"To you, sir. What is the word of the Lord?" said Eleasar Mather, standing on a wooden box at the corner of the Market Street, dressed in faded black with his Geneva bands and the widest brimmed hat Belasyse had ever seen.

"The word of the Lord is for all people for all time. He does not distinguish on a man's colour, race or the language he speaks," said Belasyse, eying the minister contemptuously.

"Except those who worship a false religion, for they shall be dammed and go to hell!"

"Christ never said that. He said 'love thy neighbour as thyself. Bless them that curse you, persecute you and say all kinds of evil about you because of me, for great will be your reward in heaven'. I will let you decide on my views, as I have on yours, minister. A relaxing ale is better than your venom," said Belasyse, as the group around the minister left in agreement and made their way to the inn.

"What may I get you, sir?" asked the landlord.

"A pot of warm cider if I may and is there any food available?"

"Most definitely, sir; always busy on market day. I have turkeys roasting on a jack, or a magnificent venison pie by the oven. How about a generous slice with roasted potatoes, fried greens, corn and a rich gravy, sir?" asked the landlord with practised salesmanship.

"Sold. How much is that?"

"Seven pence, sir. Do make yourself comfortable. I'll bring the cider and your lunch over directly." Belasyse sat next to the large fireplace, noting the brick ovens above and by the side. Roasting turkeys on iron jacks, the landlord's wife slicing off another portion for the hungry traders. "Here we are, sir." The landlord brought over the pot and a pewter dish for his lunch with a good portion of golden pie. The burning fir wood adding a present perfume to the atmosphere in the inn. Belasyse noted the carving on the cruck beam. 'He who is merciful shall be saved for the Lord so doth love the compassionate', and he reflected upon his mission.

"Good day, sir," said two children emerging from a door to his side.

"Hallo. Where are you off to?" asked Belasyse amenably.

"The market, sir. There is a stall selling fruit and has apples covered in maple syrup; they're really yummy but a penny each."

Belasyse looked at the two children and beamed. "Here," he said and gave the little girl a sixpence. "I remember when I was your age, we used to have them covered in honey."

"Thank you, sir," they both said, jumping up and down with excitement and rushed off to the market to buy their treats. The ironmonger made his way over to Belasyse's table, who caught the movement out of the corner of his left eye and his right hand slipped down to the butt of his pistol. He needn't have bothered.

"That is very kind of you, sir. My children will be so pleased at your generosity."

"It's a pleasure. I have two myself and birthdays and treats are so important," said Belasyse.

"Very true, sir. We are both fathers who want peace for all our family, don't we?" said the ironmonger.

"That we do," said Belasyse and the ironmonger touched

his forelock in respect and made his way back to the smithy to continue his work.

"I think you may be mistaken in my teachings," said Mather walking up to Belasyse, who took a deep breath.

"Many have put words into the mouth of Christ that he never said and quote them as gospel. That can be very misleading, if not dangerous. God gave his only son into the world, not to judge it, but to save it through him and I hope that you will be preaching Christ's words of reconciliation to all men, whatever they may be or believe in?" asked Belasyse.

"They may be reconciled on earth or in heaven, as long as they listen to our correct preaching of the word of god."

"Or your twisted interpretation of it," countered Belasyse and left.

Abigail's delivery wagon trundled down the path, expertly guided by Kellogg's careful hand, with the goods for Belasyse's return journey and materials for her house. As it rounded the bend of the cart way, at the large cottonwood tree overhanging the track, Kellogg spotted three men drinking from a tin pot. One of them looked up and motioned to his two companions. "What do we have here? Rations? I am plenty starving; how about a side of beef or some ham?" And the three men lurched into the middle of the road. Kellogg pulled the reins. He had dealt with drunks back in London and knew the unpredictability of them. He took one of the loaves he had purchased for Belasyse, one less wouldn't harm, and he passed it to Cleeson, carefully watching the drunks.

"Give me your money!" he said and grabbed Kellogg's outstretched left arm. Kellogg jumped off the seat and landed on him and Cleeson collapsed. Kellogg rolled quickly away as Cornelius brought the large tin pot full of ale down on his friend's head, missing Kellogg. "Sod it," he exclaimed, as the ale flew up all over his face and Kellogg knocked him out with an expertly placed right hook and rounded on Throw who looked at his two unconscious friends.

"Forget it." And off he went, as quickly as his legs could carry him.

Abigail's look of panic was replaced by one of admiration. "Mr Kellogg, sir, that was a display! We won't be seeing them again, I am sure of it. That was so brave of you. The Lord has sent me a saviour," she said touching his forearm. Kellogg mounted the waggon and off they went to Abigail's house, mightily pleased at his display.

"Mr Kellogg, the children will be so happy that you are going to build them a treehouse to play in. I just hope I have not asked too many favours from you."

"You may ask as many favours from me as you wish," said Kellogg to Abigail with a protective look, as they pulled up. Kellogg helped Abigail down and their eyes locked as he gently lowered her to the ground and he replaced a strand of hair under her cap and gently stroked her cheek. "If there is anything I can help you with please ask; it is my pleasure."

"Let me cook you lunch before you take the goods to the ferry," said Abigail and slipped her hand in his and beckoned him to the parlour. "May I offer you a jug of ale?"

"I would be delighted," said Kellogg, knowing he could spend the rest of his days looking after her.

Throw stopped running and realised he and his friends had overdone it. Still, plans go awry and no one was dead and a pound was three months' wages each.

"We're close, very close; you have been invaluable in the hunt for these men, Maverick. We may be socially different and I assure you I judge a man on his words and deeds and you have carried out the mission very well so far. We wait until the morrow. Stay in the barn and build a veritable fort here with the hay bales, just in case we are found out. Build a wall, set fire to it, knock it down when any enemy gets close, and you have fire and smoke, the perfect escape mechanism. This evening we will go over our plan for Sunday morning. We are all now bound up in a wheel of fire and if we are not prudent, we will burn on it. Remember, we get them, you get paid. Keep your eyes on the prize," said Belasyse. "I am sure a fine house in the city of Boston will be a fitting stamp of your loyalty to the King."

"That is my desire, sir," said Maverick, "and I thank you for getting us this far; a remarkable achievement of leadership." Maverick had thought of running for it at the fight between the settlers and the Dutch troops but the baron had the gold in his saddlebags, otherwise he would have gone. He was crafty that baron. If the worst case came about he could use the ferry to move down the river to Springfield, he had a contact there, and ride back down the Boston Post Road. *Wait! That's an idea; Belasyse and I find, then hang the regicides, go back to Kellogg's house, I shoot the baron and take the reward. Kill that swiving idiot of a ferryman and scatter the shillings, making it look like the two dead men had done the deed and fought over the money. The villagers will check the cart way and they won't find anyone. As it's the Sabbath they won't go far. They will check on Monday and by then I will be far away and no one will know I was even here.* "I appreciate your trust. You can rely on me, sir," said Maverick. *Just wait, you upper crust berk. I'll show you who's the cleverest here.*

CHAPTER 20

He Who Laughs Last

Belasyse awoke as his pocket watch started sounding and squeezed it gently shut. *How much I hate these early starts.* He jumped straight out of bed. *Get going straight away; learnt that the hard way. The best time to launch an attack is at dawn.* He splashed cold water over himself and rubbed his body down, exercising all the while. He donned his clothes and walked downstairs to the fireplace. He shovelled the embers into a bucket and placed some kindling wood in the centre and surrounded it with logs, struck the flint tinder and the linen rags caught alight. He placed the cast iron jug on the grate with a cauldron of water. He used part of the hot water to shave. Everyone would be in their Sunday best and he didn't want to stand out. He woke Maverick and Kellogg, then returned to check his weapons. Twin braces of double-barrelled pistols, the musketoon and his broadsword completed the offensive material. He donned a cuirass and looked at the pot, its steam rising, and added roasted coffee beans, ground to perfection. Remember, John, no mistakes.

"We must be alert, so no breakfast for anyone," said Belasyse. "Mr Kellogg, all I need is the ferry waiting with the mares, loaded with the supplies, at one hour after sunrise. We cross and haul it back to its mooring, chain it up and no one will suspect you used it. As there is no trade on the Sabbath, most people will still be in bed."

"I'll be there, John."

"Maverick, we first go to the Tilton household. He is the town magistrate, therefore he will have had much interaction with the townsfolk and I am sure will have some knowledge of these men, whether by accident or design. He will come with us to the house of John Russell, the minister. He above all knows where these men are hiding. When he sees my authority and the magistrate as our 'guest', we will have the two men, who between them know every person in the village, therefore where they are hiding, I am absolutely sure of it."

"And if they don't know or won't say, then what do we do?" interjected Maverick, worrying he may not get his reward and the villagers will discover them.

"I'll ask for divine guidance, as well as showing them these nooses I prepared last night and if necessary hang them in front of their own door. It is dawn in a few minutes. Joseph, please get the goods and horses prepared. Maverick, we go on foot."

"Why not on horse, sir?"

"For their hoof marks would be traced to our mutual friend's house and we don't want that, now do we?" said Belasyse, as Kellogg smiled in gratitude. He had been worried since the baron first appeared at his house; the last thing he needed was to flee if this whole operation went wrong, and lose his property. For if it did, the villagers would have to kill everyone connected with it and it was a weight on his mind. Still, he should not worry, the baron had a plan for everything.

"You will go first using any existing footsteps; I follow in yours with this bucket of hot water. I pour a good amount in each footprint, melting the evidence, so no one can trace us to Kellogg's house, whilst dropping some ground pepper behind us." Both men frowned. "It totally messes up a dog's nose. Most of the snow will be slush or melted by nine so there should be no trace. When we cross the main track to the right where Minister Russell's house is situated and then break the bucket into kindling wood." Kellogg grinned in respect at Belasyse's thorough research.

Belasyse took six cuts of beef from the flank he had bought in the market and wrapped them in linen cloth and opened the window shutters. It was nearly dawn and the pale sun would soon rise above the horizon.

"Maverick, remember, the calmest men win. Take the two shovels, your weapons and we move."

Kellogg poured the hot water from the cauldron into a wooden bucket and passed it to Belasyse. They carefully exited the house, Kellogg with the horses and supplies to the ferry. Maverick and Belasyse gingerly made their way across the meadow, through the woods and up to the track on the side of the common, like dancers learning their first moves. A slop of water every few seconds was the only sound they made as they crossed the long common used for grazing animals and the militia for drill, musket and pike practice. Up the right-hand side to magistrate Tilton's house. Suddenly a bark from an alert dog stirred the air, Belasyse froze, withdrew a cut of beef from his pocket and threw it as far as he could in the direction of the dog. Then another cut, to ensure a good breakfast for the animal and its silence. They both gingerly made their way to the porch of Peter Tilton's house that Kellogg had directed them to. Belasyse did a thumbs up in the gloom and Maverick started to break up the bucket into pieces, as he pulled on the bell cord.

"Good morning, Mr Peter Tilton? I do apologise for waking you so early on the day of our Lord, but I am an agent of his Majesty the King and I don't mind if I come in," said Belasyse. Both men pushed past Tilton and closed the door behind them, looking around to ensure no one else was there. Pistols combed the room as Tilton's early morning drowsiness vanished, frightened to have two armed men in his house. Belasyse gathered himself and withdrew the royal proclamation.

"My name is Baron Belasyse. I am charged by his Majesty the King to apprehend and bring to justice the regicides of his late father and all those attained by Parliament, in the encouragement in that foul and bloody murder, along with all persons who aided and abetted them. So, under the authority invested in me, I hereby do arrest you for high treason," and Belasyse handed Tilton his coat and hat from the stand, as Maverick stood at the bottom of the stairs, pistol in hand, trying to look as menacing as possible. Tilton eyed the baron – thick wool-lined boots, well-worn caramel dyed woollen britches, embroidered shirt, thin red jacket, a long, beaver-collared coat and a round capotain hat. Two pairs of double-barrelled pistols and a broadsword by his side and a musketoon slung over his back. This man was not here for Sunday service.

"Do you have an arrest warrant?" stammered Tilton, only half-dressed and amazed at such an accusation at nearly six in the morning of the Sabbath.

"I would assume that, as a man of the law, you would know that you don't need a warrant to arrest someone for murder," countered Belasyse, passing him the proclamation.

Tilton read, his legs went weak – in places unknown, directly or indirectly, conceal, harbour, keep, retain or maintain the said Whalley and Goffe, shall be regarded as traitors to the realm. He lowered the document, his eyes full of fear.

"Do you seriously think I would have gone to all this trouble if there was not more than a even chance that those indicted men were here?" asked Belasyse. Tilton looked up and stared at the baron, fear flooding through his eyes.

"Think about that. I can see that you have not replied and you're trembling with fear, which means they are here, aren't they?" Belasyse calmly took the musketoon off his back. "This is a musketoon; it has three rounds in it. An exact copy was used to kill John Lisle in Lucerne. You've heard about that, haven't you? So are they here?"

Tilton looked like a frightened rabbit and Maverick walked

slowly up to the magistrate and stuck his pistol into Tilton's groin. "The baron asked you a question."

Tilton nodded. "I, I, I promise I don't know where, I swear it. The m, m, m, minister has them," he said shaking, his teeth beginning to chatter as he stammered the words. "Per, per, please don't kill me. I did not want them here."

"Maverick, tie him up and gag him. Make sure his hands are behind his back. If you have them in front he could put them around your neck and try to strangle you or grab a weapon. Keep him close and shoot him if he tries to escape. Let us pay a visit to the minister. I am sure he has a pretty tale to tell," said Belasyse. He was in his element now and he knew it.

Off they went up the right-hand side of the common, across the main track and at the corner with the common was the minister's house. Belasyse stopped and rapped on the door of the minister's house.

"Maverick, keep your pistol in the back of this traitor and if he tries anything even remotely, like he is trying to warn anyone, shoot him! Got it, Tilton? Don't cross us. We're both good at this and I mean it."

"Yes, sir, leave him to me," said Maverick, lapping up the praise. The hour had come for another glorious moment in the King's service. A reward of two hundred pounds for both of the wanted men was at hand and he, Samuel Maverick, was going to collect it. He would be the only survivor and a grateful King was sure to reward him further. He would sail to London and once again have an audience with the monarch, and feted by the great and the good, he would hint at the disloyalty of the Boston council and was sure the King would grant him the governorship of Massachusetts.

Belasyse pulled on the bell cord and yanked it once only. This he hoped would not awake anyone else in the house. The ministers woke early, preparing their sermons for the Sabbath and Belasyse was not wrong. The door squeaked open and he gave the minister one of his ear to ear smiles.

"Sir, I do apologise at this early intrusion but I have been informed that I may attend one of your superb sermons by Mr Mather of Northampton, and wanted to ensure I had the correct place of worship."

John Russell hesitated and took in the baron for what seemed an age. Then he frowned. "I am sure you have not come at this hour to ask me that," said John Russell with a wry smile.

"In fact I have," countered Belasyse, suddenly seized by fear that he had been compromised, and looked beyond Russell, half expecting a barrage of shots. Did he know?

"You have suddenly become anxious, I suspect, therefore you are here for a different reason. So evidently you're not for a sermon, especially as Minister Mather knows it is not for another two hours, and why here and not Northampton? So whoever you are I think you should start again," said Russell.

"I am here because I have a great sense of humour," Belasyse said, looking at Russell for any reaction.

"We seem to be of the same disposition," said Russell sensing trouble. Then it hit him. My God, no! And he turned to run, as Belasyse drew a pistol.

"Halt or I fire!" Russell stopped, now knowing why these men was at his door. "Maverick, bring our guest into the house," and they all moved into the parlour.

"If I am not mistaken, Mr Tilton you are the town magistrate and you, Mr John Russell, are the town minister. I put this to you, I have it on good authority that the former Major Generals Whalley and Goffe are being sheltered in this village, possibly by yourselves, contrary to the law of England. Both men are attained by Parliament.

"I, Baron Belasyse, with Samuel Maverick, commissioners of his Majesty King Charles the Second, are charged with their apprehension. So what say you, sirs?" he said, undoing the gag around Tilton's mouth and motioning him into the front room.

Russell shuddered as if being hit by one of the shovels Maverick had over his back. He stared in disbelief. How did these men know, let alone manage the journey from England to their outpost at the edge of the known world?

"As a minister I am ultimately responsible to God and no earthly thing," said Russell, his confidence draining as he saw his friend with his hands tied and a noose around his neck and horror written all over his face.

"And I, I am with him," stammered Tilton, scared to see the King's reach was here in the form of two well-armed and motivated men. Both realised that their lives now hung upon these strangers' decisions. On the other hand there were many in Hadley who may assist them, that is, if they could be warned. Although many were still asleep, they would soon rise, but they had chosen their moment well. Not ten were awake within the village and would not leave their homes for an hour. *I wonder who will be the first to give ground?*

"If you are not responsible to any earthly thing, Mr Russell, then you are not answerable to anyone here on earth," continued Belasyse. "Which means you can commit any crime, abuse any law and not be accountable for it. All persons are responsible for their actions. Are you saying you are above any law made by man, Mr Russell?" asked Belasyse. Russell gave him a cold stare and by looking at his scarred face and determined demeanour, he would tolerate no fool and he was about his Majesty's business.

I was a fool to take these men in. I thought I was doing God's work, now the devil has come to settle the account! "I am a minister doing the Lord's work and I do as my conscience dictates and when my time on earth is done I shall stand before him and answer for my actions, as we all will, Baron; you remember that. I have nothing to say, but you are welcome to attend my service, unarmed if you please, sir."

"Maverick, check upstairs for anyone," said Belasyse, and Maverick ran up the staircase, pistol at the ready and disappeared into a bedroom, there was a cry and a slap. "There is a woman," said Maverick his head appearing over the banisters.

"Bring her down here."

"Please don't harm my wife, sir, please," begged Russell as Maverick dragged Russell's wife down the stairs, his hand over her mouth.

"Why, do you think I would? Tie her to the banisters and gag her," said Belasyse. "It's time to finish this matter. Now where are they," he said to Russell, who shook his head.

"You mangy curs. We will strike you down as we would dogs," said Maverick, his anger rising, knowing the village would soon stir and he pointed his pistol at Russell's wife.

"Dogs are man's best friend," said Belasyse. "After all, where else would you find a good warning? But as you mention dogs, how about I ask your Border collie, Mr Russell, where these men are?"

"Ask my dog?" said Russell in surprise. "Dogs can't talk!"

"Oh yes they can," said Belasyse. "You would be amazed what they can say. It's warming up a little," he said, taking off his coat, as the sun now shone fully on the spring morning, and dropped it onto the wooden floor, showing his double brace of pistols to all. "Doggy, how about a piece of beef?" said Belasyse kindly to Russell's pet, which was crouching by the parlour door confused at the unfolding events. Belasyse removed a sizable chunk from his coat pocket and cutting off a very small piece, to the dog's chagrin and placed it on his coat very slowly, in fact so slowly all were surprised, as the dog barked and barked, then snapped up the offering in an instant, hoping for the rest of the meal.

He crouched down and showed the dog the whole piece, putting it on the coat, then lifting it out of the dog's reach as the dog jumped up. "Fetch, dog, fetch Whalley and Goffe, go and fetch," said Belasyse and off the dog ran, straight behind the stairs scratching the floor and started barking for all its worth. "What have we here, a room for storage and what are we storing,

Mr Russell? Both of you stand by the side of the wall." Belasyse motioned the men to stand at the end of the corridor, with no exit – they weren't going anywhere.

"Maverick, tie Russell up."

Belasyse turned to Russell. "Strange to have a hidden room in the middle of the house, whilst your cellar is on the outside where most would look first, as I already have. I also noted the small piece of string you had tied to the inner part of the trap door to ring a bell inside your house if it were lifted." Russell's eyes narrowed, *clever sod*! Belasyse looked carefully at the floor and made out the very thin join of the wooden slats. He jammed his broadsword between the join and prised it upwards, ramming in a small crowbar very quickly, breaking the hinges and lifting up the square door to the underground room and threw in the beef. The dog jumped barking like mad as it leapt into the void. Belasyse brought out of his pocket a white linen pouch with a piece of thin black rope attached to it.

"Come out," he commanded. "I have a bag here with one pound of the finest black powder. I am going to light the fuse and you will be having a meeting with God a lot sooner than you anticipated, as well as having your friends dangle from the gallows for their treason. So make a decision."

A few seconds passed, the group stared at the opening in the floor and a ladder appeared at the top of the underground room.

"Don't even think of trying anything clever. I will kill anyone who resists and I mean it! Maverick, keep an eye out, these men are not fools, kill all of them if any make a false move," said Belasyse, pointing his musketoon at the top of the ladder, as two men rubbed sleep from their eyes in shocked disbelief that they had been discovered. "What a surprise. Let me guess, Whalley and Goffe. I must admit, you are definitely a long way from Whitehall," said Belasyse in triumph, standing in the centre of the parlour, musketoon at the ready. "What are your names? I wish to be sure of who I have."

"You know who we are, Baron," said Goffe, hate in his every word.

"Is there anyone else down there?"

"I assure there is not. May I tell you we have no desire to have anyone associated with our stay," added Whalley, hoping Dixwell could find their pistols in the dark.

Dixwell hesitated in terrified indecision. How had the King's agents come this far into the wilderness? Who told them or had they worked it out for themselves?

"Only you?" Their eyes gave it away. He pointed the two men to the ground. "Maverick, search and tie them up; careful, they are snakes in the grass."

Belasyse stared at each of them as Maverick trussed both men up like a Christmas goose. He withdrew a fuse from his trouser pocket and wrapped it around another slice of steak and lit it from the Russells' morning fire. As they all looked on he threw it into the cellar. "That is an explosive device and is your ticket to hell. You've got to be quick to get out alive or you're dog food. Everybody out!" shouted Belasyse. The two generals moved violently, trying to warn their friend, Belasyse pointed his musketoon at Whalley and shook his head. Dixwell ran up the ladder in a flash.

"It looks like my intuition paid off. Who are you, sir?" snapped Belasyse.

"My name is James Davids, a merchant form Hartford. I am here to discuss the shipping of maple syrup from New England to London. It is a fine sweet syrup good for the stomach and prevents hair loss," gasped Dixwell.

"To do that you hide in a cellar with two of the most wanted men in the realm. Do you really expect me to believe you? Do you take me for an idiot? I will count to three then I will blow your balls off with this musketoon. One…"

"Please don't shoot! I am Colonel Dixwell, former Member of Parliament and Governor of Dover Castle." He raised up his arms in surrender.

Belasyse lowered his musketoon, frowning. "Really? I thought you were dead when your house burnt down. Good ruse. If I am not mistaken, you were number thirty-eight to have signed the warrant?"

Dixwell hung his head. "Yes sir that is so."

Belasyse gave him a look of admiration. "Clever. Gentlemen, time to go. Maverick, remember to tie his hands behind his back," he said looking at Dixwell – James Davids, yes, the letters. Maverick pulled out the lengths of rope Belasyse had given him last night. He sure knew his business, this baron.

Belasyse looked at Russell's wife. "You share your home with three traitors, a poor choice of guest. Stay here and don't struggle, or else!" said Belasyse gagging her, whilst whispering in her ear, "I will speak daggers to you, but use none," and he quickly looked out the front door and checked for any early risers. Nothing, only candles flickering in one house by the middle highway to the meadow. He quickly went to the rear of the property and out the back door. Take the horse, they will think he went to visit someone, and he brought Russell's horse to the front of the house. "Let's go," he commanded and the small group left the Russell's house on the corner of the main track and started off to the cemetery down the middle highway. The early morning sun rose slowly, as they made their way to the graveyard, past the neat fields, still with last year's stubble from the maize crop rotting into the ground as natural goodness. A serene setting for the forthcoming executions.

CHAPTER 21

Blessed are the Peacemakers

The seven men walked up the path to the small cemetery. Chickens started to crow as the morning sun fully spread over the hills that surrounded Hadley. Streaks of red and bright yellow coloured the sky as they passed the barns containing cattle and sheep. Belasyse noted the gap between the graveyard and road, to bury unbaptised children, over the small ridge to the headstones, where two oak trees stood. *Perfect* thought Belasyse, and they moved to the far corner, away from prying eyes.

"Tilton and Russell, you remain here and sit on these flat gravestones; you three over here. Maverick, watch the two officials," said Belasyse and pushed the three regicides over to the two oak trees. "Do you have anything to say before sentence is passed on your bodies?"

The three men looked at each other, the fear of death in their eyes, knowing now the hunt for them was over and the King would have his revenge over them after all.

Goffe lifted his head. "If it is to be my end let me briefly say this – we wanted no more lords and ladies in their mansions, whilst the starving begged at the gate for scraps from the master's table. No more landowners with half a parish, whilst a farmer had half an acre to grub, and paying an extortionate rent on a cottage that he could never own. We wanted an equal living for all Christian men and women, enjoying the fruits of the good Lord's earth. An end to corruption, favouritism and the King's rule by decree. The court of the Star Chamber set out to destroy the King's enemies, not to deliver justice as any court should. The enclosures of public land forbid the common folk grazing their animals, a right we English have had for hundreds of years. Branding and cutting off of ears by the authority of an unelected bishop. Is that the England you fought for, Baron? How about taxes raised when the King decided. Licentiousness on a Sunday on God's day of prayer which was legally allowed in the King's book of sports – no! Rebellion to tyrants is obedience to God. This is what we fought and died for!"

"No more, Lords and ladies," said Belasyse. "Ha! Lord Fairfax, Earl of Manchester, Earl of Essex, how many lords, knights and landowners fought for Parliament? Too many to count and repeat. You call it the good old cause. Tell that to the Irish in Drogheda and Wexford. How many men were shot after they surrendered, murdered! Do you call that justice? How many did you kill with the words, God wills it? That is an example of how not to govern a nation. Provoking his Majesty with the grand remonstrance, published to the masses, abusing his wife as a Catholic and foreigner. This would have driven any man to react. Do that to all men's wives, do you? You closed theatres and taverns, horseracing and dancing were abolished, and you scrubbed the make-up off women with wire brushes. Corruption, how did you generals get your vast estates? In Maryland and Rhode Island there is religious toleration away from your vindictiveness. Here people enjoy the fruits of their own labour rather than your New Model Army looting it. Today, no more people will be a victim of your hate or religious bigotry because he plays football on a Sunday and has a beer afterwards," said Belasyse, thinking *I sound more of a Republican than they are!*

"And you, Whalley, what is your religion anyway? Faith is mercy, being just, standing up for what is right, even if those around you urge a more convenient course. Protecting the weak and never killing a woman or child. Speaking words of truth even if it costs you your life. That is faith. You sold how many of our people as slaves? Is that how you treat your fellow man? How about the outrages committed by your men after the battle of Naseby to our women. That will be your legacy. I would love to know what Jesus Christ makes of you, a man who preaches a brand of Christianity which justifies dictatorship. I think you are a long way from walking in the footsteps of our Lord. Do you have something to add before sentence is passed upon your body?" said Belasyse, venting his fury on the wanted men who had taken him so far from his family.

"If I may, Baron," said Whalley. "You are a brave man, no one can doubt that. What you have just said hurts me more that you know. We fought you at Edgehill, Newbury and Bristol, but the defence of Newark was something else. I remember it was five months of constant warfare, being outnumbered eight to one and you continued to mount an aggressive defence, nearly capturing the besieging General Poyntz, until the King ordered you to surrender. Baron, you have my respect. I know you are here under orders. What we did was wrong in many people's eyes, but may I say, with King Charles's death, a point has been made. The King, whoever they may be, must rule with Parliament, not against it. The law is in English now, not Latin or French, so all may understand the workings of the justice system. How many ordinary Englishmen had a chance in court with those languages? There is no doubt that crimes were committed by both sides and, with the benefit of hindsight, we were wrong on many things. Successful merchants now come from all walks of life, not just the rich or titled men. England has been through dreadful times, we all have suffered and I hope have learnt by our mistakes, so that England never has to go through that horror ever again."

"Ever again!" shouted Maverick "Ever again! Shoot them now.

Damn you to hell, traitors to the Crown." Belasyse gave Maverick a long hard stare and nodded to Whalley.

"Much of what you say is true. I have said before, the government and the Church must be separate and the military subject to the law," said Belasyse, warming to his theme. "The nation should not be run by religious orthodoxy or the army. It is up to the people to decide and they welcomed back his Majesty from exile with the greatest celebration since the defeat of the Spanish Armada; every year thanks are given for the deliverance from your evil ways. People now go to the theatre, dance around the maypole, go horseracing, women are further liberated and may now act on stage. A new era has dawned for England. You cannot stop progress, science and industry, and the arts flourish, when under your dictatorship they were suppressed. The people are free from you."

"I hope my wife and children have not been made to pay by the King or yourself for my involvement in the Republic," said Goffe.

"What makes you say that?" asked Belasyse.

"Because I know you have visited them," said Goffe, looking at the fur-lined coat.

"You're wise, nice coat keeps out the cold," he said. "I don't make war on the vulnerable, unlike you. Though I would have thought that a real man would have stayed behind and defended his family, if he thought the returning King was going to harm them. For what could be better for any man than to stand and fight, defending the honour of his wife, the lives of his children and the cause in which he believes? But no! You ran and abandoned your families and the cause you brutalised so many with and sailed away and hid. What kind of pathetic men are you?"

"Perfectly put, Baron," said Maverick, happy to see the regicides put in their place.

"Let me make a few points. Whalley – how much money

was owed to the soldiers? In ten years you did not pay them, but the King did in less than two. Why, because many of your so-called generals and government officials were pocketing the cash. You talk about changing the nation for the better but how many more people got the vote? None. How about the levellers who opposed your bigotry? They were imprisoned or shot. I now find you still plotting your revolution with, I suspect, only yourself as its adherents," said Belasyse.

"We fought against the tyranny of an unelected King and his bishops," said Goffe, realising Belasyse had changed whilst he hadn't.

"And replaced it with a tyranny of an unelected dictator in Oliver Cromwell and the rule of the major generals. Interesting how the mighty fall. When I hang you, there will only be a small sound."

"Have you anything to say before your sentence?" said Belasyse.

"Sir, I am John Dixwell. It must be known that I had reservations about the King's execution. Several of the jury did. John Downs had objections and he was taken from the trial, threatened and forced to continue when he complained the court was not lawful. This was said at his trial. Many were coerced into signing; you were not there. I have not shot any Royalists. I was merely a functionary for Parliament. We were threatened and intimidated by Oliver Cromwell and Axtel. They wanted the King dead and Hugh Peter was the man who preached for it. Please sir, show mercy, please," said Dixwell crying desperately.

Belasyse looked sharply at him, seeing the fear of death in his eyes, tears flowing down his cheeks, whilst on his knees begging for mercy. How many times had he seen this on half a dozen battlefields across the nation, young men, some only teenagers, begging for their lives and crying for their mothers, as shattered limbs and punctured rib cages leaking blood covered how many English meadows?

"Maverick, get them to dig their graves," said Belasyse and turned his back on the begging Dixwell.

"My pleasure, sir," Maverick said and started berating the three regicides as Russell and Tilton looked on helplessly, hands tied. "I will treat you like the slaves I buy and sell; you are the enemies of the King and a hundred pounds for each of you dead or alive. All businessmen like payment. So I will start with the main one, gold; take those rings off your fingers and put them in this pouch along with any monies you have upon your person," said Maverick throwing a small brown leather bag on the ground in front of the judges. "Move!" he shouted, levelling a pistol at Dixwell and kicking Goffe in the side of his head, as the regicides took off their rings and emptied their pockets.

Belasyse checked again for any early risers, wishing to move quickly.

"Dig your graves here," said Maverick, throwing them the two shovels.

"Mr Russell, let them have Communion before they hang," said Belasyse moving over to the two officials of Hadley, as Maverick forced the regicides to dig, whilst whipping them ruthlessly to hurry them up.

"That I will," said Russell, amazed at the situation he found himself in, but now fully aware of his predicament. "I see you're married, Baron. Any children?" asked Russell, frightened, but also fascinated in the man his guests evidently knew, as well as in admiration in tracking them down.

"What business is it of yours? I am here to administer the punishment set out by Parliament, not to discuss my personal life," said Belasyse irritated, watching the three men taking turns digging, reluctance in their every movement.

"Because my first son is named as you, John, who was commanded by Christ to look after his mother when he was dying on the cross. Will you look after their wives and children when they are gone?" said Russell.

Belasyse gave him a shocked look. "I am not their keeper."

"And neither was Judas Iscariot Christ's keeper, although he should have been," said Russell quietly.

"Look, I am not going to have a discourse on religion right now or in the future with you," said Belasyse turning around looking at Russell, his conscience pricked.

"I would not want to. I was only pointing out something like, love your enemies so you may be a son of your father, who is in heaven, just like my wife Mary Talcott. She died at the tender age of twenty-five and a perfect woman. I would not want anybody to go through that emotional hell that I had to," said Russell, with all honesty.

"Minister, I am here following orders. You have hidden three rebels and that is a treasonable offence. So I will make it plainly clear. I obey the law and you choose which ones to obey. I am the better subject of the Crown, as you are a lesser one. Clear?"

"Clear, Baron. That is why you should be here this morning ensuring fair justice and the royal prerogative for mercy. This is exactly what the King swore to when he was crowned, did he not?" said Russell.

"Oh, you're a clever one."

"A wise one in spite of my youth. You have a troubled soul and I can tell you care deeply for your family. I can imagine it must have been a strain to tell them you were going on his Majesty's service, knowing you may never see them again."

Belasyse grimaced. He had buried two wives of disease already and knew exactly how Russell felt. He remembered the day when he sat his son Henry and his daughter Mary down on the couch at their home in Worlaby and told them their mother Jane had died of a bloody flux and would never be coming home again. Just seeing his daughter's face made him cry more than she did. *God knows how much I loved her. Something in my heart died that day, and I cursed God, Christ, anyone.*

"I thought I could not be a Christian anymore," continued

Russell. "I honestly believed God had abandoned me. I don't take tobacco, work the six days and reserve Sunday for the Lord. I obey every one of the Ten Commandments. I tend to the sick, give the last rights to the dying. I thought to myself, there are so many people in this world who deserve to be punished by God for their sins; why pick on me?" said Russell, shaking his head at his loss. Belasyse looked at him earnestly and Russell saw his eyes were full of tears.

"Do you know why?" he asked, desperately looking for an answer to his two wife's death.

"Yes, I think I do. God needs help, he can't do everything. How many times have you soldiers said 'God is on my side', but I wonder if he is on yours," said Russell, looking straight at Belasyse. "Who will judge us when we die? God-fearing people, that's who. That is why they go to heaven. The good are there to judge us, all of us. There is no escape, no hiding. If we have sinned, we must ask for God's and their mercy. For if we repent, truly repent, there shall be a great joy in heaven, for if we acknowledge our sins, God shall forgive us, just as he has gathered your wives and mine in his great quest for justice and mercy."

"Blessed are the merciful for they shall be shown mercy," said Belasyse and tears started to flow down his cheeks as he thought of his children and his wife Anne. How much had he been through? The Tower, the beatings, burying his two wives, the carnage on so many battlefields, the starving children crying for bread and looking for their dead fathers. That native village and the horror he had seen. Enough! This must stop.

He turned away from Russell and saw Maverick whipping the regicides, holding a pistol in his left hand a thick leather whip in his right, swearing at them as the minister and magistrate looked on. Is this how they saw the return of the monarchy? Was this the example the King wanted to give his subjects? Is this what he stood for, had fought for and prepared to die for?

"Mr Tilton, Mr Russell," barked Belasyse, his blood boiling in righteous indignation. "I require your assistance immediately." Belasyse strode over to the regicides and took a double-barrelled pistol from his waistband and took careful aim, fired and the shot cut the whip from the hand of Maverick. Startled, he turned sharply round. "Put down that pistol or I will drop you where you stand," shouted Belasyse, shaking in anger at the evil man in front of him.

"What do you think are you doing?" said Maverick, seeing Tilton and Russell behind him, hands unbound. "I am a commissioner for the King."

"Not anymore. You're dismissed," said Belasyse bluntly. "Under the authority invested in me by his Majesty King Charles the Second, I require all your belongings," and he levelled his pistols at Maverick's groin. All stood, rooted to the spot, seeing this Lord of England, agent of the Crown, with his square jaw and cold hard look. No one expected this.

"You have to be joking?" said Maverick desperately, his eyes darting nervously in every direction. Belasyse fired again and fire poured out the barrel followed by a one ounce lead ball which tore into the sagging breaches just under Maverick's groin.

"The joke is on you because the next shot will make you less of man you are right now," shouted Belasyse, aiming another barrel. The judges looked at each other in amazement; John Russell, though, looked at Belasyse with admiration, as Maverick dropped his pistol and stripped. "Everything, every damn stich and throw that pouch of money you have to me," said Belasyse, quivering in hate he felt for this murderer and money-driven slave dealer.

"But I am naked, defenceless," said Maverick, seeing his reward disappearing into thin air.

"You are as naked and defenceless as the negroes you buy and natives you murder. Naked you entered this world and naked you shall leave it. I hope God grants you the time to reflect on your evil ways in hell. You will walk north for as long as there is daylight. I will gladly shoot you if you stop and I hope you do, because I want a chance to rid the world of a totally unscrupulous piece of garbage."

"Mercy, mercy. Please, the devil lives in the woods and it's freezing," said Maverick sobbing, seeing the bitter smiles on the faces of the judges.

"Mercy is a quality you do not possess and if the devil lives in the woods you will be in the same company. If it's cold the natives out there may have some of the blankets you sold them!" shouted Belasyse, firing a further round at Maverick's feet for good measure. He walked to the edge of the cemetery and looked over his right shoulder, seeing Belasyse as implacable as he could be, with his musketoon pointing at him, and he started walking to the tree line following the course of the river to the rolling hills in the distance, as a pack of wolves, high up on the snow-capped hills, sensed another kill.

The regicides desperate faces betrayed their horror, for they now assumed they were next, to be hunted as prey in the wilderness by the beasts or the Norwottuck Tribe. Belasyse looked at the five men before him and came to his decision.

"Mr Tilton, as magistrate of Hadley and representative of the law in this village, bear witness and John Russell minister, place your Bible on the top of this gravestone. You three men come over here," he commanded and cut the cords that bound them. "Place your right hand on the Bible and the left over your heart."

The regicides started praying, assuming now was to be their execution.

"Kneel! In front of God, do you three swear to stay in the village of Hadley so long as you all shall live?"

"Yes, we do," said all three in unison, not understanding what was going to happen to them.

"Do you swear you will never attempt to usurp the Crown or its dependents?"

"That I do," all three said, horrified from what they had just seen, knowing Maverick was going to be in all probability eaten alive.

"Do you swear to live by the law set down by the King, House of Lords and Commons?"

"Yes, I will," they replied.

"All three of you, do you swear in front of holy God, the minister John Russell and magistrate John Tilton, to attend church every day so long as you shall live and twice on Sunday, the Lord's day?"

"Yes, we are good Christians," said Goffe desperately, not wanting to be a meal for the next bear.

"And every day you will give a prayer."

"We will," they cried lustily, sensing now they might live.

"Did you, Mr Tilton, magistrate, hear that?" said Belasyse.

"Yes I did sir and note it," said Tilton now fully composed, his lawyer's mind working furiously.

"John Russell, minister, did you hear that?"

"I did," said Russell. "And I will see to it, as God is my witness."

"And you will say this prayer to our Lord Jesus Christ. Good Lord, I thank you that Baron John Belasyse let me live. I owe everything I have, including my life, to him and he should be granted a place amongst the saints, for he follows the true religion."

"Yes, I most definitely will and swear on the bible to it," shouted the three judges with their hands firmly on the bible.

"Good," said Belasyse out loud. "You have sworn to go to church every day to give a prayer of thanks and praise that your enemy, a Royalist, staunch Catholic and supporter of the Pope has just let you live."

Whalley and Goffe's jaws dropped. "What?" they said in amazement, as Belasyse mounted the horse and rode to the ferry and the track to New York, laughing all the way till tears flowed down his face.

"You can't make us do that. He worships the Pope, a follower of Satan," said Goffe to Russell and Tilton.

"Minister Russell, you can't make us do that. He is a Catholic, the devil's creed," said Whalley.

"Oh yes I can and you will, as you promised on the Bible to do so, or perhaps you lied to the baron, Mr Tilton the magistrate, myself the minister and Jesus Christ our redeemer. Maybe I should call the baron back or write to the King to say you lied." said Russell, smiling and thinking to himself, *now there was a man. Go in peace*, and he made the sign of the cross. Dixwell smiled at the baron's revenge. *I wish he had been ours.*

"Gentlemen, I suspect we could all do with a large glass of rum before prayers," said Russell, winking at Tilton and smiling at Belasyse's genius. It's over; peace in our time.

Belasyse rode to the jetty and there was Kellogg, knowing full well the baron had a plan all along and Maverick had met his deserved fate.

"All's well that ends well," said Belasyse, as he rode onto the ferry and Kellogg cast off in the morning sun. "God bless you. Go home and roast some of the coffee beans I have left, they are very costly and enjoy a good cup. Also, there is a lady at Springway who thinks you're a great carpenter and needs her barn roof fixing," said Belasyse as a goodbye, offering his hand in thanks to Kellogg.

"That I will John and may God bless you and your family."

Belasyse raised his hand in salute and rode off down the cart way to Springfield and Manhattan, admiring the beautiful sprouting foliage, as the squirrels chased each other up and down the trees, a new born fawn was being nuzzled by its mother and the soft meandering Connecticut River flowed peacefully to the Long Island sound on this beautiful spring morning – peace in our time.

Kellogg went to his home and poured some coffee beans into the roasting pan, which were followed by two hundred golden guineas. Kellogg laughed out loud and thought to himself, *I would have expected nothing less from a great man.*

CHAPTER 22

One Good Man

Belasyse presented his pass to the guard, whose eyes bugged out of their sockets.

To whom it may concern,

Baron Belasyse acts on my direct and personal orders in a matter of utmost importance to the Crown. He may pass wherever he so sees fit.

Signed Charles Rex.

"Sir, please do go through," gasped the duty sergeant, having only seen a pass like that for the Princes James and Rupert. Whoever he was, he was one of the most important people in the country.

"Thank you. I know my way," said Belasyse and turned around to the waterman. "I won't be long."

"For you, sir, I'll wait all day," said the waterman happily, knowing this was a gentleman and he would be well rewarded. It was good to hear one of his old colleagues was doing well in the plantations; he may go there himself. It seemed like there were more opportunities over the ocean than in London and these sedan chairs, there was just too much competition. Belasyse entered the Palace of Whitehall, showing the pass to the guards at the entrance to the withdrawing chamber, as usual full of government ministers and supplicants.

"Baron, so good to see you alive and well," said the Lord Chancellor earnestly. "And what news have you from the settlements as to your mission?" he asked in anticipation.

"I think its best I speak with his Majesty first if I may and let him fill you in, but I can tell you one piece of fascinating information I discovered," said Belasyse. Hyde's eyes widened, happy to be the first to hear one of the incredible stories he knew the baron had.

"I saw an animal like a deer, called a moose. It has a far bigger head than a deer, with a long snout, but what is amazing, it has five legs," said Belasyse, looking as serious as he could and went to see his sovereign whilst trying not to laugh at Hyde's flabbergasted face.

"Chaffinch, good to see you. I hope all is well," said Belasyse cheerfully. "I believe his Majesty is expecting me."

"Yes, sir, we are glad to see you back safe and sound. His Majesty has asked to see you directly and here is the key to his Majesty's private closet. You know the way, sir," said Chaffinch, *he must have had an incredible journey, that man.*

"That I do," said Belasyse, surprised at such an honour – *he trusts me implicitly.*

Turning the key and climbing the narrow stairs, hearing the clocks constantly chiming out the time. He entered the private salon, eying the great paintings, many newly returned from Europe. So the King has brought many of them back. That will have cost him – Titian, Raphael, Rubens, Holbein the finest painters in history and many had been employed directly by the royal family.

The King is cultured like his father, thought Belasyse, *but shrewder and easier going. The people love him and he has loved a few of them more than he should do. Still, it is better to have a lover as a monarch, that some maniac in charge.*

"It's good to see you safe and sound Baron," said the King, rising from his desk strewn with government papers and offered his hand in friendship. "I have received your correspondence. You have showed the highest standards of courage, fidelity and honour. The affairs of the plantations have been settled to my desire and satisfaction." The King then gave him a long look and in a shallow voice said, "And what of our miscreants?"

Belasyse said nothing, but took a small leather pouch from his right-hand pocket and emptied it onto the beautiful baroque table. Three gold signet rings tingled onto the veneered surface. The King looked at them without speaking, opened a drawer from under the table and withdrew a rectangular piece of parchment – the warrant to kill his father. He pulled over a candle, went to an ornate writing desk and picked up a silver box, from which he took out a spoon and a piece of red sealing wax. He melted a piece in the spoon over the candle and dropped three even-sized blobs onto a piece of paper, making a copy of each signet ring. Then, with a large piece of glass surrounded by a tin rim and a handle, he stood over each seal, checking them against the warrant. They all matched perfectly. "Good, it's done. It must have been an incredible journey. Do please enlighten me. I wish to know more about our positions across the ocean."

Belasyse smiled. "I may assure your Majesty my journey into the New World has been a great revelation to me. There is much we can learn from them. They are hardy folk and eschew, for the large part, luxuries we take for granted. They have an independent mind and spirit and they put up with many privations. Sire, I respect their endeavour. There is no gold, silver or precious stones. So the people for the large part have gone for reasons other than greed and they have carved out a living from the wilderness. There is also something called a barbecue which is a most delicious thing, but it won't catch on here – too much rain."

"Very interesting. Do carry on."

"When they no longer need our Army and Navy to protect them, they may go their own way, sire."

"You are a man of great human perception, Baron. You are right. Now they need us more than we need them. In the future there will be challenges ahead, but if the monarchy shows respect, listens and treats them fairly, all will be well. But if they don't and treat them with distain, rule by dictat and ignore their views, there will be trouble. I hope all my descendants are reasonable people."

"I do hope my mission is completed to your satisfaction, sire," said Belasyse.

"Definitely; no one but you could have done this. I have spoken to your colleagues, Villiers and Russell. They are good men. I have also met with your wife over my commission to you. Baron, may I ask you to move closer to Windsor Castle so I may benefit from your good counsel."

"Of course, sire. I am at your and the nation's service," suddenly he realised there was another person in the room.

In the corner, sitting on a velvet-covered chair, was a small thin man, not five foot high, with coal black eyes, dressed in a scarlet cloak, scarlet mozzetta, a scarlet zucchetto on his head and on his right hand a gold ring with a depiction of Christ on it.

"Your eminence," said Belasyse in shock. "But you, um, err, you are… I did not think your Majesty was a, err…" Belasyse didn't dare say it.

"You must have suspected," said the King jovially.

"Well, your Majesty, it's like my wife – what I think and what I know are not always the same," said Belasyse. Ha ha-ha! They all laughed and the cardinal motioned them to a table covered with an alter cloth, topped with a silver cross, a silver goblet studded with jewels half-full of wine, and a golden tray with a wafer of bread upon it.

"Gentlemen, it is time to take Communion." And both men went to the side of the table and knelt as the cardinal said, "Please join with me in saying the Lord's Prayer."

"Do you, Joseph Kellogg, take Sarah to be your wife? Do you promise to love, honour, cherish, and protect her, forsaking all others and holding only unto her?" said John Russell happily.

"I do," said Kellogg, tears in his eyes. At long last he could learn to live again. A woman to love, and a family to care for. His hard work had paid off. With the two hundred guineas Belasyse had given him, a fine home would result and he could get Abigail's boys into the Harvard School.

"If any man here have good reason why these two people should not be joined together in holy matrimony, speak now or forever hold your peace." Throw, Cleeson and Cornelius smiled. The baron's plan had worked and they shed tears at the scene. The Lord truly works in mysterious ways.

"Then I pronounce you both man and wife." And they both cried in each other's arms, for love is the wish of all good men.

"Thank God you are safe, John," said Villiers, embracing his old friend.

"Amen to that," said Russell, slapping Belasyse's back.

"It must have been an incredible adventure. We are going to have some fascinating conversations over dinner," said Villiers, relieved his friend had not only survived but had completed the King's mission.

"Thank you my good friends for your concern. How is Anne? I thought of her so often. Is she well?" asked Belasyse with a sense of trepidation.

"She is fine when we last visited. We explained about your mission for the King, but as you can imagine she was angry, though the stunning tiara from his Majesty went down well. After all, diamonds are a girl's best friend," said Russell, winking at Villiers.

"Have a great trip and reunion. You will find there is a new line of work for you at Worlaby; could be a bit demanding. We'll see you at the Newmarket races and have a good chat then," said Villiers as a goodbye as Belasyse jumped into the carriage to Grimsby.

"Do you think he got the hint?" asked Russell happily.

"Maybe; let him enjoy," said Villiers, mightily relieved that all had turned out for the best for their friend.

Belasyse walked up to his front door and rang the bell. Cavendish opened it and gasped in shock. "May the good Lord be praised. Welcome home, sir."

"Dad, Dad, thank God you are safe," said Henry and Mary Belasyse, running from the lounge to embrace their father.

"I nearly got on a ship to come and help," said Henry.

"Look at you coming to your father's rescue. Its ten boring weeks across the ocean. Where is Anne?" asked Belasyse.

"Here, John," said Anne Paulet and walked into the withdrawing room, curtsying before her husband.

"How I have missed you," said Belasyse, shaking with emotion.

"And I you," said Anne.

"Children, I wish to speak with Anne alone, if I may." Mary and Henry left the room, knowing it was to be a difficult reunion.

Belasyse bowed his head in shame in the knowledge he had again, left his beloved wife to go on a difficult mission on behalf of his King. The room was silent and Belasyse feared the worst.

"We women will never know why you men do certain things and perhaps it is best we don't. You have never cheated on me, hurt or beaten me and you have always provided a good home and you have consistently said you love me. All married women need to be reassured that their husbands love them and they have made the right decision. In that, you always have. I am your wife and I have waited for you before. I love you for what you are, a brave man of principle and unswerving devotion. I am your wife; reach for me, my loving husband, and I will always do what I can for you," said Anne and started to softly cry.

Belasyse knelt on one knee and looked at his wife, taking her by the hand.

"Whenever I thought of you, love entered my heart like the rushing of all the water in the oceans. I missed your loving embrace as God would miss his angels. Nothing, absolutely nothing, can make me happier than being beside you, and I am, madam, the luckiest man that ever walked on our saviour's earth. For if any man needed the proof that God is real, the evidence is before me." And Belasyse kissed her gently and they embraced, both of them crying tears of relief that at long last they were together again. "I'm yours, sir, but right now we have a guest."

"Guest?"

"Yes; you were away on the King's business, so we have something to say." Anne called in the children.

"Father, I am running the estate, so we have another job for you," said Henry.

"Job?" asked Belasyse frowning. *Wait, my friends mentioned something.*

"Yes, a great job, washing, fetching, dressing, waking up at midnight and looking after a lovely girl. Here is your new daughter," said Anne, pulling a cradle from behind the window dresser." O h my! Anne, you're a genius; she is so pretty," said Belasyse shocked and pleased at the same time, leaning over the cradle seeing his new daughter for the first time. "Big blue eyes and a little nose that's yours," he said with a grin. "We have to have a name. Any ideas, Anne?" said Belasyse excitedly.

"You know, I was thinking about that when you were away – here is an idea. You told us what an honour it was to serve King Charles – why don't we call her Honora?" asked Anne.

"Perfect. We can celebrate at St. Clement's tomorrow afternoon. Then we can view the plans I have drawn up for some alms houses I will have built for distressed persons, especially women," said Belasyse happily. "A glass of wine anyone?" asked Belasyse.

"Yes!" they all cried, and made their way to the dining table. Daddy was home, at last, to stay.

End

King Charles the Second ruled Great Britain for twenty-five years. Science, the arts, culture, trade and industry expanded. With the Navigation Acts and Royal Society, Britain's world influence expanded dramatically. The seeds of the Industrial Revolution had been sown. From Canada to the Carolinas most of the east coast of North America was secured for Britain. He survived the Great Plague in 1665, the fire of London the next year and assassination plots by disaffected Republicans. He was tolerant and open with his people and rewarded handsomely those who had helped him regain the throne. His court was seen as morally degenerate, but was outward looking and innovative. He had some seventeen children, none with his wife, and left the throne to his Catholic brother James, who was confrontational and difficult. He was sent packing three years later to be replaced by his daughter Mary.

Major General Whalley survived any attempt to arrest or kill him and lived out his life hiding in Hadley, Massachusetts. He was in contact with his sister and, through her, his family in England. The plan to raise the militias and declare independence was quietly dropped. He was lonely and despaired of not seeing his wife or children again. He actively traded in Hadley leaving his legacy to Minister Russell. He died around 1674 leaving few records of his life, hunted to the last.

Major General Goffe lived with his father-in-law until he

died and may have helped the residents of Hadley beat off a native attack during King Philip's war in 1675. He kept a diary with his Republican views, many of which affected future events in American history. After his father-in-law's death, he moved to Hartford using the name Thomas Duffell, as Hadley had many regular troops of King Charles' quartered in the town as protection. He was recognised by John London and fled. He returned again to Hadley and died around 1679/80, never returning to England.

Colonel John Dixwell left Hadley and returned quietly to New Haven, using the alias James Davids. He made no attempt to integrate into society and lived alone for many years, fearing the hand upon the shoulder. He married twice, first to Joanna Ling, who died a month after the wedding. Then, at the age of sixty-nine, Bathsheba How, who was thirty-one years old and bore him three children. Colonel Dixwell regretted signing the death warrant, but like many others was intimidated into doing so. He was a model citizen in New Haven and behaved with impeccable dignity and manners, and was an inspiration to many with his good behaviour and high moral standards. He did nothing to disturb the King's peace. He died on the 18th of March 1688 at the grand old age of eighty-two, his true identity being revealed to his wife on his deathbed. One of the last regicides to die, his line continues to this day.

John Davenport was dismissed from his post in New Haven and left for Boston, his life's work swallowed up by the state of Connecticut. As pastor to the first church there, he was bitter, argumentative and divisive to the end. He died in 1670.

Richard Sperry continued to farm by the side of the great west rock and raised his family in peace. He left a legacy of hard work, steadfastness, loyalty and enterprise that built the United States of America.

Captain Daniel Gookin was summoned to London to explain his actions in facilitating the escape of the regicides from London and hiding them in Boston, as well as their escape from the town. He refused and was protected by powerful men of the town council – a sure sign that the monarch was not all powerful across the ocean.

Hugh Peter was hung, drawn and quartered at Charing Cross, London on the 16th of October 1660 as a prime mover in instigating the execution of King Charles the First, the abolition of the Monarchy and the establishment of the Republic.

Samuel Maverick disappears from history. Chancer, loyal only to himself and one of the first slave dealers in the plantations, missed by none.

Samuel Kellogg lived quietly in Hadley as their brewer and ferryman. The ferrymen, called watermen and lightermen, still ply the waters of the River Thames, have a most thorough training and the oldest continual boat race in the world.

Baron John Belasyse was made governor of the city of Hull, Captain General of the King's forces in Tangier and Africa, Lord Lieutenant of East Riding, Yorkshire, and Captain of the Gentleman at Arms, amongst other important posts. He had five children and lived in the delightful village of Whitton, to the west of London, with his loyal wife Anne Paulet, dying at the age of seventy-five in 1689. He was trusted by King Charles the Second and his successor King James the Second, who made him a Privy Councillor and Lord Commissioner to the Treasury. A man of great courage and conviction, steadfast to the Crown in an age of shifting loyalties, he never wavered in his belief that the nation should be run by the monarch and the Houses of Commons and Lords, as it is today.

"Sir, loyalty comes from the heart, as does love."

King Charles the First lies in the vault at St George's Chapel, Windsor Castle, the only saint of the Anglican Church.

Today, Britain is a constitutional monarchy and is one of the most stable nations in the world.

CPSIA information can be obtained at www.ICGtesting.com
Printed in the USA
BVOW06s0220240616

453324BV00027B/174/P

9 781785 891939